Anything can happen at the fair...

"Heavens!" She wasn't quite sure how to respond, so she attempted to emulate his own flippant tone. "I daresay I should consider myself fortunate that you kissed Patsy's hand and not mine!" She'd meant to sound arch, but the voice that came out sounded petulant, even to her own ears.

"Don't tell me that bothered you!" exclaimed Philippe, looking inordinately pleased with himself.

Penelope scrambled to retrieve her position. "Of course not! If I'd wanted to have my hand kissed—which I don't!—I could find any number of gentlemen who would be happy to oblige me!"

"Of that, I have no doubt." Putting his hands on her shoulders, he drew her deeper into the shadows. When he spoke again, his voice was low and husky. "I daresay I can offer you no compliment that you have not heard, and despised, a hundred times before. So I will only say that if I were to kiss you, Miss Fair, it would not be for the entertainment of the masses. Nor, for that matter, would it be on the hand."

Perhaps it was the lingering odor of incense that mesmerized her, or perhaps it was the rhythmic stroking of his thumb against the tender spot beneath her ear. Whatever the case, she raised startled her eyes to his, and what she saw there made the breath catch in her throat. He studied her face for a long moment, then, finding what he sought, put his fingers beneath her chin and tipped it very slightly upward. Slowly, so slowly, he bent his head and lowered his mouth to hers.

Other books by Sheri Cobb South

The John Pickett Mysteries

PICKPOCKET'S APPRENTICE (novella)
IN MILADY'S CHAMBER
A DEAD BORE
FAMILY PLOT
DINNER MOST DEADLY
WAITING GAME (novella)
TOO HOT TO HANDEL
FOR DEADER OR WORSE
MYSTERY LOVES COMPANY
PERIL BY POST
INTO THIN EIRE
NOWHERE MAN (novella)
BROTHER, CAN YOU SPARE A CRIME?
DEATH CAN BE HABIT-FORMING
IN THE FAMILY WAY

The Weaver Series

THE WEAVER TAKES A WIFE
BRIGHTON HONEYMOON
FRENCH LEAVE
THE DESPERATE DUKE

Single-Title Regency Romances

BARONESS IN BUCKSKIN
OF PAUPERS AND PEERS
MISS DARBY'S DUENNA

Romantic Suspense

MOON OVER THE MEDITERRANEAN

FAIREST OF THE FAYRE

Sheri Cobb South

FAIREST OF THE FAYRE

Introduction

Come one, come all! Come to the fair! Bartholomew Fair, held in Smithfield every year from 1133 to 1855 in late summer, was a major cultural event for most of its long history. Although its purpose was originally commercial—a cloth market providing funding for the priory of St. Bartholomew and, after the Reformation, its hospital—as the centuries passed, entertainments and amusements of every sort eventually reduced its mercantile functions to a mere afterthought.

Many of the people you will meet there—Miss Harvey, the Beautiful Albiness; Mr. Simon Paap, the Dutch Dwarf, who had an audience with the Prince Regent; Miss Sarah Biffin, an accomplished portraitist despite her lack of hands or arms; and many others—were real people whose stories (as well as, in the case of Miss Harvey, their names) would, were it not for their connection to the fair, have been lost to history.

At the same time, many of the most celebrated actors and actresses of the day might be seen at the fair for a fraction of what one would pay at Drury Lane or Covent Garden, either in truncated versions of the same plays or in works written specifically for the fair—some of these latter containing political satire so scathing that they would not be tolerated at any other time.

Other performers include rope-dancers (what we would call tightrope walkers), jugglers, tumblers, and merry-Andrews —quite possibly the stage name of an actual seventeenth-century entertainer, but by the end of that century, a generic term for a clown or jester.

If carnival rides are more to your liking, take a turn on one of the big wooden swings known as the "carriage without horses" even though they look more like boats. Thomas Rowlandson's 1808 etching of Bartholomew Fair clearly shows three of these contraptions, along with what appear to be the tops of two others, as well as a prototype of the modern Ferris wheel known by the unoriginal name of the "up-and-down." This same illustration shows two other rides whose functions are not entirely clear, although one appears to share some similarities with a carousel—quite a variety of mechanical marvels, in a world without electricity or even steam-powered motion.

So, come to the fair! But keep a tight hold on your heart as well as your purse. For pickpockets and rogues of every sort abound…and anything can happen at the fair.

Prologue

Paris, 1794

"But *Maman*, I don't want to!" wailed seven-year-old Philippe Markham, *Vicomte de Valois*, only son and heir of the *Duc de Sainte-Marguerite*. "The onions, they have a smell of the most *désagréable*," he added, wrinkling his nose for emphasis. Despite fluency in both his mother's and his father's native tongues since he was in the nursery, he apparently considered these two languages insufficient to sufficiently convey the magnitude of this offense against his nostrils.

"Hush, *mon fils*," chided his mother, and although she addressed Philippe, she darted a quick, nervous glance over her shoulder toward the shabby house to whose back door a wagon containing the offending onions, along with heaps of cabbages, had drawn up. "Get in, quickly—*vite*! We have not the time to waste."

"Can I not ride on the box with André?" pleaded Philippe, glancing from *madame la duchesse* to the strapping young man seated on the box with the reins in his hands. "Sometimes he lets me drive. I should like to drive this wagon, for then I could tip these stinky onions into the ditch," he said, pondering the prospect with obvious relish.

The duchess sighed. How to explain to a child that all of Paris had become drunk on blood, when she could hardly comprehend it herself? "Not today, pet. Today we are playing a—a game with your papa. You shall hide in the wagon amongst the cabbages, and André will drive us, oh, very far. Then we will see how long it takes for Papa to find us. Does that not sound *très amusant?*"

Philippe, regarding his mother skeptically, did not answer at once. He had never understood why, at the beginning of what Papa called "the Trouble," they had left the big grey stone *château* in the lush vineyard country of the Loire Valley to live instead in a hovel in Paris. Now, several months later, he could not understand why a game would make its players so tense and strained, or would require his elegant *Maman* to dress like a peasant, with a kerchief over her glossy black hair, a threadbare shawl about her shoulders, and sturdy wooden sabots on her feet. Before he could point out these contradictions, however, a noise in the street in front of the house, faint at first but growing steadily louder, suddenly resolved itself into a series of dull thuds, like a fist—or several fists—pounding on the front door.

"*Oui?*" *Monsieur le duc*'s calm voice came faintly through the thin walls. "How may I be of service to you?"

"You are Citizen Markham, formerly the *Duc de Sainte-Marguerite?*" the visitor demanded in the guttural French of the Parisian slums.

Philippe's father chuckled. "Look about you, *mon ami!* Does this appear a likely residence for *le duc?*"

And then Philippe heard no more, for André, apparently judging that the time for persuasion was past, cast aside the reins and leaped down off the box, then picked up the young *vicomte* by the seat of his breeches and dumped him unceremoniously over the side of the wagon.

"Now, you stop jawing at your mum and get yourself down among the cabbages, where you can't be seen," he said in an accent that was pure Midlands, for André—known in his native country as Andrew—was an Englishman.

Philippe, yielding perforce to a superior power, burrowed beneath the cabbages while André lifted the duchess onto the box, then climbed up after her and urged the sturdy draft horses forward with two clicks of his tongue against the roof of his mouth. As the wagon lurched forward, Philippe shifted the cabbages slightly in order to peer between them for one last look at the house where they had lived for the last four months.

He never saw his father again.

1

London, 1814

The tall French windows of the overheated ballroom had been thrown open to allow the dancers access to the terrace at the rear of the house and the garden beyond, where the scent of jasmine hung in the air and the moonlight glinted silver on every leaf that stirred in the soft breeze of a summer evening. Anyone must have agreed that this was a setting made for romance—anyone, that is, except for Miss Penelope Fayre, reigning belle of the Season just nearing its end. Miss Fayre had no attention to spare for such fanciful notions, for she was fully engaged in trying to dissuade the young Viscount Tarne from dropping to one knee, while at the same time attempting to extract her hand from his—no easy task, as that enamored young man appeared determined to cover it with kisses.

"No, my lord, pray do not!" She backed away from him in the direction of the house and its sweltering ballroom, only to realize with some dismay that he fully intended to crawl after her on his knees. "I have told you that I cannot accept your offer, so your persistence only serves to make us both ridiculous!"

Lord Tarne had been intent upon pressing kisses into her palm (or, more specifically, onto the palm of her long kid glove), but this slanderous claim compelled him to protest so gross a misrepresentation of his suit. "Impossible! True passion can never be ridiculous. If you only knew the depth of my feelings—"

"I can hardly *not* know, since you will insist on telling me," she said tartly. "I like you very well, but you are far too young to be thinking of marriage. Depend upon it, by next Season, you will have set your sights on some other lady, and you will be very glad *not* to be leg-shackled to me. Now, will you please accept my answer so that we may part as friends with our dignity still intact?"

In truth, she feared that ship had already sailed. A burst of laughter from inside the house recalled his lordship's attention to the wide-open French windows, and the fact that they were within full view of anyone in the ballroom who cared to look. He cast a rather shamefaced glance toward the dancers, then clambered to his feet and dusted off the knees of his black stockinette pantaloons.

"Don't know what you're holding out for," he grumbled, sounding more like a sullen schoolboy than a peer—even a very youthful peer—of the realm. He cast a resentful glance over the same features he'd been rhapsodizing in badly written poetry for the better part of the summer: dark brown curls framing eyes of the same shade, a straight little nose, and a Cupid's bow of a mouth, porcelain skin, and a trim figure. "Looks won't last forever, and everyone knows you haven't a feather to fly with."

Penelope stiffened. "You need not be insulting, my lord."

"Just stating a fact. Not too many gentlemen so plump in the pocket that they're willing to take a dowerless bride, so you'd best have a care, or else you'll find yourself on the shelf. Who'll be 'ridiculous' then?"

She was spared the necessity of a response by the arrival on the terrace of a third party, a gentleman of about five and twenty. At first glance, he appeared to be an unlikely rescuer. At five feet eight inches, he was too tall to be short, but too short to be tall. His hair was neither blond nor brown, but an indiscriminate shade somewhere in between, and his eyes tended to fluctuate between blue, green, and hazel. Taken together, this collection of unclearly defined characteristics led those who did not know him well to deduce that his character was equally indecisive. In fact, nothing could be further from the truth—as Penelope had cause to know, having been acquainted with the young man since her birth.

"Is everything all right?" he asked, his gaze shifting from Penelope to her swain and back again.

"Oliver! Yes, everything is quite all right," she assured him, although the excessive brightness with which she greeted his arrival gave the lie to this claim. "But I had not expected to see you here. Tell me, have you tried the lobster patties? Heavenly! I wonder if there are any left?"

Oliver Fayre, well aware of the effect his sister's beauty tended to have on susceptible young men, was quick to take his cue. "Lobster patties, you say? No, I must have missed them. Come with me to the refreshment room and point them out." He acknowledged the rejected Romeo with a cool nod that gave her suitor no cause to hope. "Your servant, Lord Tarne," he said, then led his sister back into the house.

Once they had made their way through the crowded ballroom to the almost deserted refreshment room, he regarded Penelope with one eyebrow lifted in playful reproach. "Don't tell me; let me guess. You've turned down another one."

"Well…" The look she gave him, one of mingled guilt and apology leavened with just a hint of mischief, told its own tale.

"Say no more! But I must say, my sympathies are fully aligned with Tarne. If you didn't mean to have the fellow, then why in the world have you been encouraging him to dangle after you?"

"How was I to know he was thinking of marriage?" she demanded, bristling. "If he is old enough to marry without his father's permission, I shall own myself much shocked."

Oliver conceded this point with a shrug. "Fair enough. But what about Lord Denbury, or Sir Edwin Lassiter, or Mr. Sprague, or—"

"It's my London Season," she reminded him. "I'm *supposed* to be making myself agreeable to gentlemen."

"Being agreeable is one thing; getting a reputation as a flirt is quite another."

Penelope gave a soulful sigh. "I'm afraid it's too late. Lord Tarne says I shall be left to languish on the shelf. But, Oliver," she continued in quite a different tone, "I didn't know you planned to be here tonight. You might have escorted me, and relieved Mama of the responsibility."

"I hadn't expected to be here. In fact, I'm acting as Lord Sparling's surrogate."

"Are you indeed? It seems an odd task for a secretary," Penelope observed. If her mind had been less taken up with her own affairs, she might have noticed the faint flush that stained her brother's cheeks. "It seems to me that your leisure hours ought to be your own. Still, I can't say I'm sorry, under the circumstances."

Oliver shrugged. "Oh, I don't mind. You'd be surprised at the government business that can be transacted at these things, and if I'm ever to obtain a diplomatic post—but never mind that! Where are these lobster patties?"

She led him to a long table that groaned beneath the weight of platters filled with sweets and savories of all kinds. As he filled a plate, she turned her mind to the possible repercussions of the little scene on the terrace.

"Do you think—" She glanced about the room to ensure no one was within earshot before lowering her voice and asking, "Do you think Mama will be very displeased?"

He made a wry face. "Well, she won't be thrilled. Still, you can't be expected to marry an idiot, no matter how plump he is in the pockets. And so I shall tell Mama, if she gives you any grief over refusing Tarne. In any case," he added bracingly, "the Season is almost over, and by next year, some other lucky girl may replace you as the reigning belle of the *ton*, so *she* can deal with Lord Tarne and his ilk."

Penelope gave him a smile, but in truth, her brother's words echoed all too closely those of her rejected suitor. *Looks won't last forever… Not too many gentlemen willing to take a dowerless bride…* Granted, she was unlikely to become old haggish by next Easter, the unofficial opening of the Season. Still, the current fashion for dark hair and eyes might well give way to a passion for the angelically fair, making her own style of beauty quite passé. Perhaps more to the point, her mother might not be willing to fund another Season, especially since Penelope had squandered her opportunity by rejecting no fewer than seven offers of marriage during the one just ending.

"Look here, Penny, will you mind very much if I take you back to Mama now?" Oliver asked somewhat sheepishly, darting a quick glance toward the open doorway that led back into the ballroom. "I'm here on Lord Sparling's instructions, so I wouldn't want to be derelict in my duty—"

"I wish you would not call me by that odious nickname!"

"What nickname? Penny?" he asked, utterly bewildered. "Caro and I have called you Penny all your life, and you've never said a word."

She sighed. "No, for it never bothered me before. But someone must have overheard you, for the scandal sheets have given me a particularly hateful variation on the theme. I daresay you may not have seen it, since you spend your days at Lord Sparling's beck and call, but the *Ton Crier* has dubbed me 'the Fayre Farthing.' A *farthing!*" she echoed indignantly.

Not a penny, not even a ha'penny, but a farthing—one-fourth of a penny, and the least valuable coin produced by the Royal Mint. She'd recognized it at the time as an oblique reference to her paltry dowry; now, in the light of Lord Tarne's mocking retort, it occurred to her that a second analogy, one even less flattering, might be equally fitting. Her beauty, to which her mother had pinned all her hopes for an advantageous marriage, must be worth very little, if it could be so easily replaced by any good-looking girl who happened to capture the *ton*'s attention.

Where would she be by that time—married to the least objectionable of her suitors, or on the shelf, as Lord Tarne had predicted? Four months ago, at the beginning of the Season, she had resolved never to marry a man she did not love. But this, it had soon become apparent, was a great deal easier said than done. It seemed absurd to think that in a city of more than a million people, there was not one single man she could love, but after spending an entire Season searching for him, she had to admit that if such a man existed, he was keeping himself very well-hidden.

"Who cares what the *Ton Crier* has to say?" he asked bracingly. "Jealous cats, most of 'em."

Her brow furrowed as she considered this claim. "The writers, or the subscribers?"

"Both," he replied without hesitation.

She might have pressed him as to the source of these insights—the authorship of the popular weekly periodical was, after all, one of the *ton*'s best-kept secrets—but, seeing her brother's increasingly nervous glances toward the door, she recalled guiltily that she was keeping him dancing attendance on her while he was supposed to be carrying out an assignment for his employer.

"You go ahead," she told him. "I can find my way back to Mama on my own."

"I'm obliged to you." He began to turn aside, then paused to add another lobster patty to his plate. "And remember, if Mama gives you any grief over rebuffing Lord Tarne, you have only to send word to me," he added, then quitted the refreshment room with unflattering speed.

* * *

Upon their return to the tall, narrow house in Upper Gower Street that was their temporary Town residence (hired for the Season at quite a reasonable rate, situated as it was on the fringe of Mayfair rather than in the heart of that fashionable district), Mrs. Fayre and Penelope trudged wearily up the stairs toward their bedrooms. As they reached the first-floor landing, however, their ascent was interrupted by a soft voice calling from the drawing room.

"Mama? Penelope? How was the ball?"

Mrs. Fayre veered away from the staircase and joined her eldest child in the drawing room, her weariness forgotten. "She has refused *another* one!" she announced.

"Oh, dear." Mrs. Caroline Fayre Cummings directed a sympathetic smile toward her younger sister, entering the room at that moment in her mother's wake. "Who was it this time?"

"Lord Tarne," Penelope said mulishly.

"A viscount!" moaned Mrs. Fayre, collapsing onto the sofa and digging her plump, beringed fingers into fashionably coiffed locks that were now more silver than gold. "A viscount who will be an earl someday, although that may not be for years, for his father, Lord Harkness, is not yet fifty, and the men of that family seem to be remarkably long-lived—not that it makes any difference to us, for she has turned him down!"

"But, Mama, surely you would not wish her to accept a man who would not make her happy," protested Caroline, whose own blissful marriage to a country vicar had ended three years previously with her husband's death—albeit not before their meager savings had been exhausted by his medical care, forcing his young widow and three-year-old son to cast themselves upon her mother's charity after surrendering the vicarage to the new incumbent.

"One can be just as happy with a rich man as with a poor one," Mrs. Fayre pronounced, although how she could possibly know this when she had never been married to a rich man was a question Penelope dared not ask. "And even if he were not a viscount, how could she not be happy with a man who is so truly devoted to her? Such compliments he pays her! Such pretty attentions! Why, he has sent her so many bouquets of flowers, I vow the house smells like a florist's shop!"

She cast a wistful glance toward the mantelpiece, where vases of roses, lilies, and peonies vied for prominence.

"He pays extravagant court to me because it is fashionable to do so, Mama," Penelope explained patiently. "He does not think of me as a person at all, but merely a prize to be won, like a"—she groped for a suitable analogy—"like a pig at Bartholomew Fair!"

Mrs. Fayre blinked at this unexpected revelation. "I didn't know one *could* win a pig at Bartholomew Fair. Only fancy—one might have enough meat to last the whole winter! Does it require any particular skill to win, or is it purely a matter of chance?"

"You mustn't mind Penelope, Mama, for she is mixing her metaphors," Caroline said, fighting not entirely successfully to suppress a smile. "The pig would be the competitor, not the prize."

Mrs. Fayre turned to stare in dismay at her youngest child.

"Penelope, my dear, you cannot mean to tell me his lordship likened you to a pig!"

"Well, no, I daresay he is not as bad as all that," conceded Penelope, giving credit where it was due. "But you may depend upon it, the moment it becomes fashionable to dangle after some other lady, he will be the first in line. Why, he all but told me so!"

"*No!*" breathed Mrs. Fayre, shocked to her very core. "I'm sure he never said such a vulgar thing! No true gentleman would ever be so ungallant—especially not a viscount!"

The Fayre sisters' eyes met, and they exchanged furtive smiles at their mother's conviction that a man's rank rendered him incapable of ungentlemanly behavior.

"Not in so many words," Penelope admitted. "He only reminded me that a fresh crop of young ladies will be launched on the marriage mart next Season, and that if I persist in rejecting offers—or perhaps only if I persist in rejecting *his* offer—I will be supplanted and will end my days as a spinster on the shelf."

Mrs. Fayre sighed. "Well, and he's not wrong, dearest, you must admit. Life is not easy for unmarried ladies, and it can be especially cruel to unmarried ladies with no fortune."

"I am not trying to be disobliging, Mama, but it seems to me that life is not particularly easy for married ladies, either, given the precarious positions in which you and Caro were left by your own husbands."

A sharp intake of breath drew Penelope's gaze to the sofa where Caroline sat stiffly.

"It is true that James was not wealthy, and his long illness depleted what savings we had," Caroline said with great deliberation. "But make no mistake, Penelope: I would gladly have spent twice—no, ten times as much, if by doing so I might have kept him alive for one more day."

"I—I'm sorry, Caro—" Penelope stammered, the wind quite taken from her sails. "I never meant—"

"I know you didn't, you goose," her sister chided her gently. "I only meant to point out that although no one is guaranteed a 'happily ever after'—you're quite right about that—marriage to the right person is worth any price. And now," she added bracingly, glancing at the ormolu clock just visible amidst all the floral tributes, whose hands were inching toward three o'clock, "since little Benjamin invariably awakens before seven, I think I had best seek my bed."

"Lud, yes, and so should we all," agreed little Benjamin's fond grandmama, shooing her daughters toward the stairs. "I vow, I don't know where that child gets his energy, for his poor father was always the most *restful* of men…"

Leading the way up to the second floor, Mrs. Fayre kept up a flow of fond reminiscences of Benjamin's babyhood, a circumstance that allowed Caroline to fall back and ask her sister in an undervoice, "Are you all right, Penny?"

Penelope heaved a sigh, but refused to allow the *Ton Crier* to nettle her. "Aside from the fact that I've disgraced myself yet again, I'm quite all right. Oh, Oliver was there. At the ball, I mean," she added, seizing upon a chance to change the subject.

"Oliver? What was he doing there?"

"Representing his employer, or so he said. Really, Caro, what kind of man expects his secretary to attend social engagements for him?"

Caroline shrugged. "Lord Sparling's kind, apparently. I don't think I've ever met the marquess—James and I didn't move in such exalted circles—but I was a little acquainted with his daughter at school. She was a few years younger than I, and very well-liked, but wild to a fault."

Grateful to be no longer the center of attention, Penelope encouraged Caroline to recount anecdotes from her schooldays in which Lady Diantha Sparling figured to some degree, and in this manner contrived to reach her bedchamber without being obliged to further defend her actions in refusing an undeniably advantageous match—at least, she acknowledged with a sigh, until the eighth suitor made her an offer.

2

The funeral cortège was so small that anyone passing by might have been forgiven for overlooking it entirely, consisting as it did of only the distinctive six-sided pine box borne on a wagon drawn by two black horses, followed by two men who accompanied the vehicle on foot. One of these was a slender young man in his late twenties with jet-black hair, his black-eyed gaze fixed upon the somber vehicle with a look of grim determination. The other, a giant of a man some fifteen years his senior, was as fair as the younger man was dark, and bore the appearance of one who would have been much more comfortable sitting on the coachman's bench with the reins in his hands than trudging behind on foot. Both men were clad in somewhat shabby tailcoats with black armbands affixed to the sleeves, but the fact that the elder followed behind the younger made it clear that it was the latter who was the chief mourner. Occasionally, one of the more observant of the passersby noted the wagon's sad cargo or perhaps recognized the significance of the black ostrich plumes crowning the heads of the horses, and paused on the pavement to remove his hat as a mark of respect for the unknown deceased—a gesture which the young man solemnly acknowledged with a nod.

And this, he thought bitterly, *is how the* Duchesse de Sainte-Marguerite *and Baroness Markham should be laid to rest. It will not always be so, Maman*, he silently promised the coffin's occupant.

Someday, he would remove his mother's remains to the family vault, either the one on the Markham estate in Leicestershire or perhaps, if the war between his two countries would ever end and some form of order be restored in France, even to the Sainte-Marguerite estate in the Loire Valley.

Perhaps.

If the big, steep-roofed grey house had not been burned to the ground in the name of liberty, equality, and fraternity.

The wagon had arrived at the burial ground by this time, and soon the coffin was removed from the vehicle and lowered into the deep hole that had been prepared to receive it.

"'Man that is born of woman hath but a short time to live,'" intoned the priest, "'and is full of misery...'"

And a large part of Maman*'s misery was self-imposed*, thought Philippe, feeling the old frustration rising within him, *for it was so unnecessary*.

"'...we therefore commit her body to the ground; earth to earth, ashes to ashes, dust to dust...'"

Granted, the Leicestershire estate of the Barons Markham was not so vast as the *Duc de Sainte-Marguerite*'s holdings in France's Loire Valley, but it had been his father's, and was now rightfully his. In fact, it was to this estate that they had intended to return after their escape from France during the Terror of '94. But then the faithful André (or rather Andrew, now that he was back on his native soil) had returned from a reconnaissance mission to Markham Grange with a report that the late Lord Markham's younger brother was now in possession of both the land and the title.

With this fresh disaster, all the fight had gone out of the duchess. She had seen too much during those terrible months in France, and even though they were back in England, she could not seem to summon the fortitude to take up the cudgels in her seven-year-old son's defense, not even to secure his inheritance. Instead, *madame la duchesse* had chosen to live out the rest of her life in obscurity in the market town of Leicester, subsisting on the pittance she'd earned from doing fine needlework for ladies far less well-born than herself, her meager wages subsidized by whatever Andrew could bring in from odd jobs. Even after Philippe—called Philip now that he had returned to the country of his father's birth—had achieved his majority, by which time he contrived to eke out a living by imparting to others those rudiments of swordsmanship he still remembered from his own long-ago lessons, she had pleaded with him so piteously that he had refrained from making use of these latent skills in an attempt to reclaim his heritage, albeit not without reluctance.

"'...in sure and certain hope of the resurrection...'"

But his mother was dead now, and could not be hurt, physically or emotionally, by anything that might result from his efforts to claim what was rightfully his. The title of *Duc de Sainte-Marguerite*, with all its ancient privileges, might be forever lost to him, but that only made him all the more determined to take his place as Lord Markham of Markham Grange.

"...honor and glory forever. Amen."

"Amen," murmured Philippe, although anyone privy to his thoughts might have been forgiven for wondering whether this was a reverent response to the priest's closing prayer, or a determined confirmation of his own long-delayed quest.

* * *

"The Findlays' butler is removing the knocker from their door," Penelope observed with a sigh, idly tracing a raindrop down the glass with her forefinger as she watched the procedure from the drawing room window overlooking the narrow street. "Everyone seems to be going to Brighton. At this rate, there will be no one left in Town by the end of the week but us."

"If the only alternative is driving to the coast in this weather, I would much prefer to stay here," put in Caroline, looking up from the copy of *Mother Goose's Melody* she was reading to her son.

"Surely it won't rain throughout the entire month of August," protested Penelope. "In any case, it would be lovely to visit the sea, even if one could only look at it through the windows."

She looked to her mother for confirmation, but Mrs. Fayre only shook her head.

"I'm afraid it isn't possible. I've taken this house until Michaelmas, and I can't afford to break the lease. Nor can we afford to pay for two houses until the end of September, so don't ask," she added quickly, effectively silencing her daughter's arguments before they were uttered.

Penelope might have asked why, if they couldn't afford it, her mother had kept the lease on the house for fully two months after the Season had ended, but she suspected she already knew.

Mama had cherished hopes of hosting a betrothal ball during the Little Season in October, when the *ton* would return to London for the autumn session of Parliament—a ball financed, if not directly by the bridegroom himself, then certainly upon the Fayre family's expectations as spelled out in the terms of the marriage contract. The late summer months, Penelope supposed, were to have been spent in buying her bride-clothes.

Caroline interrupted her reading of "Hey, Diddle Diddle" to offer some encouragement to her sister. "Come now, Penny, spending the last days of summer in London won't be so very bad, you know. There will still be many ways you may amuse yourself, and without the crowds one finds during the Season. One can always walk in St. James's Park, or peruse the newest offerings at Hookham's Library, or attend the theatre, or look in the windows of all the Piccadilly shops, even if one can't afford to buy anything. In fact," she added diffidently, "I had thought to visit the linen-draper's to buy fabric for a new dress, or possibly two."

"*Two* new dresses, Caro?" Penelope chided playfully, seizing upon the chance to change the subject, at least until she could marshal her arguments to put to her mother at a more opportune time. "Such profligacy!"

"You must admit there are bargains aplenty to be had at this time of year," Caroline pointed out, flushing slightly. "Between the fact that their clients are departing London in droves and the upcoming competition from the cloth traders at St. Bartholomew's later this month, the linen-drapers are almost *forced* to lower their prices if they hope to sell the last of the inventory they laid in for the Season."

"Really, Caroline, I had no idea you were so knowledgeable about trade," said Mrs. Fayre, not at all certain she approved of her elder daughter's unexpected expertise.

"You forget that I was married to a vicar, Mama," Caroline reminded her with a smile. "His parishioners naturally confided their concerns to him, and *he* naturally confided *his* concerns to me. You would be surprised at the knowledge I have gleaned over the years."

Penelope hardly heard this exchange, for she had fixed upon one of Caroline's words. "St. Bartholomew's!" she breathed rapturously, the window, the rain, and the departure of their neighbors all forgotten. "Oh, Mama, may we go to the fair? Please, *please* let us! I've heard so much about Bartholomew Fair, but have never been. Oh, pray say we may go!"

"Good heavens, no!" cried Mrs. Fayre, appalled. "Whatever would you find to admire in such a place? Why, one hears the fair abounds with pickpockets and rowdies and vices of every kind—"

"So does Covent Garden, for that matter, but we go to the theatre there anyway," Penelope countered with unassailable logic. "As for the fair, what does one *not* find there? Rope-dancers and magicians and puppet-plays, and big wooden swings that one may ride in, and games to play, and fairings to win, and—"

"—And no place for a lady," Mrs. Fayre said firmly.

Penelope sighed. How could she ever make her mother understand that this was a large part of the fair's appeal? For here was a place where she would not have to worry about attaching an eligible gentleman—or, for that matter, worry about discouraging those gentlemen, eligible or otherwise, whom she had not the slightest desire to marry—but a place one could go for the sheer enjoyment of it, with no thought for the future. But Mama would hardly approve of such sentiments, even if she were capable of explaining them. No, the only thing that might satisfy her mother's notions of propriety was also the thing that would rob the outing of its joy: a gentleman's escort. Unless…

"Perhaps Oliver could take us there," she suggested.

Caroline observed in a murmured *non sequitur* that little pitchers had big ears, and Penelope glanced down at her small nephew, who had apparently lost all interest in aeronautical bovines and eloping tableware, and was now following the discussion with rapt attention.

"Surely no one could object to my going—*there*—with my own brother," she continued in less enthusiastic tones. "Besides, I daresay he would like to visit the—*that place*—too."

Her mother did not attempt to dispute this claim, but nor did she endorse the idea. "Yes, I daresay he would. But you forget that Oliver's time is not his own. His first responsibility must be to Lord Sparling, his employer. He hasn't the leisure to go gadding about Smithfield just because his sister wishes it."

Penelope opened her mouth to speak, but could think of no counterargument. She thought instead of her brother the last time she had seen him. He had obviously been torn between his responsibility to his sister and his duty to the employer on whose instructions he had been present, and while it had not been through any fault of her own that she had needed him to come to her aid on that occasion—not unless one considered her rejection of yet another marriage proposal a personal failing—there was no denying that she had placed him in an uncomfortable position. She could not do so again, and this time quite deliberately. Still, there was one other possibility, although she suspected Mama would like this one even less.

"Caro doesn't require an escort, since she is a married lady, or has been." She turned pleading eyes on her sister, who, at the age of seven and twenty, had long since reached her majority, and so possessed the further advantage of not requiring their mother's permission for any excursion she might wish to undertake. "Perhaps she and I could take—" She broke off, unwilling to raise false hopes in Benjy's six-year-old breast.

"I'm afraid I can't either, Penny," Caroline said, albeit not without sympathy. "I have taken a position of my own, you see, as governess to the Earl of Westermain's children."

Penelope's dark eyes grew round, Bartholomew Fair and its delights temporarily forgotten. "Caro? You're going to be a—a *governess*?" She turned to her mother for confirmation, but found that Mrs. Fayre, having made her point, had quitted the room, taking her grandson with her with promises of raisins from the larder. "Does Mama know?"

Caroline nodded. "I had to discuss the matter with her, of course, for I'm afraid Benjy's care will fall to her, since I will be residing beneath Lord Westermain's roof. You must see that I had to do something," she added quickly and, to Penelope's ears, defensively. "Mama's widow's jointure is small enough without compelling her to stretch it to support two more people."

"But Benjy," Penelope protested. "How can you bear to leave him?"

"That is the worst part of it." Caroline stroked the open book in her lap as if it were her son's fine blond curls. "But Lord Westermain's position with the War Office keeps him in Town for most of the year, and I shall have a half-day free every week, and a full day once a month to take whenever I please, so it is not as if I won't be able to see him at all. Heaven knows it isn't a perfect plan, but I don't believe such a plan exists, and in the meantime, I must do something, especially since—since it won't be long before he'll be going off to school, hard as that is to believe," she concluded brightly.

The abrupt change in her tone was jarring, and Penelope wondered what it was that her sister had stopped herself from saying. *Especially since you keep rejecting suitors? Especially since Mama may be forced to fund another Season for you in the hope that you may eventually find a man you might deign to accept? Especially since you refuse to pull your own weight?*

"But—But Oliver sends funds every month—"

"He sends what he can, of course, but secretaries aren't paid as much as all that. Besides, someday Oliver is going to want to marry, and he can't possibly support a wife and a family of his own when he sends most of his wages to his mother and sisters. It wouldn't be fair to expect him to provide for us indefinitely."

"I—I didn't know," Penelope said, rather stunned by all these revelations. "Oh, I know Mama is always saying that we must economize, but I didn't realize things had come to such a pass."

"We contrived to rub along well enough until this past spring," Caroline assured her, but Penelope was not deceived.

"Until my Season had to be funded," she said slowly, still trying to take it all in. For besides the hire of a house in a respectable part of Town, she'd also had to have a wardrobe capable of sustaining her through five months of near-constant dinners and dances and parties—sometimes two or three in one night—without her ever appearing to wear the same garment twice. And while she had danced and laughed and flirted and rebuffed eligible suitors, her mother and siblings had worked and scrimped and saved and told themselves that everything would come right again once she made a good—"good" in this case meaning "rich"—match.

Except that she hadn't. She'd had her opportunities—seven of them, in fact—but she hadn't.

"I—I didn't know," she said, although this sounded like a feeble excuse even to her own ears. "Why was I never told how—how desperate our situation had become?"

Caroline put her hand over her sister's and gave it a squeeze. "Never mind it, Penny. Mama did not wish to burden you with such a thing, and you only nineteen years old. In any case, she would not want you to marry a man you dislike, be he never so wealthy."

Penelope nodded distractedly, but her thoughts were elsewhere. She could almost hear the whispered discussions between her mother and siblings after she had gone to bed, discussions deliberately withheld from her because "Penelope isn't old enough to understand," or, worse, "Penelope shouldn't have to worry her pretty little head over such things."

To do them justice, they had probably not thought of it as deception; to them, no doubt, they were shielding her from adult concerns. *But I don't* need *to be shielded*, she thought with growing indignation. *I'm not a child anymore!*

No, she was almost twenty years old, and it was high time she took up the burden of adulthood and did her part to rescue her family from ruin. She would accept the next eligible offer of marriage she received, no matter what her feelings toward the supplicant might be.

But first, she would carry out one small act of rebellion, one little statement of defiance before submitting to her fate.

She would find a way to visit Bartholomew Fair.

3

"Caro," Penelope said hesitantly, rolling up a pair of delicate silk stockings with great concentration, "may I ask you a question?"

The two sisters were alone in the elder's bedchamber, packing Caroline's belongings in preparation for her removal to Lord Westermain's town house while their mother kept Benjamin occupied in an attempt to distance him as much as possible from these reminders of his mother's approaching departure.

"Of course." Caroline looked up from the serviceable brown merino gown she was folding to regard her sister with a mischievous smile. "That is, you may certainly ask, although whether or not I can answer may be another matter entirely."

Penelope either failed to take the joke or chose to ignore it, for her expression was serious, and her voice held a note of urgency as she asked, "What is it like? Being married, I mean."

Caroline studied the lovely, anxious face for a long moment. "By that rather comprehensive question, am I to understand that you want to know what married people do?

That is, what will be expected of you as a wife?"

Penelope nodded, blushing crimson.

Caroline took a deep, fortifying breath, trying to determine what, and how much, to tell her younger sister. She was firmly of the opinion that sending young women to their marriage beds wholly ignorant of what would take place there was hardly conducive to marital bliss; nor, on the other hand, was overwhelming them with too much information all at once. In the end, she resorted to a question of her own. "What has Mama told you?"

"She said a lot about doing one's duty as a wife, but as for particulars—" Penelope tucked the rolled stockings into a corner of the battered portmanteau that stood open on the bed, then picked up a petticoat of fine if somewhat threadbare cambric. "Mama called it 'a woman's burden,' which gave me the impression that it must be quite horrid. But Sophie de la Tour—she was at school with me, you know; her parents were French *émigrés*—she told the girls at school about a very handsome footman with whom she had a tryst, and *she* says…" There followed a breathless description of the precocious Sophie's amorous intrigues, at the end of which Penelope concluded, "But she is French, so I daresay she might have exaggerated. Some of the girls say she is rather *fast*, you know."

"Fast?" echoed Caroline, her eyebrows arching toward her hairline. "I should think she could give points to any entrant in the Royal Ascot! Still, what she told you is essentially correct."

Penelope wrinkled her nose. "But that sounds disgusting!"

"It does, doesn't it?" Caroline agreed, laughing. "And it is true that it may be rather uncomfortable at first, but—"

"Uncomfortable in what way?" interrupted Penelope, the petticoat in her hands quite forgotten. "Embarrassing, or painful?"

"Either, or perhaps a bit of both," Caroline said, albeit not without sympathy. "But that is only at first. If a man will be very patient and loving with his wife, and if a woman will concentrate on bringing pleasure to the man she loves instead of dwelling on her own discomfort, they may very soon discover that it is not uncomfortable at all, but instead something very special belonging just to the two of them."

"The man she loves," Penelope echoed softly. Recalling the task at hand, she folded the petticoat in half, then in half again, studiously avoiding her sister's gaze. "But what if she *doesn't* love him?"

Caroline laid the brown merino in the portmanteau and sat down on the edge of the mattress, taking her sister's hand and pulling Penelope down to sit beside her. "I'm sorry you're being put in this position, Penny," she said. "Perhaps if I had made a more advantageous match years ago, you would be spared the prospect of a loveless marriage now. But we didn't know, James and I. We had no idea that Papa would leave Mama so inadequately provided for, and there was no indication then of the illness that would take James's life."

"Caro!" Obeying a sudden impulse, Penelope threw her arms around her sister and hugged her tightly. "Of course you couldn't know! How can you think I would blame you for that?"

Caroline held her sister close for a long moment, stroking the dark curls so different from her own fair ones. "No, I know you would not. But, Penny, listen to me." She gently extricated herself from Penelope's embrace so that she might look her in the eye. "There are many people who might envy what Mama calls poverty, and yet they contrive to be happy in spite of their lack."

Penelope nodded in understanding. "Because they married for love," she said wistfully.

"That is true in some cases, but not all. I have known couples who were very happy together even though theirs was not a love match. But such marriages can only prosper when there is genuine affection between the husband and wife. Friendship may suffice in place of romantic love, but romantic love can never replace mutual respect."

"Surely no woman would love a man she could not also respect," Penelope protested.

Caroline gave a short laugh. "You would be surprised at the flaws of character a woman can overlook, provided a man's face is handsome enough. Of course, a man may do the same thing for the sake of a beautiful woman, but his situation is different. When a woman marries, she quite literally puts her life in her husband's hands, heart, body, and soul. Don't give yourself to a man you cannot trust to take the greatest care of them. To be trapped in marriage to such a man would be a—a poverty of the soul for which no amount of money could compensate."

Penelope made a noise which in a less beautiful young woman would have been called a snort. "I wish you could convince Mama of that."

"Never mind Mama. In the end, it is you, and not she, who will have to live with the man."

"Caro"—Penelope's fine dark eyes grew wide as a new thought occurred to her—"have you ever thought of marrying again?"

"Certainly not!" Caroline exclaimed, perhaps a bit too quickly. "I've had my chance at matrimony, and my time for marriage is long past."

"You're not so old as all that!"

"Pray do not talk nonsense." Caroline stood up abruptly, snatching up a dove-grey morning gown and briskly folding it. "In any case, I shan't have time for courtships and flirtations, for I shall be fully occupied in teaching Lord Westermain's children."

"If you were to marry again, you wouldn't have to become a governess," pointed out Penelope, warming to this theme. "You could stay at home with Benjy instead."

"And there's the rub," Caroline said. "Few men are willing to take on the responsibility of feeding, clothing, and educating another man's child. Then, too, there are Benjy's feelings to be considered. What would he think of me setting another man in his father's place? You see, I haven't the luxury of thinking only to please myself."

"Neither do I." Rolling her eyes, Penelope returned to the original subject with a sigh. "I have to think of pleasing Mama."

Caroline smiled, but kept to herself the observation that, although it was true that successful marriages might be built upon foundations of respect and friendship, no one who had once known wedded love could possibly settle for less.

* * *

One by one, the days of August slipped by. Caroline

removed to Lord Westermain's house to take up her position as governess, and although Penelope accompanied her mother to such amusements as were still to be found in London, her sister's absence left a hole that no amount of entertainment could fill. On those infrequent days when Caroline was freed from her responsibilities in the schoolroom, she not unnaturally wished to spend as much time as possible with her young son. And while it was true that Penelope was always delighted to see Oliver whenever he returned to the bosom of his family on his own free days, there was no denying the fact that, as Caroline had said, a man's situation was different.

Still, Penelope had one secret to which not even Caroline was privy. For at that very moment, she was awaiting the hackney that would bear her—along with Patsy, the upstairs maid who also served as abigail to the three Fayre ladies, and Jim, the greengrocer's son with whom Patsy was "walking out"—to Smithfield and Bartholomew Fair. Despite her sister's assurances, Penelope considered herself honor-bound to accept the next eligible marriage proposal she received; she could do no less, now that she knew the truth about her family's finances and recognized how many opportunities she had wasted. Today's trip to the fair would serve as a last taste of freedom before she resigned herself to her duty and gave herself—body and soul, at least, even if she could not give her husband her heart—to the man who would rescue her family from penury. She wished she had thought to ask Caroline if gratitude would suffice as a foundation for marriage.

In any case, she had not long to ponder the question, for at that moment a hackney hove into view, drawing to a stop as

Jim waved his arm to flag it down.

As it turned out, the question of how to get to the fair had been solved with surprising ease. Patsy had returned from her half-day just in time to dress the Fayre ladies' hair before dinner—Mama was determined that they should still dress for dinner every night—and as the maid had performed this task, she had hummed a little tune under her breath.

"You seem happy tonight," Penelope remarked, recognizing the lilting melody as "Johnny's So Long at the Fair." "You must have enjoyed your half-day."

"Oh, yes, miss!" Patsy readily agreed. Her eyes met her mistress's in the mirror, and Penelope noticed the girl's rosy cheeks and shining eyes. "Me and Jim—he's my young man, you know—we spent the whole morning and most of the afternoon at the fair."

Penelope gave a sigh of pure envy. "I wish I could go! But Mama won't hear of it. What was it like?"

Patsy had needed no further persuasion, but launched into a rapturous description of rope-dancers and play-actors, of dogs trained to jump through hoops and a clever pig who could count and do sums, of boat swings that made one feel as if one were flying and booths where one could buy succulent roast pork and fresh gingerbread, at last concluding with, "I would go back tomorrow if I could, for I'm sure one could go every day and still not have time to see it all!"

As she'd listened to these transports of delight, Penelope had conceived a plan.

"If you really want to go back tomorrow," she said thoughtfully, when Patsy finally wound down, "perhaps there is a way."

Patsy shook her head regretfully. "That there's not, miss, for I won't have another half-day for two weeks, and the fair only lasts for two more days."

"Yes, but you won't have to wait for your next half-day. You have only to accompany me on a shopping trip."

"Shopping, miss?" Patsy echoed, all at sea.

"Except that instead of going to Bond Street," Penelope continued resolutely, "we shall go to the fair."

Patsy wrung her hands, torn between duty and desire. "I don't like lying to the missus," she said, in a tone that clearly invited Miss Fayre to persuade her.

Penelope did not disappoint. "It's not really lying," she said coaxingly, ignoring the little voice in her head that whispered otherwise. "We *will* be shopping, only we'll be shopping for gingerbread and fairings instead of stockings and gloves."

"I don't know, miss…" Patsy's agitated hands twisted the folds of her skirts.

"If Mama finds out—that is, if there is any trouble, I will take full responsibility," Penelope promised, pressing a hand to her heart as an indication of good faith.

"Well…"

"Of course," Penelope went on, judging it time to deliver the *coup de grâce*, "we will need Jim to go with us, as protection against the criminal element with which, according to Mama, the fair abounds."

"I didn't think it was as bad as all that, miss," the little maid protested. "Still, I won't say I wouldn't feel a deal safer with Jim there with us, he being a man and all."

And so the thing was done. Over dinner, Penelope had asked her mother's permission to go shopping upon the morrow, and was relieved when this was granted without her being obliged to embroider her request with outright falsehoods about torn stockings or lost gloves. After that, it had only been a matter of walking around the corner out of view of the house, so that Mama would not see them enter a hired hackney, much less the fact that this vehicle set off in quite the wrong direction for the fashionable shops in Bond Street or Piccadilly.

Leaning back against the squabs to avoid being seen through the windows, Penelope resolved not to dwell on the more dishonest aspects of the scheme, but instead to concentrate on experiencing the glories of Bartholomew Fair to the fullest, storing up a day of memories to warm her heart over the long course of a cold, loveless marriage.

4

*O*hhh!"
Gazing in wonder at the transformation of what was usually open ground (not for nothing had Smithfield been named for the "smooth field" outside the walls of the medieval city), Penelope breathed a sigh of pure ecstasy.

A temporary city of booths had been erected cheek by jowl on the site, forming an almost unbroken ring around the perimeter. Inside the ring, a double row of tall booths built up on stilts stood back-to-back, separated from the outer ring by a wide avenue of what had once been mown grass, now looking rather the worse for the many feet that had trampled it during the fair's first day. Beneath the booths, tables had been set up wherever their owners could find a place, some offering fresh gingerbread or succulent roast pork for sale, others inviting fairgoers to risk their pennies on games where one might win such prizes as oranges, ribbons, handkerchiefs, or whistles.

The cloth market that had once drawn merchants from all over England and even some parts of Europe could still be found here, near the street to which it had given its name—

Cloth Fair—but the mercantile beginnings of the fair had long since yielded pride of place to more frivolous attractions.

And what attractions they were! One booth was papered with posters announcing the comic genius of Merry Andrew, along with feats of balance and dexterity displayed by a team of acrobats and tumblers all the way from Russia; another promised a reenactment of the story of Judith and Holofernes, performed entirely by puppets. A barker on a raised wooden platform announced that a new musical play in three acts would be starting in only ten minutes, and urged all those with a taste for the dramatic arts to purchase a ticket before all seats were filled. Meanwhile, another, striving to outdo his fellow in volume, invited fairgoers to feast their eyes on a collection of exotic animals from all over the world, while overhead, the talents demonstrated by a rope-dancer—a young woman who performed upon a rope strung from the church tower to the corner of the nearest booth—were scarcely more astonishing than her costume: a tight-fitting bodice of gold satin that made the most of her slender but curvaceous figure, worn with scarlet knee-breeches cut very full through the hip and thigh and tied with knots of ribbon, leaving her lower limbs bare save for spangled stockings that caught the sunlight and threw it back.

Nor were the attractions limited to the circle of booths. One could see a comic play at the George Inn Yard featuring the very same actors one would see at Drury Lane, for a fraction of the price. Enterprising residents of Long Lane and Cloth Fair sold ale and gingerbread from their back doors, while nearby pubs such as the Hand and Shears housed such human wonders as the Beautiful Albiness or the famous Miss Biffin, a skilled painter of miniatures in spite of her complete lack of hands or arms.

And the people! Ladies and gentlemen clad in silks and satins promenaded along the broad avenue separating the rows of booths as if they were taking the air in St. James's Park, and Penelope, recognizing several of these persons, avoided making eye contact and resolved to give them a wide berth. A man on tall stilts, standing head and shoulders above even the tallest of the fairgoers, tipped his hat and bowed with exaggerated courtesy to a family all dressed in their Sunday best, from the stout, red-faced father to the six children and even the baby in its mother's arms. Some little distance away, a woman in a low-cut satin gown made coy advances to a fellow whose weathered complexion and bow-legged stance suggested that he was a sailor returned to port. Suddenly, the man on the stilts was almost knocked off his balance by a youth, dressed in rags and none too clean, who darted through the crowd with a prosperous merchant huffing and puffing in hot pursuit and shouting "Stop, thief!" whenever his breath would allow it.

A smattering of applause broke out as the stilt-man regained his footing (or whatever one called it), and he acknowledged his audience's approval with an elaborate bow, clutching the brim of his tall hat to his heart. As he straightened, he spied their little party and blew a kiss in their direction, sending Patsy into fits of giggles and prompting Jim to playfully put up his fists, provoking laughter as well as more applause from the crowd.

Penelope hardly noticed this exchange, for she was still dazzled by her surroundings. She wanted to see and do it all, and hardly knew where to begin. With so many delights clamoring for her attention, it was perhaps fortunate that Patsy and Jim, having sampled a number of these the day before, took charge of their itinerary, charting a clockwise course around the field that would allow them to revisit favorite attractions as well as take in new ones.

They marveled over a magic lantern show that portrayed the fall of Troy (during which Penelope reasoned with herself that Mama could surely find nothing to object to in so educational a presentation), then exclaimed with delight at the discovery of the raree show, a long wooden box punctuated at intervals with holes through which one might, according to the announcements painted in bold red letters on the box, view scenes from the battle of Trafalgar. Upon being informed by the barker that this treat would require a payment of one ha'penny each, Jim gallantly paid not only for himself and Patsy, but for Miss Fayre as well. Penelope might have objected—she suspected that she might be more able than he to afford the expense, despite Mama's claims of poverty—but as she had no desire to embarrass the young man (and certainly not in front of his sweetheart), she accepted with a good grace and resolved to repay his kindness at the first opportunity.

She had not long to wait. As they walked away from the raree show, exclaiming over the detailed model of HMS *Victory*, right down to the tiny figures swarming about her miniature deck, they drew abreast of a large theatrical booth with "Richardson's" painted in bold letters over the proscenium arch. Here a man stood on the edge of the makeshift stage, calling to fairgoers and demanding in lurid accents to know if they were brave enough to face the Skeleton Spectre.

Patsy ran to examine the posted broadsheet. "*Monk and Murderer! or, The Skeleton Spectre,*" she read aloud with ghoulish zeal, then, seeing that her beau had come up behind her, clutched his arm and exclaimed with a shudder, "I'm sure I would be scared to death!"

"I would be there to protect you," Jim pointed out, patting her hand reassuringly. "I wouldn't let the Skeleton Spectre get you."

While they debated (in flirtatious tones) Jim's ability to best the Skeleton Spectre in a fight, Penelope drew a little apart and spoke to the barker.

"How much for the three of us?" It was unlikely that the young lovers would have heard, caught up as they were in each other, but Penelope pitched her voice low all the same.

"One shilling each—but for you, miss, half a crown for the lot." If he thought it odd that a young lady would pay for their admission while her companions flirted—both of them clearly of an inferior status to hers, and one of them a man, at that—he gave no sign.

"Why, thank you!" Penelope said warmly, digging in her reticule until she found the large silver coin, which she dropped into his outstretched palm. "And if you will not let them know I paid, I would be much obliged to you."

"Anything you say, miss," he declared gallantly, and strode over to the pair still standing in front of the broadsheet, where Jim was doing his best imitation of a spectral monk. "If you'll step inside, the show will be starting directly," he announced, waving them toward the curtain flap in a grand gesture.

"How much—?" Jim began, reaching once more for his coin purse.

"For these two lovely ladies?" The barker shook his head. "Not a farthing. Their presence is an honor to my establishment."

In spite of her earlier protestations, Patsy was all eagerness, and her occasional giggles in the darkened theatre suggested that Jim was as good as his word. From the murderous monk they progressed to the up-and-down, an ingenious device something like an enormous cartwheel fitted with wooden seats along its rim that lifted passengers up into the air and down again as the wheel turned on its axis. Alas, as they drew nearer, it became clear that the seats were only wide enough for two people to sit comfortably side by side. Once again, Jim rose to the occasion, insisting that, since he had ridden the up-and-down with Patsy only the day before, that pleasure should now belong to Miss Fayre.

The young women took their seats in the contraption, Penelope covering her nervous anticipation by telling herself that, after the murderous monk, the up-and-down could hold no terrors for her. Still, she could not deny a certain feeling of relief when the barker lowered a hinged table of sorts across their knees, rendering it very nearly impossible for them to tumble out.

"It's very kind of Jim to surrender his place to me," Penelope told her companion, resolving *not* to look down when the machine came to a stop with their seat at the highest point, leaving their feet dangling over the void. "Especially when he must be wishing me at Jericho."

"Not at all!" Patsy, made of sterner stuff than her young mistress, leaned over the arm of the seat and waved enthusiastically at her earthbound swain, who observed their progress from his lowly vantage point on *terra firma*. "How could he, when you are making it possible for us to visit the fair again? Tomorrow is the last day, and who knows? By fair time next year, we may be married, and me in the family way."

"Are things as serious as that?" Penelope asked, taken aback. Marriage seemed suddenly to be everywhere. "Well, then, let me be the first to wish you happy."

Abandoning her beau for the nonce, Patsy turned back toward her mistress. "We're not formally betrothed," she confessed, looking somewhat sheepish. "But I'm thinking a Christmas wedding would be nice."

"*Very* nice," Penelope seconded warmly. "Jim seems to be a very agreeable young man."

"He's well set up, too," Patsy continued, practically swelling with pride. "His father is a greengrocer—but you know that, for I first met Jim when he came with a delivery of beans and lettuce for Mrs. Fayre—and since Jim is the only son, it'll all belong to him someday."

"Oh?" It occurred to Penelope that this was the fate of all women, whatever their class, this tension between the desires of their hearts and the necessities of life.

Something of her thoughts must have shown on her face, for Patsy quickly put in, "Not that I'd marry him for no other reason but that. The Good Book says it's better to live in the corner of an attic than to live in a fine house with a quarrelsome man." She frowned over this pronouncement, then added an amendment. "That is, it says 'a quarrelsome woman,' but it takes two to quarrel, so I reckon the same thing goes for men, too."

"I'm sure you and Jim would be happy together anywhere," Penelope said, then added mischievously, "And at the first opportunity, I promise to give you sufficient time alone together for him to declare himself."

The opportunity was not long in coming. Shortly after she and Patsy had exited the up-and-down, the three young people caught the sounds of fiddle and fife, and followed the music to a large tent bearing a placard that invited passersby to come inside and dance, for the modest fee of only a ha'penny per person. Penelope glanced at her maid and saw the look of pure longing on the girl's face. Surely after spending the last five months helping her and her mother prepare for four or five balls per week—sometimes even two or three in a single night—Patsy deserved the chance to do some dancing of her own.

"Why don't you two go inside and dance?" she suggested, earning a glowing look from Patsy and a grateful one from her swain.

Jim's brow puckered. "Are you sure you don't mind?" he asked, duty clearly warring with inclination.

"Not at all. I'll stay here and"—she cast a quick, appraising look about, weighing the attractions on offer in the nearby booths—"and watch the fencing, shall I?"

Patsy and Jim agreed to this plan with a fervor that was hardly flattering, but Penelope took no offense. She promised to obey Jim's admonitions that she not allow her reticule to dangle from its strings, but instead hold it tightly clutched in both hands so as not to fall victim to the thieves with whom the fair abounded. She urged them to enjoy themselves, and after watching them pay their admission and disappear through the flap into the tent, she turned and joined the crowd gathered at the base of a raised platform on which two men matched swords with feral intensity.

It soon became clear which of the fencers was the more skillful, as well as the popular favorite. Younger than his opponent by a decade or more, he appeared to be in his late twenties, and although his height was scarcely above the average, he possessed a lean, sinewy strength and an elegance of movement that held the audience in rapt attention. Eschewing the tailcoat, waistcoat, and cravat that were *de rigueur* for men's daywear, he wore only a plain white shirt tucked loosely into the waist of his breeches, his long, full sleeves buttoned at the wrist and his collar open at the throat. The fine cambric was now dark with perspiration, and the damp fabric clung to his skin in a manner that made Penelope's face grow warm.

The clash of steel on steel jerked her mind back to the matter at hand. The young fencer had disengaged his blade from that of his opponent and was now slowly circling his panting adversary with the air of a panther stalking its quarry, the point of his blade darting in and out in swift, sharp feints as if it were a live thing.

No one observing the match was ever quite certain of what happened next, or whether it was simply part of the act. The fencers were now perpendicular to the length of the booth, the bigger man with his back to the crowd, the younger facing it. Suddenly the younger man's eyes grew blank, his gaze fixed upon some point in the middle distance. His blade still parried the thrusts of his opponent, but his movements were like that of an automaton, his attention clearly elsewhere.

Then the larger man whacked the edge of his sword against that of the crowd's favorite with a force that made a few of the spectators nearest the booth instinctively duck their heads for fear their champion would lose his grip and his sword with its wicked blade come sailing into the crowd. Nothing so dramatic occurred, but there was no denying that the blow had awakened the young fencer from whatever spell had held him mesmerized. Gritting his teeth in a rictus grin, he launched into so aggressive a volley of thrusts that his opponent, forced into a backwards retreat, was hard-pressed not to step off the edge of the platform. On the very brink of the precipice, he dropped his sword and clutched his arm just above the elbow—and with this, the drawing of first blood, the contest was over.

The crowd reacted with wild applause, and Penelope so far forgot herself as to loop the strings of her reticule over her arm so that she might have her hands free to join in. The young swordsman acknowledged the crowd's appreciation with a deep bow, then ran the fingers of his free hand through his straight black hair, raking the damp strands back from his forehead and motioning for his defeated foe to join him.

"*Mes amis*," he announced in perfectly accented French, as his erstwhile opponent retrieved his sword and joined the champion at the front of the platform, "a show of appreciation, if you please, for my opponent and very good friend, Monsieur André de la Marche."

The crowd did not disappoint. The vanquished combatant made his bow and said, with no trace of French in his own speech, "As you can see, my poor skills pale beside those of Monsieur Philippe Valois."

If the crowd's appreciation of André was enthusiastic, the applause with which they greeted Philippe was nothing short of ecstatic. André was obliged to wait fully thirty seconds for their enthusiasm to expend itself—which he did with a patience suggesting that this was not the first time his victorious rival had been met with such a demonstration of approval.

"I wonder," he went on, once the applause had abated enough for his voice to be heard, "if there is anyone amongst you who might pay a shilling to pit his own skills against those of *monsieur*, with a crown piece"—he held up a large silver coin for their inspection— "as the prize if you best him in the duel. Will you, sir? Will you?"

André pointed to random men in the audience, most of whom were quick to demur, until at last, a group of young men, all of whom appeared to have been tarrying too long at the ale booth, succeeded in badgering one of their number into accepting the challenge. Scattered applause and a great deal of raucous laughter accompanied him as he climbed the stairs and paid the requisite shilling, whereupon André made a great show of accepting the young man's payment and presenting him with his sword. Following his lead, the young man took possession of the weapon with mock solemnity, then waved it through the air in a few experimental passes.

"If you will take your places, *messieurs*," André began, directing the new challenger to stand on a spot indicated by a large red X painted on the boards of the platform. "*En garde!*"

Even as he opened his mouth to give the "*Allez!*"

command to begin, he was interrupted.

"A moment, *s'il vous plaît.*" Raising his arm to belay the command, Philippe strode across the platform to where his opponent stood with sword at the ready. "In order to make certain it is a fair fight…" he said almost apologetically, then plucked the bead from the end of his opponent's blade and tossed it carelessly into the crowd, leaving his own torso vulnerable to the deadly point of his opponent's rapier.

A frisson of anticipation rippled through the crowd as they recognized that the danger to Monsieur Valois had just increased exponentially. In the light of this realization, *monsieur*'s next action seemed rash to the point of recklessness. Reaching into his sleeve, he pulled out a large square of black cloth resembling a handkerchief one might carry while in deepest mourning. But he did not mop his brow, or blow his nose, or any of the other things one might expect a man to do with a handkerchief. Instead, he gave it to André, who folded it once, then twice, until he'd made a long, thick strip, then—the audience gasped—tied it over Monsieur Valois's eyes like a blindfold. Having completed this task, he took the champion's arm and led him to his place on the platform, then stepped back and gave the commands.

"*En garde!*" he said once again, and then, "*Allez!*"

He had hardly given them the command to begin when the young challenger slashed wildly with his blade, forcing Philippe to leap back, instantly on the defensive.

Penelope covered her face with her hands, not daring to look. Still, she could not block out the ringing sound of steel on steel, and when a sudden shout rose up from the crowd, she was compelled to peer through her fingers at the combatants in spite of her inclinations. The challenger was still on the attack, having driven Monsieur Valois all the way to the end of the platform and, finally, down onto his knees, frantically parrying the flashing blade and its deadly tip. The crowd fell silent, holding its collective breath as it awaited the end. Would the young man show mercy, or, goaded by the earlier laughter of the crowd, would he be satisfied with nothing less than the champion's death?

Surely not! Penelope thought, horrified at the prospect of coldblooded murder being done before her very eyes. This wasn't a real fight, only a bit of sport for the amusement of the fairgoers. Even if the challenger had any murderous intentions, duelling was still illegal, and she recalled hearing somewhere that a special magistrate was always designated for the sole purpose of ruling on any disputes that might arise over the three days of the fair, an arrangement amusingly if obscurely dubbed piepowder court. If *she* knew that, when she'd never been to the fair in her life, then it must surely be common knowledge— common enough, anyway, to discourage the kind of senseless violence she feared.

And then, even as these frantic thoughts flitted through her head, Philippe surged to his feet, driving his stunned opponent before him in retreat from a blade that seemed to be everywhere at once. If the cheers of the crowd had been appreciative before, their response to this sudden change of fortune now bordered on delirium. But Penelope hardly heard the voices of the spectators pressing against her from all sides. She was conscious of nothing save for two rows of gleaming white teeth bared, incredibly, in a smile—not the rictus grin of a man putting forth great physical effort, but a smile of pure joy, the smile of a man doing what he loved—and knowing he excelled at it.

He's laughing at us, she thought with growing indignation. While they all watched with bated breath, fearing that at any moment his opponent's blade might find its mark, he was having the time of his life, knowing himself to be the superior of any man who might be persuaded to part with one shilling in the hope of winning five.

Feeling curiously betrayed and not a little foolish for having been so completely taken in, she did not wait to see the *denouement,* but turned and squeezed her way past the spectators, muttering apologies and deaf to any responses save for that smug, French-accented voice announcing, "Now, *mes amis,* is there anyone else who wishes to try his skills against mine?"

5

"D'you mind telling me what *that* was all about?" André demanded, lowering himself with a groan to sit on one of two camp stools.

The show was over, at least for the next twenty minutes, and the two fencers had repaired to the shadowy space beneath the platform, a dark cavern illuminated only by the narrow strips of sunlight filtering between the boards above their heads. The sounds and smells of the fair all around them still penetrated their sanctuary, but even the illusion of privacy was a welcome reprieve.

"I know you don't like the blindfold trick," Philippe said, abandoning his French accent as he dragged up the second stool and seated himself on it with the same unconscious grace that characterized all his movements. "But the crowd always loves it, and it's not as dangerous as it looks. I have only to determine whether my challenger is a slasher or a jabber, and plan my attack accordingly."

"I daresay this fellow was a slasher," André said, drawn into a discussion of strategy in spite of himself.

"Oh, yes. I knew it the moment he took the sword in his hands." He picked up his second-best rapier and, putting his finger to the bead that covered its sharp tip, idly pushed its two ends together until the fine Damascus steel bowed in a graceful arc. "You saw the way he waved it around. It's a curious phenomenon, but when one's eyes are covered, one's other senses become sharper. I can hear the wind created by the blade as it slashes through the air."

"And the—what did you call the other one? The jabber?"

"The jabber betrays himself with the quick intake of breath that precedes his thrust."

"One of these days," André predicted grimly, "you're going to get quite a surprise when you play off those tricks on a young man who's your equal."

Philippe shook his head. "I daresay it's possible, but unlikely. Pistols are the duelling weapon of choice these days, and few of the young bucks have ever held a sword, much less studied how to use it." He gave André a speaking look. "You ought to know that, from our ill-fated attempt to open a *salle* in Warwick."

André gave a reminiscent sigh. "Aye, they were hardly beating down our door."

"So you see, as long as my challengers are mostly young men wanting to impress their sweethearts, I'm actually quite safe. It's the man of middle age, who learned to fight with the sword during the last century, and who has kept up his skills— it is he who would pose the greater threat." He considered this last statement, then repeated, in quite a different tone, "Yes, it is a man of middle age who poses the real threat."

"That's as may be. But I wasn't talking about the blindfold trick, or the one where you fence with first your right arm and then your left. What the devil made you stand stock-still in the middle of a match? *That's* what I would like to know."

"I wasn't standing stock—"

"Oh, your blade was still moving," André said, readily conceding the point. "But your brain might have been a million miles away, for all the attention you were paying. You realize I could have run my sword right through you—and you'd have been well-served if I had!"

"But you decided to have mercy on me, and merely gave my blade such a whack that it all but jerked my arm out of its socket," Philippe said, grimacing as he massaged the arm in question.

"Maybe so, but you still haven't told me why it was necessary for me to take such an action."

"There was—" Philippe frowned, seeing again a slender figure in a plain but obviously expensive gown of yellow sprigged muslin, a heart-shaped face with wide brown eyes, framed by dark curls beneath a straw bonnet trimmed with yellow roses. Clearly a well-bred and apparently a well-heeled young lady. What was she doing wandering about Bartholomew Fair all alone? "—A girl."

André rolled his eyes with the air of one who has heard it all before. "Of course there was! Are you sure there was only one?"

"Believe me, this one would be enough for any man." He shook his head as if to banish the image. "But it doesn't signify. I'm well aware that I have nothing to offer a girl—*any* girl."

Suddenly restless, he rose from his camp stool and ducked through the curtain closing off the back of the booth, determined to see what he could of the fair before the next performance.

* * *

Outside the crush of people surrounding the fencing booth, Penelope stopped to take stock of her surroundings. She could not go far, certainly not out of sight of the tent where the dancing was taking place, for Patsy and Jim would expect to find her there when they returned, as she'd promised. But she had no idea how long that might be, and she had no intention of wasting her time at the fair doing nothing but standing around waiting for them. She brightened at the sight of a toy-booth enticing young fairgoers with riches ranging from the ever-popular "Bartholomew babies"—elaborately dressed dolls clad in miniature versions of the latest fashions—to the wooden swords coveted by small boys for generations.

In fact, there were two boys clamoring for just such a prize at that very moment, one pointing out the weapon of his choice while a smaller boy, probably his younger brother, tugged on the dark skirts of a woman who was most likely his mother. Or his governess, she amended, noticing that the clothing of the boys' elder sister, a girl in her teens who would certainly break hearts in the not-too-distant future, was of a considerably finer quality than that of the woman.

Benjy would love to have such a sword, she thought, feeling a sudden rush of affection for her little nephew, who sometimes cried for his Mama at night when he thought no one was awake to hear. As she considered how best to bestow such a gift upon the boy without arousing her own Mama's suspicions, she was struck with the thought that the smallest of the children clustering about the booth might even have *been* Benjamin: the slight, thin figure, the tousled curls of pale gold, the impatient little hand now twisting in the grasp of the slender woman wearing a dark pelisse and a close black bonnet…

Good God! It is Benjy—and he's with Caroline!

Penelope fought back the rising tide of panic that held her in its grip as tightly as Caroline's hand held her young son. This was not her sister's half-day—she always spent them with her son at the hired house in Upper Gower Street—so Caroline must have taken Lord Westermain's children to the fair as a special treat. *And after she wouldn't take me, the slyboots!* Still, Penelope conceded that to accompany the children on such an outing might comprise part of a governess's duties, and to include one's younger sister in addition to one's own son in the party might well stretch even the most good-natured employer's forbearance to the breaking point.

In any case, Penelope reassured herself, she had never met her sister's charges, so they posed no immediate threat. Benjy, however, was quite another matter, for he would certainly come running at the sight of his aunt. She must not let him see her, and therefore must do nothing that might call attention to herself—including, she told herself sternly, making a mad dash in the opposite direction, no matter how tempting such a course of action might be. Instead, she forced herself to turn away from the toy-booth with an air of indifference, all the while considering where she might go that would be simultaneously in Patsy's view and out of Caroline's.

Her speculative gaze fell upon a small table which she had previously overlooked, lost as it was amongst the raised booths that towered over it. It was set—if one could call it that—with three porcelain cups turned upside-down and arranged in a row, and was presided over by a short, stout man holding a long pole from which fluttered lengths of grosgrain ribbon in every color imaginable.

Seeing her interest, he called to her in a singsong cry. "Guess the cup and win a prize!" He swept his arm in a gesture that directed her gaze down the length of the brilliantly adorned pole and onto the plain wooden table with its three cups. "Come and play, lovely lady! Win a ribbon to wear in your bonny brown hair!"

Penelope hurried over, although she was less interested in winning a prize than she was in silencing the man's importunities before Caroline could become curious as to the identity of the "lovely lady" on whom he lavished increasingly extravagant compliments.

"Yes, all right, I'll play," she said breathlessly, resolutely turning her back on the toy-booth and its patrons. "How much is it?"

"For you?" He made a gallant bow. "Only a farthing—or, if you prefer, three for a ha'penny."

She groped in her reticule and withdrew a copper coin, then dropped it into the palm of a plump, none-too-clean hand. "Three, then. What should I do now?"

Somewhere behind her, a man's voice murmured something too softly for her to hear, but the hastily smothered guffaw that followed told her all she needed to know. Her cheeks burned, but she refused to give the men the satisfaction of knowing she'd heard the vulgar jest, let alone been put out of countenance by it.

"Something about guessing a cup, you said?" she continued with an admirable pretense of serenity. "Are these the ones?"

"That's them, miss." He stuck the lower end of the beribboned pole in the ground, much as an explorer might plant the flag of his native country in the soil of a foreign land. Then he leaned over the table and lifted the center cup to reveal the small round marble made of green glass that had been hidden beneath it. "I'll put the ball under one of these three cups, then you watch as I mix 'em up. If you can pick out the cup that has the ball underneath, I'll give you whichever ribbon your heart desires."

"That sounds easy enough," Penelope said thoughtfully, pondering the small green sphere as if she half-suspected it of harboring some trick through which to deprive the credulous player of her precious ha'pennies.

"Aye, nothing to it." As his hands went deftly to work, the stout man shook his head, apparently marveling at his own lack of business acumen. " 'Jack,' I tells myself sometimes, 'you'll never make any money if you keep giving away ribbons to every pretty girl you see at the fair.' But here I am the next year, sure as check, and when I close up here tomorrow, me and my ribbons'll be off to Stourbridge next morning, just see if we ain't."

Penelope made no reply, for she was fully absorbed in watching the cups beneath the pudgy hands, the center cup changing places first with the cup on the left, then with the cup on the right, then with the left again. She had not expected so large and ponderous a man to move so very quickly, and by the time his hands finally stilled, she had lost any sense of which cup concealed the little green ball.

Still, he looked up at her expectantly, so she pointed very much at random to the cup in the middle and asked, "That one?"

"Let's see, shall we?"

He lifted the cup with a flourish, and Penelope, letting out an "Oh!" of disappointment at finding nothing underneath, was surprised to hear a chorus of sympathetic exclamations joining her own; she had not realized that a considerable crowd had gathered to watch.

She had no time to wonder at this, and still less time to scan the group to ensure that her sister was not amongst their number, for Jack had paused only long enough to disclose the marble hidden beneath the cup on the left before returning all three cups to their original positions and beginning once more to mix them up. Penelope studied his movements with an intensity that her former dancing master might have envied, but although she made her selection this time with a good deal more confidence than she had felt on her first try, there was no green marble beneath the cup on the right. Instead, it was the center cup that would have won her the prize.

On her third and final attempt, she had a good deal of help in making her selection, for the assembled spectators were not shy in offering advice.

"The one in the middle," urged a bespectacled young man in the sober apparel of a clerk, who had spied Penelope as he and a friend were passing by en route to the exotic animal booth, and had instantly lost his heart to her. "Pick the one in the middle."

"No, no! The one on the right, there's the ticket."

"The left one!" called a faded young woman with a baby on her hip and a child clinging to her skirts. "Choose the left one!"

"The right!"

"The left!"

"No, the middle!"

She stretched out her hand and was just about to make her selection when a new voice, low and French-accented, spoke almost in her ear.

"You could always say 'Your right sleeve.'"

6

Penelope had assumed—if she'd thought about the young swordsman at all—that he must still have been at the fencing booth, playing off his tricks on some new mark. It was disconcerting (though not as distressing as it should have been) to find him standing practically at her elbow.

"Y-Your right—?" She glanced uncertainly from Philippe to Jack, and back again.

"I'll thank you to keep a still tongue in your head, you damned Frog," growled Jack, his previous good humor quite vanished.

"Such language, Jack," chided the Frenchman, clicking his tongue in disapproval. "And in front of a lady, too. Really, I'd expected better of you."

Jack gave a skeptical snort. "That's rich, coming from you!"

Philippe's smile never wavered, but something in his expression grew wintry. "Would you perhaps care to elaborate, *mon ami?*"

Jack obviously recognized the change in the Frenchman's demeanor, for when he spoke again, it was in a very different tone. "Well, we all do it, don't we?" he said defensively, sounding very much like a small boy caught with his hand in the proverbial cookie jar. "You're no better, with those parlor tricks of yours."

"Are you saying the ball is *not* up your right sleeve?"

Quick as a flash, he grabbed Jack's arm just above the wrist with his left hand, holding it in a grip of steel while he thrust his free hand into the deep, turned-up cuff of Jack's coat sleeve. A moment later, a small green ball fell onto the table, bounced twice, then rolled slowly across the worn surface until it bumped lazily against the rim of one of the three cups beneath which it was supposedly concealed. Silence reigned for a full second as the spectators pondered the significance of the small green sphere now resting against the china cup. Then, as if in response to some cue, the crowd burst into raucous laughter.

"You've been outwitted, Jack!" one man said, apparently compelled to point out the obvious.

"Aye, the Frog's got the better of you!" chortled another.

"Give the lady 'er ribbon!" commanded one gallant soul. "God knows she's earned it."

Others quickly took up the cry, unwilling to see a chit of a girl—and such a pretty one, at that—taken advantage of. In the end, it was Philippe who settled the matter.

"Come, man, give the lady her prize and have done with it. This crowd will settle for nothing less, and once they're satisfied, they'll disperse and you can go back to fleecing your fellow man with impunity."

"That's what *you* say," Jack grumbled resentfully, reaching for his pole of ribbons nevertheless. "You think they won't blow the gaff to everyone they meet?"

Philippe conceded the point cheerfully. "Oh, *naturellement.* And some of those people will be determined to try it for themselves, either to see if it's true, or just to see if they can catch you in the act. In any case, no one is likely to haul you before the piepowder court for the sake of a ha'penny ribbon." He turned to Penelope. "Which one do you want, Miss—?"

She ignored the implied question, addressing herself instead to Jack with an air of great dignity. "I should like the coquelicot ribbon, if you please."

Alas, dignity was wasted on Jack. "You'll have to tell me in English." He cast a resentful glare at Philippe. "You want French, you'll have to take it up with the Frog."

"Coquelicot *is* English! It's that one"—she pointed at the ribbon in question— "the poppy red."

"You want poppy red, you ought to say poppy red," Jack muttered under his breath. Still, he detached the ribbon from the pole and surrendered it to Penelope with a good grace.

"Thank you." Having taken possession of her prize, she walked away with her head held high and her nose in the air, although whether this performance was for Jack or the "Frog" was a point she preferred not to examine too closely.

She had not gone far when she heard herself hailed in French-accented English.

"Stop! Wait, Miss—you did say it was Miss, did you not?"

Penelope had said no such thing, and told him so. "And," she added, nettled, "why you should make such an assumption quite escapes me."

"Oh, I don't doubt you've had offers aplenty," he

observed, falling into step beside her. Then, perhaps seeing some hint of her dilemma reflected in her countenance, he added hastily, "My dear child, I meant no insult. Quite the contrary, in fact."

"I'm not a child, and I'm not your 'dear'!"

He sighed. "Too true, alas. Still, I can't help wondering exactly whose dear you are. Surely there must be someone in your life—if not a husband, then a parent, or perhaps an elder brother—who would warn you about the dangers of going to the fair alone."

This observation called Mama's warnings vividly to mind, and she said, perhaps a bit too vehemently, "I'm not alone!"

He made no attempt to dispute this claim, but turned very pointedly to look first left and then right, as if searching for an escort who was nowhere to be seen.

"My maid and her beau are with me." She hadn't intended to volunteer this information, but thought that—in this instance, at least—preserving her incognito was less important than making it clear to this disturbing young Frenchman that she was not utterly without protection.

"Are they?" asked Philippe, much interested. "What is it like, having invisible servants? I should think privacy would be a concern. One could never tell whether they were present to overhear one's conversations."

Penelope choked back laughter in spite of herself. "Of course they're not invisible! But I thought *they* deserved some privacy—they *are* courting, after all, and I'm sure they must have been wishing me at Jericho—so I told them that if they wanted to dance, they could visit the dancing-booth while I amused myself nearby. When they tire of dancing, they'll come back to me, and we can visit some of the other booths. What?" she asked, seeing him shaking his head.

"They may tire of dancing, but they won't tire of each other," he predicted with grim certainty. "I'm afraid you may find yourself deserted."

She bristled. "Patsy would never leave me alone here!"

"My dear girl, she already has! Even if she and her swain do come back for you," he put in quickly, anticipating her argument, "it seems a pity that your companions may enjoy themselves at leisure while your time at the fair must be limited to those attractions within sight of the dancing-booth. *Vraiment*, it makes one wonder who is the mistress and who is the maid."

"That's not true!" she protested perhaps a bit too emphatically. "I've been having a wonderful time: I've seen the tumblers, and the rope-dancer, and the reenactment of Trafalgar, and the play with the Skeleton Spectre, and I've ridden the up-and-down, and—and—"

"And had a ribbon off Jack's cup-and-ball game," Philippe concluded, glancing down at the length of colorful grosgrain she was tying to the top button of her pelisse. "Let's not forget that."

"And for that I have you to thank," Penelope acknowledged somewhat sheepishly. "I didn't know—I never thought he might not be honest. He seemed so very agreeable."

"My dear child, of course he did! How else is he to entice people into parting with their copper?"

"I told you before, I'm not a child!" she protested, flaring up once more.

"So you did," he said meekly. "Of course, now that we are

out of the shadow of the booths, I can see how old haggish you are."

Most young ladies would have been insulted to be so described, but to one who had spent the last several months hearing her eyes likened to stars and her teeth compared to pearls (and, in the case of one young cleric who had thought to advance his cause by quoting from the Song of Songs, her hair to a flock of goats descending from Mount Gilead), this disparaging remark was oddly refreshing. She choked back a laugh.

"Of course, if you really want to thank me," he continued, pressing his advantage, "you may do so by telling me your name."

"Very well," she said, acceding to this request. "It's Fayre."

"It is," he agreed. "After all, you know my name, so it is only fair that I should know yours."

She shook her head. "No, I don't mean it's 'fair.' It's *Fayre.* My name is Fayre."

"How very appropriate! 'Miss Fair' visits the fair."

She realized he thought she had given him a false name, but even as she opened her mouth to correct his continued misunderstanding, she realized this was exactly what she should done: given him a false name or, better yet, refused to have given him any name at all. It was not at all the thing to engage in conversation with young men to whom she had not been properly introduced, and certainly not the sort of young men who traveled the country as itinerant swordsmen performing at fairs. For that matter, it was not at all the thing to steal away from home to go to Bartholomew Fair with no one to accompany her but a servant and her beau, two people who were, as he had said, far more interested in each other than they were in playing chaperone. Still, that was exactly what she had done, so it seemed a bit late in the day for missishness now.

"So, 'Miss Fair,' what do you think of your namesake? Apart from being taken advantage of by unscrupulous cup-and-ball men, that is."

Her face lit up, temporarily depriving her companion and not a few of her fellow fair-goers of breath. "I think it's wonderful! Especially the up-and-down." She laughed in pure elation at the memory. "I felt almost as if I were flying!"

"I notice you make no mention of the boat swings, which are said to produce a very similar effect. Then, too, there are exhibitions that might interest you: the equestrian performers, for instance, or the Amazing Pig of Knowledge who can count and do sums, or the Beautiful Albiness, or—"

"Oh, no!" For a moment, Penelope had been sorely tempted to abandon Patsy and Jim to their own devices, and allow this intriguing young Frenchman to introduce her to those attractions she might otherwise miss. But as he outlined the delights in store for her, she felt compelled to object to one. "I should not like to see the Beautiful Albiness at all!"

"If you fear being outshone, I can assure you that hers is a very different sort of beauty from your own," he said dryly, and it seemed to Penelope that a hint of something like contempt had crept into his voice.

"Of course I don't fear being outshone! But how she must hate it, being pointed out and stared at, all because of the way she looks—" She grimaced at the memory of a very young man with spots who had attempted to peer down her décolletage whenever the movements of the cotillion had brought them together, and an elderly roué who had leered at her in a way that had made her feel as if she'd forgot to put on her stays

Philippe's shout of laughter jerked her out of these unpleasant recollections. "If that is how you feel, then you must certainly meet her!"

Without waiting for her consent, he took her arm and steered her away from the cup-and-ball game and the dancing-booth. She went without protest, but as they drew abreast of the fencing-booth, where André appeared to be demonstrating various moves for the benefit of a group of young boys who had apparently persuaded their parents to buy them wooden swords from the toy-booth, her steps slowed.

"Is it true what Jack said?" she asked, studying her jean half-boots with great interest. "Does everyone cheat?"

He pondered the question for a long moment before answering. "I cannot speak for everyone," he said at last. "To be sure, there are some who do, for what else is one to make of Jack? But if I may be forgiven for boasting, I can assure you my skills are such that I have no need for cheating."

"So you couldn't see through your mask after all?" asked Penelope, relieved out of all proportion by this claim.

"Indeed, I could not."

"Then how did you——?"

He raised his hand, cutting off the question before it was asked. "But you cannot expect me to give away all my secrets!"

"I wouldn't tell anyone," she said coaxingly.

"Certainly, you would not," he agreed, laughing. "For then

they would know that you stole away to the fair, and that you fell into conversation with a gent—with a young man to whom you have not been properly introduced. I will say only that when I cannot use my eyes, I must use my ears, and the soles of my feet. Will that suffice?"

She gave him a sidelong look. "I daresay it must, for I surmise that is probably all the answer you will give me."

He sketched a small bow. "You surmise quite correctly," he said, making her giggle.

"Forgive me," she said, suddenly serious, "but I thought fencing was a skill for wealthy men." A faint glimmer of something like hope stirred in her breast, and she asked, "*Are you a wealthy man?*"

He shrugged. "Who can say, these days? One hears of vast fortunes being won and lost every night in the gaming hells of London, while in France, one may own a vast fortune one day, only to be left without a *sou*—or, worse, a head—the next. There is a great crowd attending the fair today, is there not?"

Penelope recognized this sudden *non sequitur* as a blatant attempt to change the subject, but let it pass, suspecting that she had touched him on the raw.

By all accounts, the size and scope of the fair had grown exponentially since its twelfth-century beginnings, and the wholesale cloth trade for which it had originally been granted a charter was now no more than an afterthought. The Bartholomew Fair in this year of 1814 was almost wholly given over to pleasure—a trade so thriving that its attractions could no longer be contained within the boundaries of the "smooth field" from which the section of London just north of the City derived its name. The various inns and pubs bordering the fairground had been quick to meet the demand, and many of the fair's wonders were now to be found in private establishments along its periphery, from theatrical performances and horse-riding exhibitions in the yard of the Greyhound Inn to wonders of nature both animal and human presented in the private rooms of nearby pubs.

It was within one of these latter—the George, by name—that one might, for the modest sum of one shilling, behold the lady known far and wide (according to the placard prominently displayed in the window of this establishment) as the Beautiful Albiness. For half a crown, one could not only see the lady, but even purchase an engraved portrait and have it inscribed in her own fair hand.

Penelope was inclined to balk outside the door of the George, but Philippe resolutely paid two shillings for their admissions and gently but firmly steered her inside, assuring her blithely that she and the lady whose charms were on display would be quite enchanted with one another. With this glib prediction, he flung open the door to the private parlor with a flourish, and Penelope beheld the Beautiful Albiness.

Much as she objected to anyone being stared at simply because of their appearance, Penelope found it difficult to obey her own vociferously stated precepts. The lady in the private parlor was not much older than Penelope herself, and although she was seated, it was evident that her figure must be universally pleasing—neither too tall nor too short, neither too stout nor too thin.

But her skin was the pure white of porcelain, its delicate

hue reflected in her high-waisted gown of white muslin. Flesh and fabric alike contrasted strikingly with the black velvet cloth draped over the sofa on which she sat. Save for a few short curls at her temples, her long, silky hair was worn loose over her shoulders, and was as white as her skin. More striking still were her eyes, which were of a silver-grey hue so light as to appear almost colorless, and which were framed by eyelashes that gave the impression of having been dusted with freshly fallen snow. Penelope found herself recalling the watercolor image of a winter princess reproduced in a book of fairy tales she'd had as a child.

"Why, Philippe!" exclaimed the young woman delightedly upon recognizing her newest client. "Don't tell me my favorite performer at the fair has abandoned me for another! I thought you were going to marry me and take me away from all this." The wave of her pale hand took in the parlor and its furnishings, from the sofa she sat on to the paper that covered the windows lest passersby peek in and see the Beautiful Albiness for free.

Philippe gave a regretful sigh. "I could not find it in myself to deprive England's male population." Dropping Penelope's arm, he strode across the room and raised the white hand to his lips with exaggerated gallantry. "Miss Harvey, allow me to present 'Miss Fair.' The two of you have a great deal in common."

"Miss Harvey." Penelope dipped a curtsy, painfully aware of having been caught out in the same behavior which she deplored. "I'm very pleased to meet you."

The Beautiful Albiness rose from her seat to make a curtsy of her own. "Likewise, I'm sure."

"Miss Fair," Philippe continued, addressing himself to Miss Harvey, "finds it appalling that women should be stared at merely because of their appearance."

"Not just women," Penelope objected. "No one should be obliged to endure such an indignity!"

Miss Harvey's lips twisted in a droll moue that invited Penelope to share in the joke. "Pray save your breath, Miss Fair. Men think they have only to say we are beautiful, and we will forgive any rudeness on their part."

"Yes!" exclaimed Penelope, surprised and gratified to hear her own frustrations with the London Season expressed so succinctly. "And in addition to forgiving them, the odious creatures think we ought to feel flattered by their attentions!"

Miss Harvey nodded sagely. "And can't understand why we don't realize what a compliment they are paying us. I can see you know exactly how it is!"

"I've never been exhibited at a fair," Penelope conceded, suddenly self-conscious as she recollected the difference in their respective stations. "But I've just had my first Season, and at times it felt as if I were being put on display."

"Like the horse market here at Smithfield," agreed Miss Harvey. "Has anyone asked to examine your teeth? I wouldn't put it past them."

Penelope choked back a laugh. "No, but pray be careful about saying such things out loud. I shouldn't want to give anyone any ideas."

Philippe shook his head sadly. "We men are beasts, one and all. If I promise not to examine your teeth, will you both do me the honor of allowing me to treat you to gingerbread? Miss Fair has become separated from her companions, and I have taken it upon myself to introduce her to the delights of the fair," he explained to Miss Harvey. "Since she is no doubt growing hungry by now, my duty is clear. Do say you will join us!"

"Thank you for the invitation, but I'm afraid I must decline." Addressing herself to Penelope, she explained, "I rarely go out in full sun, for the light hurts my eyes."

Penelope thought it was a great pity that Miss Harvey was obliged to stay all day at the fair without being able to enjoy it, and said so. Miss Harvey was quick to correct this misapprehension.

"Oh, I shall certainly enjoy the fair, but I shall do it later, after sunset." Her gaze drifted toward the paper-covered windows. "After all, you can't really say you've seen the fair until you've seen it at night, under all the lights."

They took their departure a few minutes later, yielding their place to a merchant's family eager to part with their silver in exchange for a look at the Beautiful Albiness.

"I can understand your abhorrence," Philippe told Penelope as they passed a pub offering fairgoers a look at a man only thirty inches high as well as a calf with two heads, quite as if they were equals. "But I know several of these people—many spend every year from spring to autumn traveling the country from one fair to the next—and for most of them, this is their best chance of avoiding the workhouse. In fact, many of them would not be welcome even in the workhouse. Little Simon Paap, for instance, could hardly keep pace with the treadwheel, and so would probably be reduced to begging for his bread. Instead, the Prince Regent saw him at the fair and was so taken with him that he held an audience at Carlton House, where Simon was presented to the entire royal family. And Miss Biffin, who has neither hands nor arms, is a talented portraitist whose patrons include the king as well as the Earl of Moreland, who sat for her to take his likeness."

"Oh," Penelope said, quite daunted.

"Of course, not everyone is so fortunate," Philippe conceded. "Those who are exhibited only to line the pockets of their handlers usually fare the worst. The 'Hottentot Venus,' for instance." He cast a scornful glance at a booth adorned with a poster featuring the image of an African woman with exaggeratedly large buttocks. "Her situation is little better than slavery, poor woman. And yet, for those with the freedom to choose, it's not a bad life, following the fairs."

The stout woman behind the counter appeared to be another of Philippe's friends, for they exchanged the familiar small talk of old acquaintances as he paid for the gingerbread and gave Penelope her portion.

"It must be an adventure, in any case, seeing different parts of the country and meeting different kinds of people," she said, resuming their conversation as they turned away from the gingerbread seller and joined the crowds swarming about the broad avenue of beaten earth that separated the rows of booths. "But don't you ever get tired of it? The—the *rootlessness*, I mean. Do you never think of settling down in one place?"

"Sometimes," he said, and his gaze grew distant, as if he were looking at some place very far away from the noise and the bustle of the fair—a place where, she knew instinctively, she could not follow.

And so she did not press him, but instead asked some innocuous question about his acquaintance with the gingerbread seller, and the conversation turned to less fraught topics. They walked for some time in companionable silence, fully engaged in savoring the moist, spicy cakes that certainly lived up to the promise of their tempting aroma. It seemed to Penelope that there was something particularly pleasant about conversing with a man so very ineligible that she need not give the snap of her fingers for his opinion of her, or hers of him.

All too soon, however, this idyll was interrupted by a feminine shriek.

"*There* you are!"

Turning with a start, Penelope saw her maid hurrying toward her, with the devoted Jim at her heels.

"We looked *everywhere*," Patsy continued breathlessly, although her blushes suggested that their search was not quite so diligent as she implied. "When we came out of the dancing-booth and you weren't there, I was imagining the most *dreadful* things!"

Covered with mortification, Penelope dropped Philippe's arm and pressed her hands to her cheeks. "I'm so sorry! I had meant to stay nearby, indeed I did. I watched the fencing for a while, but then I saw Caro—er, Mrs. Cummings. My sister," she added as an aside to Philippe. "And although I love her dearly, I'm not at all certain that she wouldn't consider it her duty to tell Mama. I'm not supposed to be here, you see," she confessed, quite unnecessarily. "Mama thinks I've gone shopping."

Philippe's eyebrows rose, and when he spoke, there was the merest tremor of laughter in his voice. "*Sacré bleu!* How could she have come by such a notion?"

Penelope resolutely ignored him. "But I couldn't bear to waste my day at the fair in hiding! I thought the cup-and-ball game might serve, at least until she had moved on, so I stopped to play, only Jack cheated, and then Philippe—that is, Monsieur Valois"—she gestured toward her companion—"Monsieur Valois is the one at the fencing-booth, and since he travels with the fair, he knows all the people in it, and he knew Jack was cheating. So he made Jack give me the prize he'd cheated me out of, and when he—Monsieur Valois, that is, not Jack—when he offered to show me about the fair—well, I accepted."

Her conclusion held a trace of defiance, for her companions had listened to this rambling speech with eyes widening in incredulity at the sight of Patsy's wellborn mistress being squired about Smithfield by a strange man of dubious background.

The strange man himself must have been aware of the awkwardness of her situation, for he retreated a step, bending gracefully in a bow that encompassed the little group. "And now that you are reunited with your companions, I will yield to their prior claims."

Instinctively, Penelope clutched his sleeve. "Oh, but must you?" She had spoken impulsively, but once the words were out, she blushed at her own brazenness. "That is, I'm sure you could point out all the best attractions to us," she amended, with a truly admirable attempt at flippancy.

"I am honored by your kind invitation, Miss Fayre, but I fear I must return to my own booth before poor André fears I have abandoned him."

With a final nod of farewell, he began to walk away, and it seemed to Penelope as if her previous enjoyment of the fair had suddenly turned to dust and ashes. She was still trying to make sense of this abrupt change when he stopped and turned back to address the group.

"Some people say," he observed in a tone every bit as indifferent as hers had been, "you haven't really seen Bartholomew Fair until you've seen it at night."

Without waiting for a response, he strode off in the direction of the fencing-booth, and was soon swallowed up in the crowd.

7

"Well?" Jim asked, regarding his female companions with quizzical expectancy.

Penelope had insisted that they leave the fair shortly after Philippe's departure, lest her mother wonder at their long absence and begin to suspect they had *not* gone to peruse the fashionable shops of Piccadilly after all. In fact, the attractions of the fair had suddenly seemed rather flat—so much so that, aside from wishing she'd had the opportunity to have her fortune told, or to ride in the big, boat-like swings, she was able to abandon it with very little regret. Now they were once again seated in a hired hackney, being borne southwestward away from Smithfield and into the more fashionable and, to at least one of the party, more staid environs of Mayfair.

"That was an invitation to come back tomorrow night, if ever I heard one," the young man continued. "I believe Miss Fayre has made a conquest. What do you think, Patsy? Ought I to defend her honor by measuring my steel against his?"

Although Patsy squealed in flirtatious terror at what would be her beau's likely fate were he to propose such a contest to the

Frenchman, Penelope responded to this sally with no more than a half-hearted smile. While she knew her honor to be uncompromised, she had no doubt that her mother would view an itinerant swordsman as the very last man whose attentions she ought to encourage.

They weren't "attentions," she insisted, arguing with herself mentally. *He thought I was alone, and only wanted to protect me. His actions were those of a gentleman, even though his profession is not.*

And if those actions might have been denied to a plainer female, well, what of it? The men of her own class were no different in that regard, as evidenced by the number of young ladies left to languish against the wall at every private ball or Almack's assembly. In fact, far from lavishing extravagant compliments upon her, he had seemed to regard her appearance with indifference, perhaps even contempt, as when he'd thought her reluctance to gape at the Beautiful Albiness had sprung from an unwillingness to be outshone by that young woman's ethereal charms. Far from feeling chagrin at her apparent failure to captivate, Penelope had found his indifference almost a welcome change. Almost.

Patsy and Jim were so fully absorbed with one another that they didn't seem to notice her uncharacteristic silence, and so she was left alone with her thoughts until the hackney drew to a halt on the same corner at which they had boarded a similar vehicle only a few hours earlier. Jolted out of a most unsatisfactory introspection, she hastily thanked Jim for his escort and accepted his proffered hand as she stepped down from the carriage, then she and her maid (after Patsy and her sweetheart had exchanged a somewhat more protracted farewell) retraced their steps to the hired house.

Here maid and mistress parted ways, with Patsy descending the curving stair to the service entrance below street level while Penelope entered the house through the front door. She passed the door to the drawing room and, glancing inside, beheld her mother standing before the mantel, a folded piece of parchment clasped to her bosom and a beatific expression on her face.

"*There* you are! Such wonderful news, and you nowhere in sight, why—" Her rapt expression yielded to one of puzzlement, and her eyes fixed upon some point in the general direction of her daughter's chest. "Penelope, my dear, what in heaven's name are you wearing?"

Too late, Penelope remembered the coquelicot ribbon she'd tied to the top button of her pelisse. The bright poppy hue might as well have been a flag announcing her disobedience to the world.

"Isn't it a pretty color?" Penelope ran her fingers through the long, fluttering ends, looking admiringly down at her prize, although her apparent fixation might have had more to do with avoiding her mother's gaze than with taking any pleasure in the sight. "It's called coquelicot, and it's all the rage just at present, you know."

"But *not* with a pelisse of primrose yellow, I think," said Mrs. Fayre, frowning at the offending addition to her daughter's toilette. "Very nice for trimming a hat or a bonnet, however, and just when—my dear, you will scarcely credit it! We have been invited to Markham Grange for a hunting-party!"

"But Mama, we don't hunt." Penelope, pointing out the obvious, was at a loss to account for her mother's enthusiasm for a sport she had often denounced as not only expensive, but dangerous into the bargain.

Mrs. Fayre waved a hand in airy dismissal. "Good heavens, child, what has *that* to say to the matter? The Grange is in Leicestershire, you know—the seat of the Barons Markham for generations! And Lord Markham," she added in a voice heavy with meaning, "is a widower."

Penelope could hardly believe what she was hearing. "*Lord Markham?* Why, Mama, Lord Markham is *old!*"

"Nonsense! I daresay his lordship isn't a day over forty, and with *such* an air! And just that touch of silver at the temples that lends a man such distinction! They say he hasn't so much as looked at another woman since his wife and son died, so I never *dreamed*…" Her mother prattled happily on, blissfully unaware that her daughter's heart had suddenly abandoned its usual location, and had taken up residence in that young lady's sturdy half-boots.

This is it, then, Penelope thought. She had rationalized her clandestine visit to Bartholomew Fair by insisting that it would be her just (if premature) reward for accepting the next eligible offer she received. But with so many of the *beau monde* having departed London for Brighton or their country estates, she'd consoled herself with the thought that she was unlikely to receive such an offer until the following spring, when next year's Season began. Perhaps, she now realized, she'd even secretly indulged the hope that the family finances would not permit of a second Season in London, and so she would never be compelled to make good on her self-made bargain at all.

"When is the party to be, Mama?" she asked, keeping her

voice steady with an effort, and schooling her features into an expression of pleasurable anticipation.

"Not until the first of November." Mrs. Fayre handed her the invitation so that she might read the glad tidings for herself. "Thank heaven, for it gives us time to order new clothes! We didn't bring your riding habit to London, for setting up a stable in Town was out of the question, and I could never have held my head up if you'd been obliged to promenade in the park dressed in that old thing in any case, for it was made for Caroline, you'll remember—although she has grown so thin since poor James took ill that I daresay—but that is neither here nor there! You must have a new riding habit, as well as a new pelisse warm enough for the cooler temperatures, perhaps trimmed in fur with a muff to match—chinchilla, perhaps, or ermine..."

Penelope made no reply, for she was hearing a very different voice, a masculine voice with the faintest of French accents. *You've never really seen Bartholomew Fair until you've seen it at night...*

* * *

"A lecture on *astronomy?*" Mrs. Fayre echoed incredulously, regarding her daughter with displeasure. "Really, Penelope, I can't think what's come over you. First you spend the Season behaving like the most arrant flirt, and now you appear to be turning bluestocking! How you can ever hope to find a husband—you, who of all my children might have made the most brilliant of matches! I vow, you might as well plunge a knife into your mother's bosom!"

As if in demonstration, she pressed a hand to the bosom in

question. Penelope listened to her mother's protests in shame-faced silence, unwilling to add further embellishment to the story she'd spent the past twenty-four hours concocting—the story that would, she hoped, make it possible for her to return to Bartholomew Fair, and to the intriguing young Frenchman she'd met there. *Perhaps*, she thought sheepishly, *Mama had not been entirely wrong when she'd derided it as a bad influence.*

Meeting no resistance from her youngest child, Mrs. Fayre took advantage of the unexpected silence to expound at length, finally concluding with the observation that, after having rebuffed some of the most eligible gentlemen in London, it would be just like her daughter to throw herself away on a penniless scholar.

"Caroline married a penniless scholar, and she was quite happy with him," Penelope pointed out. "And you can hardly deplore a match that resulted in Benjy."

This proved to be a happy gambit, for Mrs. Fayre was instantly diverted. "Poor little Benjy," she said with a heavy sigh. "To lose his father in such a way, and then, just when I'd hoped Caroline might be persuaded to look about her for a suitable stepfather for the poor little mite, what must she do but go off governessing! If she is so eager to teach children, she might begin by teaching her own!"

"And so she has done, Mama, for the last two years and more," Penelope reminded her. "But she can hardly instruct Benjy in Latin, for she hasn't any herself. So she must have money to pay for his lessons."

"*Latin!*" The single word held a world of scorn. "Much good *that* will do him!"

"But he must have it if he is to attend Eton or Harrow," her daughter pointed out reasonably, "along with philosophy, and mathematics, and—"

"I'm sure mathematics must be the same no matter where one learns them," insisted Mrs. Fayre, unconvinced.

Penelope readily conceded the point. "Mathematics would be the same, yes. But where else is one to make friends with the sons of dukes and earls? The same friends," she added while her mother considered this point, "who, once they are grown men, may remember Benjamin Cummings with fondness, and be willing to help him establish himself. Recall that it was just such a friendship that led to Oliver becoming secretary to Lord Sparling."

"My poor, dear boy!" Overcome with emotion, Mrs. Fayre withdrew a handkerchief of fine cambric from her sleeve and loudly blew her nose into its folds. "When I think of my unhappy son, forced to support his mother and sisters when he ought to be thinking of marrying and having children of his own!"

"Oliver has never seemed particularly unhappy to me," Penelope said, dispassionately considering this claim.

"Only because men don't talk about these things," Mrs. Fayre observed sagely. "But believe me, my dear, a mother *knows*. And when I see my poor boy, the sole support of his family, and all because his sister cares for nothing but balls and parties, and won't lift a finger to ease his burden—"

"*Mama!* How can you say such a thing, when the whole purpose of those balls and parties has been for me to find a husband? I'll lift as many fingers as you wish, but at least allow me the luxury of choosing who I am to lift my skirts for!"

"*Penelope!*" cried Mrs. Fayre in shocked accents. "Wherever did you learn such vulgar language?"

Irrepressibly, a dimple appeared in Penelope's cheek. "From Caroline."

"I'll swear she never did so! In fact, I should have said she would be the *last* of the three of you to say such a thing."

"She was only telling me what I might expect as a married lady," Penelope said, torn between guilt at having unwittingly exposed her sister to their mother's displeasure, and relief at the knowledge that so long as Mama was complaining about her elder daughter, she was less likely to examine too closely the misdeeds of her younger one.

"That is for your husband to do," Mrs. Fayre pronounced primly. "Why, I remember when I was first married—"

At this juncture, however, Mrs. Fayre's recollections were interrupted by the arrival of her poor, dear boy, Oliver himself, entering the drawing room unannounced.

"My son, my son!" she exclaimed blissfully, enveloping him in a maternal embrace. "I vow, I was never so pleased to see anyone! Here is Caroline gone for a governess, and now what must Penelope do but plague me to allow her to attend a lecture on astronomy tonight!"

"Astronomy?" He glanced at Penelope for confirmation, and was apparently satisfied by what he saw. "I'll admit, I never thought of Penelope as particularly bookish, but—"

"Oliver! How can you say so?" chided Penelope, playfully indignant. "The first thing I did after arriving in London was take out a subscription to Hookham's library."

He bent a mischievous look upon his sister. "Minerva Press romances don't count, my dear." Turning back to their mother, he picked up the thread of their interrupted conversation. "Still, Mama, many ladies these days take an interest in scientific subjects. Penelope was educated in the globes, just the same as any other young lady, so it's not so far-fetched to think she might extend her study of the celestial globe to the actual sky. Some even equip themselves with a spyglass or a small telescope for just such a purpose, so if all she asks is to attend a free lecture on the topic, I should say you've got off remarkably lightly."

Mrs. Fayre wrung her hands indecisively, and Penelope noted without surprise that her brother's arguments, by virtue of his being male, carried a good deal more weight than her own.

"But my dear boy, we can't have people thinking her a—a *bluestocking!*" She spoke the word in a hushed voice, as if she were repeating a profanity she'd overheard on the streets.

"Would you prefer them to think her a shameless flirt who cares for nothing but dancing and clothes?"

This home question so perfectly echoed her own previous complaints that Mrs. Fayre was left with nothing to say. She heaved a sigh of resignation.

"Very well, Penelope, go to this lecture you're suddenly so keen to hear." On a more hopeful note, she added, "There may even be a few eligible gentlemen there, for now that London is so thin of company, there is such a dearth of entertainment that they may find nothing else to amuse them."

"Oh Mama, *thank you!*" cried Penelope, showing every intention of throwing herself upon her mother's bosom.

"But" —Mrs. Fayre wagged an admonishing finger in a

fruitless attempt to quell her daughter's effusions— "you must take Patsy with you, for I have no intention of chaperoning you to such an affair. Why, I should very likely die of boredom."

Penelope assured her mother quite truthfully that she would never ask her to make such a sacrifice. Mrs. Fayre paid no heed, for she had turned a speculative gaze upon her son. "Oliver, I don't suppose you could escort Penelope to this lecture?"

To Penelope's surprise, Oliver flushed crimson. "I'm afraid not, Mama. I'm, er, otherwise engaged."

"I can't honestly say I'm surprised," Mrs. Fayre grumbled. "Say what you will, Lord Sparling works you a great deal too hard."

Oliver neither confirmed nor denied this charge, saying only, "He pays me very well for my trouble."

"And so he should, for he gives you a great deal of it. But you will stay for tea, will you not?" she asked, reaching for the bell pull.

He shook his head. "Not today, Mama. I was only in the area on an errand for his lordship, and thought he would not object to my stopping by for a moment. But I must be getting back."

"So soon? Why, you've only just arrived!" A noise from the floor above put a halt to her protests. "And there is Benjy wakened from his nap. Penelope, my dear, will you—"

"I'll show Oliver out," Penelope offered hastily, before she could be dispatched to the nursery.

Mrs. Fayre rose and shook out her skirts. "Yes Oliver, I suppose you must go now, before Benjy sees you and starts begging you to play bounders or blind man's buff. If ever a child needed a man in his life—! Caroline would be better served looking for him a stepfather instead of flitting off to be a governess to other men's children…"

She was still complaining as she left the room and started up the stairs.

"Did Caro flit?" Oliver asked in mild curiosity. "I wish I might have seen it!"

Penelope swatted her brother's arm affectionately. "No, of course she didn't. It was heartbreaking, really, watching her tell Benjy goodbye and bid him be a good boy for Mama. Whatever Caro's reasons, no one can accuse her of making such a decision lightly."

He stopped as they reached the front door and regarded his sister quizzically. "And what of *your* reasons?"

"What do you mean?" asked Penelope, all innocence.

"Astronomy lectures?" He raised one skeptical eyebrow. "Since when?"

She peeped mischievously up at him through her lashes. "You made it sound so reasonable that I'm almost tempted to go to one someday."

"Cut line, Penny. I daresay you're planning to go somewhere tomorrow night, but I'll wager astronomy forms no part of your plans."

"No. In fact, I'm going to Bartholomew Fair!" She told him the whole story, including the hunting-party invitation and her determination to accept any marriage proposal that might result from it, and how Bartholomew Fair was, to her, a brief celebration of freedom, after which she was resolved to do her duty by contracting a loveless marriage. Curiously enough, she made no mention of the very obliging Monsieur Philippe Valois. Still, her account held more than a trace of defiance, as if daring her brother to inform their mother of her plans.

He refused to take the bait, however, only saying, "I wish I could convince you that these machinations are unnecessary. Mama wouldn't expect you to marry anyone you dislike."

"Oh, wouldn't she just?" scoffed Penelope.

"If she tries to force you into such a marriage—good God, I can't believe we're talking about Mama this way!—in any case, Caroline and I will support you, I promise."

"I'm sure you would," Penelope allowed generously, then added, "but you won't be here, will you? Neither will Caroline. How can you expect to help me when you won't even know what's happening to me?"

This home question effectively silenced him, and it was only after a long moment that he said, "About your going to the fair, though… I suppose there's nothing I can do to stop you, since, as you say, I won't be here. Still, I wish you had some other escort than a maid scarcely older than you are."

"Patsy is almost twenty-one," she insisted, as if the achievement of one's legal majority represented the epitome of wisdom and maturity.

Oliver made no answer to this, but reached for his coin purse and withdrew a large silver coin, then dropped the crown piece into the palm of her hand and curled her fingers closed around it. "I daresay you'll want to purchase some fairings to remember your big adventure by. Still, for God's sake keep your wits about you, and be sure you hold back enough money to cover the cost of a hackney ride home, in case you should need it. So don't spend it all on fripperies," he concluded in mock severity, and tweaked one of her curls just as he'd done when they were children.

"Oliver," she said impulsively, "what do you know about Lord Markham?"

"Nothing, really," he said, after considering the question. "I believe he came into the title when his elder brother was killed in Paris during the Revolution. His nephew, Freddie Markham, was at school with me. Freddie hadn't a lot in his brain-box, but he was a very good sort of fellow. About his uncle, though, I'm afraid I can't tell you much. Why do you ask?"

Penelope shrugged. "No special reason. Oliver, do you ever think about marriage?"

His eyebrows rose. "My own, do you mean, or marriage in general?"

"Either. Both. It just occurred to me that moving in Lord Sparling's circle must bring you into contact with a great many marriageable young ladies, and I wondered if you'd ever met one you should like to marry. I know his lordship's daughter is very pretty—"

Oliver cut her off with a short laugh. "Lady Diantha Sparling wouldn't look at me if I were the last man on earth."

And with this pronouncement, he kissed his sister's cheek, told her to make his farewells to their mother, and took himself off.

8

If Bartholomew Fair had been impressive by day, it was magical by night. The tall theatrical booths were still there, as were the humbler food and drink booths that lined the perimeter of the grounds. But now the broad avenue that separated them was strung with colorful Japanese lanterns, their lights flickering and bobbing with every breath of wind that stirred. The performances taking place on the high, makeshift stages were illuminated from above by still more lanterns, and from below by a row of improvised footlights consisting of candles burning in small tin buckets. It seemed to Penelope as if a marvelous fairyland had sprung up, if not quite in the middle of London, then certainly amongst its nearest suburbs.

It appeared that many Londoners shared this view, for there were even more people here tonight than there had been in the light of day. Great crowds pressed close to the stage where Mr. Richardson's players enacted a scene from *The Friend Deceived*, enticing spectators to pay their sixpence and come into the booth to see the play in its entirety. Somewhere nearby, cries of "Stop! Thief!" suggested that the swindlers, dodgers, and pickpockets who made the fair notorious were present as well, taking advantage of the darkness to ply their dubious trades more effectively.

Penelope had scarcely a thought to spare for any of them. All her attention was fixed on a point at some distance down the long row of booths, where a brilliantly lit sign summoned fairgoers to witness "incredible feats of derring-do" demonstrated by the "Blade of Paris," the master of swordplay having come all the way from France in search of a challenger worthy of his steel. As for her companions, Patsy and Jim saw nothing to wonder at in her eagerness to reach this booth, each incorrectly assuming that she shared their own enthusiasm to see Jim try his luck against the Frenchman.

They reached the fencing-booth just in time to see Philippe press the tip of his blade to the chest of his most recent opponent—an act which would have skewered the young man, had it not been for the bead covering the deadly point. The crowd burst into rapturous applause, which Philippe acknowledged with a deep bow. He then turned to salute his vanquished foe, inviting the crowd to join him in paying tribute to the other man's courage, if not his skill.

Lastly, André stepped forward to issue the usual invitation. "Is there anyone else who is brave enough to pit his skills against those of Philippe Valois, the Blade of Paris? Only tuppence to challenge him, with this crown piece to the winner!" He held up the large silver coin for everyone to see.

Jim thrust his hand up. "I will!"

"Ah! We have a challenger!"

He beckoned for Jim to come forward, and the crowd

parted to allow Jim, followed closely by Patsy with Penelope bringing up the rear, to reach the steep wooden stairs leading up to the stage. Penelope was content to watch the contest from the foot of the stairs, but Patsy, now that the moment was at hand, was much inclined to cling to her beau's arm.

"You will be careful, won't you?" she pleaded.

Jim promised to do so, then promptly forgot all about this pledge as he reached the top of the stairs, paid his two pennies, and accepted the rapier from André.

"What is your name, sir?" asked Philippe, transferring his own weapon from his right hand to his left in order to shake hands with his challenger.

"James Michael Foster," said Jim, apparently feeling that only his full name was sufficiently impressive for the occasion.

"You are a fencer?"

"Er, no," Jim confessed sheepishly, drawing a ripple of laughter from the crowd.

"What, then, is your occupation?"

"I'm a greengrocer."

Philippe turned to the spectators with a Gallic shrug. "Greengrocer, fencer, what is the difference?"

The laughter was louder this time, and Philippe quickly waved them into silence. "No, no, no! If there are not the greengrocers, then how are we fencers to eat? Also, I believe there is one here who finds this greengrocer worth more than any number of fencers. Is this not so, *mademoiselle*?"

Patsy nodded, pressing her hands to her flushed cheeks in rather pleased embarrassment.

"*Très bien*. I shall not be too hard on him, then, *non*? I shall cut him into only two or three pieces instead of nine or ten.”

Patsy did not look notably reassured, and Jim's smile was rather uncertain, as if he were beginning to question the wisdom of this attempt to impress his sweetheart. But there was no time to withdraw from the challenge even if he had been inclined to do so, for André was showing the two combatants to their places and explaining the rules of the contest. Having done so, he stepped back and gave the commands to begin.

"En garde…prêt…allez!"

And then the contest began, André's voice drowned by the ringing of steel against steel. Philippe's manner—self-confident to the point of audacity—made it easy for Penelope to overlook the fact that his physique was unremarkable. His height was not above the average, and although he possessed a certain wiry strength, he lacked the musculature of Jim, whose formative years had been spent lifting heavy crates of cabbages or sacks of potatoes. Now, to her dismay and Patsy's delight, Penelope found that Jim was not only holding his own against a far more experienced opponent, but was actually driving him back, compelling the Frenchman to retreat step by step across the boards. The crowd responded, first with surprise and then with enthusiasm, and those who had previously sided with Philippe now transferred their allegiance to Jim. Penelope could only breathe a silent thanks that her rescuer had not seen fit to don a blindfold for the match, and shuddered at the picture conjured by the thought.

And then, just when it appeared Philippe could not take another step without tumbling off the raised stage, he went on the offensive, baring his teeth in a grin as he swept Jim's blade aside with one lithe movement and thrust his rapier forward in the direction of that startled young man's chest. The fickle spectators roared in surprised delight at having been, like Philippe's opponent, so thoroughly hoodwinked, and Penelope was surprised to find her fists clenched so tightly that her fingernails had left crescent-moon creases in the palms of her soft kidskin gloves.

With Philippe on the attack, the end came very quickly. At the conclusion of the contest, he shook hands with his laughing opponent and, after exchanging a few words with him, turned to present him to the crowd.

"I give you," he announced, "James Michael Foster, the Gallant Greengrocer!" As the audience applauded Jim's effort, Philippe strode up to the edge of the platform to where Patsy stood just below, regarding her beau with naked adoration. Philippe dropped to one knee and held out his hand to her. "I believe you will find him unharmed, *mademoiselle*. Of myself, however, I am not so sure." A ripple of laughter greeted this sally, which turned to loud hoots and still more applause as he lifted Patsy's hand to his lips.

Patsy blushed crimson at this unexpected attention, and Penelope was conscious of an uncomfortable sensation that she greatly feared was envy. Philippe, apparently oblivious of having evoked such turbulent emotions, turned his attention to the crowd at large, inviting anyone who dared to pay their tuppence and try if they could improve upon Mr. Foster's performance.

Penelope failed to notice whether anyone accepted this challenge, for she followed her companions as they withdrew from the crowd, Jim pausing occasionally to accept congratulations from first one spectator and then another, in between recounting his exploits to Patsy—a tale that certainly lost nothing in the telling. Penelope wasn't quite sure what she had hoped to gain from visiting Philippe's booth a second time, but there was no denying her disappointment at not having achieved her aim, whatever it had been.

He might at least have acknowledged my presence, she thought with rising indignation. But no, he had ignored her, choosing instead to drool all over her maid's hand.

Penelope was not vain—in fact, over the course of her brilliant London Season she had come to view her acclaimed beauty as more burden than blessing—but she was not accustomed to meeting with indifference from the men she met, and she found Philippe's sudden lack of interest bewildering. Jim had seemed quite certain that the Frenchman had fallen captive to her supposed charms, but nothing in Monsieur Valois's conduct toward her on this second meeting would appear to support this claim. Had he, in retrospect, regretted giving her cause to believe his interest was more deeply engaged than was in fact the case? How mortifying, if that were so!

Such was her tumultuous state of mind as they approached the popular attraction known as the "carriage without horses." This boat-like vehicle, large enough to accommodate two couples seated face to face, was made of wood and hung with stout ropes from the crossbar of a wooden frame some twenty feet high from which it swung back and forth, to the evident delight of its passengers. Some half-dozen of these contraptions were positioned at intervals along one end of the open field that constituted the fairground, and each had its own queue of would-be riders, all eager to take their turn.

"*There* you are!" a familiar French-accented voice called breathlessly from somewhere behind her.

Penelope turned and saw Philippe hurrying in their direction—no easy matter, as he was obliged first to swerve to avoid a collision with two stout men who appeared to have spent too long at the ale booth, and then duck out of the way of a pieman carrying his wares on a large tray balanced somewhat precariously on his head.

"I was beginning to think I would have to search for you all over Smithfield," he continued, addressing himself to Penelope. "I hope I have not kept you waiting."

She opened her mouth to inquire frostily why he should suppose her to have any expectations of him at all when Jim spiked her guns by asking with a grin, "What, no more challengers? I expect I set a standard too high for anyone else to make the attempt."

"Very likely," agreed Philippe, returning his smile. "In any case, I have left André to do battle on my behalf."

"We were just going to ride the carriage without horses," Patsy put in. "Won't you join us? Each one seats four, you know."

"I would not miss it," he said emphatically, then turned to examine the great wooden swings, some swooping back and forth in wide arcs while others stood temporarily still in order to disembark its existing passengers and take on new ones. "Which one has the shortest queue, do you suppose?"

After some discussion, they made their choice. As they worked their way through the crowd in its direction, Philippe took Penelope's arm and steered her around a remnant of gingerbread trampled into the grass by the passage of many feet.

"You are displeased with me," he said, lowering his voice just enough that the noise of the crowds around them would prevent their words from reaching Patsy and Jim, who were walking just ahead of them.

"What makes you say so?" she asked somewhat defensively, disconcerted at having her thoughts so easily read.

"If Jim had not spoken first, you would have annihilated me with a word," he said, his white teeth flashing in a knowing smile.

"I—I didn't like the way you mocked Jim." Since Jim himself clearly bore the Frenchman no ill will, this excuse sounded lame even to her own ears.

Philippe's smile evaporated, and his black eyebrows arched toward his hairline in real concern. "Did I do so? If this is true, I will beg his pardon."

"You let him think he was winning," she insisted, although she felt as if the ground were suddenly crumbling beneath her feet, as unstable as her argument.

"Would you have me embarrass him by defeating him in ten seconds or less?"

She regarded him uncertainly. "*Could* you have done so?"

He shrugged, but answered her question with one of his own. "And what pleasure would the crowd derive from watching a bully swordsman publicly humiliate his opponent? Perhaps they would prefer to see the challenger do well, at least for a time. Perhaps, too, some of them will say, 'had he done *this* instead of *that*, he might have won. I, who have seen this, shall challenge the Blade of Paris myself, and I shall win.'"

"At tuppence each," she concluded dryly.

The Frenchman made her a little bow. "Just so. After all, one must eat."

Penelope did not attempt to dispute this point, instead merely observing, "When you fought Jim, you didn't wear a blindfold like you did yesterday."

"Oh, so you remember this from yesterday?" he asked, looking immensely pleased with himself. "But this was before we met! Dare I hope that you feared for my safety?"

Too late, she realized her error. "I had to do *something* while I waited for Patsy and Jim!"

"Yes, and the fair offers so little to interest one, does it not? I do not wonder that you abandoned me in favor of Jack. But to answer your question, or rather, the question you did not ask, I did not wear a blindfold during my match with Jim because everyone watching could see that he was not my equal. I do not say this to boast, but merely to observe that few grocer's sons are schooled in the art of the sword. But when an arrogant young *aristo* stands in need of a lesson in humility, then I am happy to don the blindfold and serve as his instructor."

A trace of bitterness colored his words, and Penelope recalled stories she'd heard from persons of her mother's generation, stories of liberties taken by the French aristocrats of the *ancien regime* and the terrible vengeance wreaked upon them by the revolutionaries they had once oppressed. Philippe must have been only a child at that time, but surely even a child would have his own memories of those violent times. Had he suffered at the hands of those aristocrats? What would he think of her if he knew that she aspired to marriage with one of their English counterparts?

She might have done a bit of delicate probing, had they not at that moment caught up with Patsy and Jim, and now joined the queue for their turn to ride in one of the great swings. Their conversation grew strained, as she was now fully conscious that they might be overheard, not only by the maid and her beau, but by anyone else nearby who cared to listen. The silence gave her time to think, however, and when the motion of the swing slowed to a stop, she took advantage of the confusion caused by recent passengers disembarking and new ones being assisted to board.

"You said you hoped that you had not kept us waiting," she said to Philippe, her tone faintly accusatory, "as if we were expecting you to join us."

"I told you yesterday that you haven't really seen the fair until you see it at night," he reminded her. "Did you think that, having discovered you had taken my advice, I would make no attempt to join you?"

At a loss for words, Penelope tried to cover her confusion by looking jaded, but succeeded only in looking adorably con-fused. In truth, she didn't know quite what to make of him. She would have known how to deal with extravagant compliments, but on the few occasions when Philippe had made mention of her vaunted beauty, he had not couched it in flowery phrases, but only as a matter of fact, giving no hint of whether he admired her or not; he had behaved with equal gallantry to Miss Harvey, the Beautiful Albiness, and even the woman selling gingerbread, who was fifty years old if she was a day and weighed fifteen stone at the least reckoning. To be sure, he had tossed out a clear invitation to return to the fair, but this had not been directed at her exclusively. Nor, for that matter, had it been *her* hand that he had kissed when the opportunity had presented itself.

She was spared the necessity of making a reply, for suddenly it was their turn to climb into the big wooden structure, and all her attention was fixed on boarding the contraption without breaking her neck—no easy task, as it swung gently on its fulcrum with every movement she made. Having accomplished this modest goal, she sat down on one of the benchlike seats and arranged her skirts, only to be thrown into further confusion when Philippe sat down beside her, so near that their shoulders almost touched. Patsy and Jim climbed in next—not even at so egalitarian a venue as Bartholomew Fair would a maid take precedence over her mistress—and once they had settled themselves on the facing seat, the swing was set in motion, gaining in velocity and altitude with each arc until Penelope was obliged to put a hand to the crown of her bonnet to prevent its being tugged off her head by the wind created by their movement.

Higher and higher it went, and then, at its apex, the swing seemed to pause for one brief moment before plunging downward so suddenly that it seemed to Penelope as if her stomach had been left behind at the top of the arc. Her breath caught in her throat and, instinctively, her free hand clutched the nearest support. She did not realize until the swing began its next ascent that this was Philippe's arm.

"I—I'm sorry," she stammered, appalled at her own boldness. She would have released his arm at once, but he took her hand and drew it through the curve of his elbow, covering it with his own.

"I'm not. In fact, I rather liked it." His hand tightened on hers as the swing plunged downward once more. "It's quite safe, you know."

But safety, she saw with sudden clarity, was vastly over-rated. Some risks were eminently worth the taking.

"It's wonderful!" She smiled raptly up at him, and the moon and all the stars shone in her eyes.

9

What shall we do next?" Jim asked, quite as if the world had not just tilted on its axis.

The swings had gradually slowed to a stop, and the four had somewhat reluctantly disembarked. Now they stood once more on *terra firma*, surveying the brightly lit booths and debating their next course of action.

"We could see the exotic animals," Patsy suggested, gesturing toward a booth whose entrance was flanked by posters, one of a fiercely roaring lion and the other of a large grey elephant, its long trunk curved upwards.

"You two go ahead," Philippe said with a glance at Penelope. "I thought I might take Miss Fair to see Madame Theodosia."

"Who is Madame Theodosia?" Patsy asked.

"She's a fortune-teller," Jim answered. "I noticed her booth yesterday."

Patsy clapped her hands in anticipatory glee. "Oh, yes! Let's have our fortunes told!"

This proposal found no favor with her beloved. "Why

should we pay good money to be told what we already know?"

Patsy made no attempt to deny this wisdom of this argument, declaring instead for the exotic animals of Polito's Wild Beast Show. Left to their own devices, Penelope and Philippe made their way toward the fortune-teller's booth.

Madame Theodosia's tentlike booth was not difficult to find. It was smaller than most, since only one patron was allowed inside at a time, but it was certainly eye-catching despite the much larger booths dwarfing it on either side. Its crude wooden façade was covered with scarlet satin and emblazoned with a large, rather unsettling poster depicting a wild-eyed beauty with jet-black hair, both hands hovering with fingers splayed over an eerily glowing orb from which clouds of white smoke billowed. Long strands of beads hung from the booth's opening in place of a door, their facets sparkling in the light of the lanterns overhead with flashes of red, purple, and blue. Penelope regarded the bead curtain uncertainly, trying to decide how best to knock—or, failing that, how else to request permission to enter.

Philippe, at least, had no doubts on this head. He swept the curtain aside, setting its beads clashing together, and called into the dark interior, "Madame Theodosia? Are you there?"

"Of course I'm here," a voice grumbled, a woman's voice thick with an accent Penelope could not identify. "What do you want?"

"I've brought you a charming customer," he said, glancing at Penelope. "She wishes to have her fortune told."

"Send 'er in, then." She sounded rather impatient, as if he should have known to do this without being told.

Penelope gave him a brave if somewhat tremulous smile, then ducked through the opening in the curtain he still held.

Seen from inside, the scarlet cloth covering the walls appeared blood-red in the feeble light of two tallow candles set in gleaming pewter candlesticks. The noises of the fair seemed oddly muted, and the air within the small chamber was redolent with the heady odor of burning incense. Penelope had the curious sensation of having been whisked away from the fairgrounds entirely and set down inside a Romany camp.

As her eyes adjusted to the darkness, she saw that the tentlike chamber was unfurnished save for a small table and a pair of three-legged stools. The table was covered with a black cloth and contained, in addition to the two candles, two stacks of cards, one rather larger than the other. There was no sign of any glowing orb, smoke-emitting or not, and Penelope was not sure whether to be disappointed or relieved by its absence.

The space's only other occupant, she deduced, must be Madame Theodosia. If Madame had ever looked like the painted image outside, that likeness had long since faded. To be sure, the eyes that glittered in the candlelight were indeed dark, and the hair visible beneath the woman's colorful scarf was as black as jet. But the hooded eyes were set in a face lined with wrinkles, and the dusky tresses were threaded with silver. Far from her painted representation, Madame Theodosia was at least sixty years old.

Penelope had not long to ponder this discovery, however, for the woman asked, in a thick accent, "So you wish to know what your future holds?"

Penelope nodded. "Yes, if you please."

The fortune-teller regarded her with one black eyebrow raised. "Sometimes it is better not to know these things."

"I can see where it might be," Penelope said thoughtfully. "Still, I should like to—to be prepared."

"Ah, well." Madame Theodosia gave herself a little shake that set the gold hoops at her ears dancing. "Sit down, then, and we'll begin."

Penelope obediently sank onto the stool the older woman indicated, while Madame Theodosia seated herself on its counterpart on the opposite side of the table. She picked up the smaller of the two stacks of cards with one hand, and stretched out the other hand, palm up, across the table.

"Cross my palm with silver, my dear, and we'll see what the cards have to say."

Penelope tugged open the drawstrings of her reticule and withdrew, albeit not without a pang, the crown piece her brother had given her the day before. "Will this do?" Following the woman's instructions, she bisected the open hand with the edge of the coin first this way and then that in a crisscross pattern, then placed it in the hollow of the deeply scored palm.

"Yes, very well."

Having secreted away the coin with the skill of a conjurer, Madame began laying out the smaller stack of cards face up in three rows of seven cards each. Penelope was surprised to discover, not the familiar red and black hearts, spades, diamonds, and clubs she knew from playing ombre with Mama and Caroline on those rare occasions when she had no other engagements, but curious pictures of people dressed in vaguely medieval costume: the Emperor, the High Priestess, and the

Hermit were there, as were personifications of abstract concepts such as Strength and Justice and heavenly bodies such as the Sun, the Moon, and the Star. More ominous were the winged and horned Devil and the skeleton on horseback labeled Death.

"Look over the cards, and choose the one that most speaks to you," instructed Madame Theodosia.

Penelope looked up from her perusal of the cards. "Do you mean the one I like the best? Or the one I think is most like me?"

"The one that most speaks to you," repeated the old Romany woman, unhelpfully.

Clearly, she was on her own. But which one should she choose? She looked somewhat wistfully at a card bearing the legend "The Empress." Unlike her stern masculine counterpart, the face looking up from the tinted pasteboard wore a serene smile, and her head was adorned with a crown of stars. In the background, a deer drank from a flowing stream. Everything on the card spoke of peace and serenity—and nothing could have been further from Penelope's own state of mind.

Her gaze fell on a card called "Strength," and her hand hovered over it for a moment as she studied the figure of a lady in flowing robes stroking the mane of a fierce lion. She would certainly need strength to go through with a marriage of convenience to an as yet unknown man. Still, there was one thing about the card that puzzled her.

"Which one is supposed to represent strength?" she asked, shifting her gaze from the cards on the table to the woman seated opposite. "The lady, or the lion?"

The fortune-teller nodded, and the gold hoops in her ears

winked in the candlelight. "Which one, indeed? Will the lady tame the lion, or will the lion devour the lady? An excellent question."

Despite her approval of the query, however, the old Rom woman made no attempt to answer it. In the end, Penelope decided, there was only one card that fit.

"This one," she said, and picked up the card labeled "The Fool."

The old woman nodded sagely. "An interesting choice. What made you decide on this one?"

Penelope sighed. "Because I feel like a fool. I had a choice to make—I knew I had—but because I put it off, I—I wasted my chances, and now the decision is out of my hands."

"It may please you to know"—Madame Theodosia swept up the twenty remaining cards in one deft movement—"that the Fool has nothing to do with your wits, or lack of them. It represents innocence, and the beginning of a journey."

"A journey?" Penelope thought of the hunting-party invitation that had sent her mother into such transports, and felt slightly ill. "A journey to where?"

Again the black eyebrow rose. "That depends. Let us see what the cards can tell us."

She placed the smaller stack of cards on top of the larger, then shuffled them together with an agility that seemed to defy her age. The rings on her gnarled fingers flashed in the candlelight as she placed The Fool face up in the center of the table and laid out ten cards face-down on the table in a crisscross pattern, with four on the left side of the Fool ("These represent your past," she explained), one above it, one below ("These two are the present"), and another four on the right side.

"And these suggest the future," she concluded. Having completed the spread, she turned over the card nearest to the Fool on its left. It portrayed two children in the garden of a cottage, playing amidst six large golden goblets. "Besides the cards you have already seen, the tarot contains four suits: wands, cups, swords, and pentacles. This card is the six of cups. Like the Fool, this card also suggests innocence, this time in your past. You had a happy childhood, yes?"

"Very happy," Penelope agreed. So happy, in fact, that she tried not to think of those days, as her memories only made her present situation, as well as Caroline's and Oliver's, all the more intolerable.

Madame Theodosia turned over the next card, and Penelope recognized it as one of the more disturbing of the cards she'd been instructed to choose from. Instead of the pleasant scene on the six of cups, this one showed a tall tower crumbling beneath a dark sky streaked with flashes of lightning. The legend at the bottom read, "The Tower."

"This card indicates destruction. Some disaster has stricken your family."

Penelope nodded, thinking of her father's death—not only the loss of a beloved parent, but the family's radically changed circumstances in the aftermath, from the sale of her father's stables to their own removal to hired lodgings in the village, and the sight of strangers living in the house that rightly belonged to Oliver. The memories were so unpleasant that she was relieved when the fortune-teller turned over the next card.

"It's upside-down." Instinctively, Penelope reached for the

card to orient it in the same direction as the others.

Madame Theodosia put out a warning hand. "No, don't touch it. The meaning changes when a card is reversed."

"What does it mean, then?" Penelope tilted her chin, the better to examine the card in which a young man regarded a bush bearing seven large gold coins. Each coin was marked with a five-pointed star.

"The seven of pentacles represents reaping the rewards of one's labors. Reversed, it suggests a reluctance to work, perhaps refusing to see that one's circumstances require it."

"Oh," Penelope said in a small voice. She had accused her mother and siblings of treating her like a child, but perhaps they'd had good reason. Perhaps she had *acted* like a child, clinging to the memory of more prosperous days and refusing to accept the fact that those days were gone—and that only she had the power to bring them back.

She had not yet fully processed this thought when the fortune-teller turned up the next card, revealing a smiling man surrounded by goblets of the same type shown on the earlier card, the one with the happy children.

"The nine of cups," pronounced Madame Theodosia, "speaks of frivolity and the pursuit of pleasure."

Penelope thought she had never heard a better description of Bartholomew Fair. Or, for that matter, of the London Season. *And while I waltzed at Almack's,* she chided herself, *the bailiff was practically at the door.*

"Mind you, pleasure-seeking is not always a bad thing," the old woman continued, as if Penelope had spoken her thoughts aloud, "but like anything else in this life, it can be misused. Too much merrymaking may be nothing more than an attempt to avoid one's responsibilities, or to ignore unpleasant circumstances. Perhaps the remaining cards will tell us if this is the case."

Having shown Penelope an all too accurate portrait of her past, Madame Theodosia turned her attention to the cards above and below the Fool—the cards which, she claimed, would reveal the inquirer's present situation.

I don't need cards to tell me that, Penelope thought, but leaned a bit closer nonetheless. Then the next card was revealed, and she gasped. The picture on the card was that of a woman standing alone, blindfolded and with her arms tied behind her back. Eight swords, each almost as long as the woman was tall, were driven into the ground around her, surrounding her like a high fence. *Or a prison.* The thought rose unbidden to her brain, confirmed almost at once by the old Romany woman.

"You feel trapped," she said. "Like the woman on the card, you can see no way out of your present circumstances. But there may be hope yet. Let us see what else the cards can tell us."

The card directly below the Fool portrayed a man with an armload of long wooden sticks. His face was turned away, but his stooped back suggested the weight of his burden.

"The ten of wands," said Madame Theodosia in her heavily accented English. "You have an obligation to someone, a responsibility you fear is too heavy to bear. But look." The rings on her gnarled fingers winked in the light as she pointed to a detail Penelope had not noticed before. In the background, a cluster of buildings indicated a village or small town, presumably the man's destination. "You have not much farther to go. The end of your journey is rapidly approaching, and will soon be in sight. Shall we see what your future holds?"

Without waiting for Penelope's assent, she turned over the first of the "future" cards, the one directly to the right of the Fool. The High Priestess, a woman in flowing blue draperies, was revealed, although this card, too, was upside-down, just as the Seven of Pentacles had been. *Reversed*, the Romany woman had called it.

"You have a secret." The fortune-teller sounded almost accusatory, and her black eyes, glittering in the candlelight, were inscrutable.

Penelope could hardly deny it. "Mama doesn't know I'm here," she confessed. "But surely that would be the present, would it not?"

"You may soon have another secret, or be charged with keeping a secret for another. Perhaps the next card will shed some light."

But the next card, when it was revealed, was equally cryptic. It portrayed a man in flowing robes, his arms outstretched before a table on which lay a sword, a pentacle, a cup, and a wand—each of the four suits. The man's splayed fingers seemed to suggest that he wielded some power over the objects or what they represented.

"The Magician." The old Romany woman nodded sagely. "Here is a man who knows what he wants—and knows how to get it. He is a man of passion, perhaps even danger."

The man I shall marry, Penelope thought, with a hollow feeling at the pit of her stomach. He did not sound like a very admirable man, for all his determination. Was that the danger

Madam Theodosia spoke of?

"Wh—What kind of danger?" she asked rather breathlessly.

"The cards do not speak in such detail," was the not very satisfactory answer. "They only suggest and, sometimes, warn."

"Is this card meant as a warning, then?"

The bony shoulders rose and fell in a shrug. "Perhaps; perhaps not."

While Penelope considered this vague response, Madame Theodosia turned over the next card. "Ah, here is a card that may be more to your liking. The Knight of cups signals a lover's approach."

"A man of passion and danger," Penelope said in a flat voice.

Madame Theodosia looked up at Penelope through her black brows. "Some women find such men attractive."

Some women are not being forced to marry them, Penelope thought. But no, that was not right. She wasn't being forced; she had made a bargain with fate that she would accept the next eligible offer she received, if only she could experience Bartholomew Fair first. And so she had, not only once, but twice. Surely she was now doubly obligated to accept whatever future Fate had in store for her. Still, it would be nice to have some idea of what to expect.

Almost as if the fortune-teller had read her thoughts, Madame Theodosia chose that moment to turn over the penultimate card, and Penelope's eyes widened. To describe its design as strange would have been an understatement. No persons in medieval garb looked up from the brightly colored pasteboard. Instead, a disembodied hand emerged from a cloud, its fingers cupped about a large gold coin embellished with a five-pointed star. Below the mysterious hand, a lush garden bloomed along the lower edge of the card, and a mountain range comprised the far horizon.

"Its appearance may be startling, but you have nothing to fear," Madame Theodosia assured her. "This card predicts wealth, and the beginning of a new life."

"A new life as a married woman?" Penelope asked, knowing and yet dreading the answer.

The old woman's black eyes keenly assessed the questioner, taking in every detail of Penelope's brown hair, glinting with chestnut lights in the candlelight, her porcelain skin, and her large dark eyes, the pupils so dilated in the dimness that they appeared to be inky black pools.

"Very likely," she said dryly. One beringed finger tapped the one card remaining face down on the table. "This last card may be considered the most important card of all, since it reveals the outcome, the result of all the cards that have come before."

Preparing herself for the worst, Penelope straightened her spine, then nodded. "I understand."

She had not been aware that she was holding her breath until she let it out. For, to her relief, the tenth and last card was lovely. A colorful rainbow adorned with ten goblets arched across the top half of the card, while the bottom half showed a man, a woman, and two children playing in front of a house that was presumably their home.

"The ten of cups is one of the most positive cards in all the tarot," Madame Theodosia said in a congratulatory tone. "It represents family, contentment, prosperity, and happiness. A very lucky card indeed, yes?"

"Yes," Penelope agreed tonelessly, recognizing that she was to be the means, not the recipient, of this most desirable of outcomes. Suddenly it was all too much. The musky odor of incense made her senses swim, the smoke made her eyes sting, and the shadows cast by the dipping and bobbing candle flames seemed to close in about her like living beings. There was no offer of escape here. She might have saved her crown piece, for the cards had not revealed anything that she had not already known.

By making an advantageous marriage, she would make her family happy.

She must learn to be content with that.

* * *

Philippe had been leaning patiently against one of the satin-draped posts supporting Madame Theodosia's booth, but he straightened at once when the beaded curtain stirred and Penelope emerged.

"Well? I trust Madame Theodosia did not disappoint?" He had spoken playfully, but his smile quickly faded when he saw the expression on her face. "What is wrong?"

"Why, nothing!" she said a bit too brightly. "Why should anything be wrong?"

If he heard this question at all, he chose to ignore it. "If that woman has said anything to distress you—"

"No, not at all," Penelope insisted, although there was something in her voice that suggested quite the opposite. "She says I am to marry a wealthy man. Isn't that what every girl dreams of?"

"Every girl's parents, perhaps," he said, frowning thoughtfully at her. He took her hand and drew it through his arm, but did not release it. His fingers closed over hers as he steered her into a dark niche formed by the gap between Madame Theodosia's booth and the much larger one adjacent to it. "But it is my understanding that girls often dream of something very different for themselves. Tell me, are you being pressured into agreeing to such a match?"

Penelope shook her head, but her hand twisted under his, and her fingers clung as if to a lifeline. "No, not—that is, Mama had hoped that I would find a husband while we were in London, but as for there being any particular gentleman who— but Mama would never expect me to marry a man I could not quite like. Only I didn't meet any man I could love, either, and I must marry *someone*."

Philippe considered her dilemma for a long moment, then asked, "How old are you, Miss Fair?"

"Nineteen."

"There you are, then. You have plenty of time." Seeing she was not convinced, he added in mock solemnity, "Surely someone will turn up before your looks fade—another year or two, perhaps."

"But that's just what I *don't* have," she insisted. "That is, I thought I did, but then Mama said she cannot afford another Season for me, and in the meantime Caroline—my sister, Mrs. Cummings; she is a widow, and she has the dearest little boy!— but she has been obliged to take a position as governess in order to send Benjy to school, and my brother, Oliver, can never marry so long as he is obliged to support Mama and me out of his wages, and—and I might have accepted any one of *seven* marriage proposals and made things easier for all of them, only I didn't understand just how matters stood—or perhaps I didn't really want to understand—and I wasted my opportunities. So I made up my mind that I must accept the next eligible offer I receive, no matter how—how objectionable the gentleman who makes it," she concluded miserably.

He considered this impassioned speech for a long moment before deducing, "This visit to the fair, then—it is in the way of a last taste of freedom?"

"Something like that," Penelope confessed. "How did you know?"

"Let us say that I have enough experience of fairs to know that gently bred young ladies are rarely allowed to attend them with no more chaperone than a maid and her beau—delightful people, to be sure, but perhaps understandably more concerned with their own courtship than they are with your safety"—his lip curled scornfully— "else you would not be left alone with no other escort but an itinerant swordsman."

"I'm quite safe," she pointed out bitterly. "I'm to marry a wealthy and titled gentleman, remember?"

He regarded her thoughtfully for a moment, then said, "Miss Fair, no one can tell you your future; you must make it for yourself." Seeing she was not convinced, he added in an exaggerated whisper, "Besides, Madame Theodosia is really just plain Mary Shadwell of Yorkshire."

Penelope's eyes grew round. "Do you mean *she's* a fraud too? Just like Jack?"

He looked away from her, his gaze encompassing the row of brightly lit booths for a long moment before his attention returned to her, and he shrugged. "We're all frauds, in our varying degrees."

"But not you," she cried in real alarm. "Never you!"

His gaze fell, and he idly kicked at a discarded pork bone lying on the ground at his feet. "My dear girl, I'm the biggest fraud of the lot."

A thoughtful frown creased her brow as she considered this claim. "You're not really French?"

He was startled into a bark of rather humorless laughter. "If *that* were all! No, I am French, but a great deal of my childhood was spent in England. Or one may say that I am English, and a great deal of my childhood was spent in France." He made an ironical little bow. "You may call me a citizen of the world," he said, in a flippant tone that did not quite ring true.

"What, then?"

"Suffice it to say that I am the last person to give anyone advice on marriage, least of all someone like you."

"Heavens!" She wasn't quite sure how to respond to these self-recriminations, so she attempted to emulate his own flippant tone. "Do you mean to say you have a wife and family tucked away somewhere, pining for your return? I daresay I should consider myself fortunate that you kissed Patsy's hand and not mine!" She'd meant to sound arch, but the voice that came out sounded petulant, even to her own ears.

"Don't tell me that bothered you!" exclaimed Philippe, looking inordinately pleased with himself.

Penelope scrambled to retrieve her position. "Of course

not! If I'd wanted to have my hand kissed—which I don't!—I could find any number of gentlemen who would be happy to oblige me!"

"Of that, I have no doubt." Putting his hands on her shoulders, he drew her deeper into the shadows. When he spoke again, his voice was low and husky. "I daresay I can offer you no compliment that you have not heard, and despised, a hundred times before. So I will only say that if I were to kiss you, Miss Fair, it would not be for the entertainment of the masses. Nor, for that matter, would it be on the hand."

Perhaps it was the lingering odor of incense that mesmerized her, or perhaps it was the rhythmic stroking of his thumb against the tender spot beneath her ear. Whatever the case, she raised startled her eyes to his, and what she saw there made the breath catch in her throat. He studied her face for a long moment, then, finding what he sought, put his fingers beneath her chin and tipped it very slightly upward. Slowly, so slowly, he bent his head and lowered his mouth to hers.

Penelope had been kissed before. Over the course of her brilliant London debut, more than one suitor, overcome at finding himself unexpectedly alone with the object of his desire, had taken full advantage of the opportunity, seizing her in his arms and planting sloppy kisses on whatever part of her face happened to be nearest at hand—or at mouth, as it were. In truth, she had found these expressions of passionate devotion more than a little revolting.

But this…

This was something else entirely. She knew instinctively that, unlike her struggles to free herself from those unwelcome proofs of her swains' devotion, any show of reluctance on her part would lead to her instant release.

And so she was careful to make no move that might lead to so erroneous an interpretation, but closed her eyes and surrendered to bliss.

10

Penelope awoke the next morning to a feeling of loss, as of a beautiful dream interrupted, replaced by an overwhelming sense of dread. She opened her eyes and found that the sky above her window was just beginning to grow light. It must be very early; a glance toward the fireplace, its black maw just recognizable in the still-dark room, confirmed that Patsy had not yet come in to sweep out the grate and light the fire that was needed to drive out the morning chill even in late summer.

The thought of the maid stirred a chord of memory in Penelope's sleep-fogged brain. Patsy…something about Patsy…

Suddenly it all came flooding back: the fair…the kiss…the bright lights…the kiss…the sights and sounds and smells…the kiss…most of all, the kiss…

The kiss for which he had instantly apologized, as if the most wonderful experience of her life were some shabby little tryst they should both be ashamed of.

"I had no right," he'd said, immediately after begging her pardon. "Not when I have absolutely nothing to offer you."

"Some girls," she'd said somewhat breathlessly, "don't care

about things."

"Miss Fayre—" he'd begun, only to be interrupted by Patsy and Jim, exclaiming at having finally found her after what had apparently been a prolonged search.

There had been no further opportunity for private conversation. Patsy had said, quite rightly, that they had best return to the hired house in Upper Gower Street before Penelope's mother began to wonder at her daughter's absence, and Philippe cited his own need to relieve André at the fencing booth. They'd said their goodbyes in full view of not only the maid and her beau, but the dozens, perhaps hundreds, of fairgoers passing by on their way to whatever amusement or food stall had caught their eye. Now she would never know what he might have said, for that had been the last night of the fair. Today the actors and rope-dancers and animal exhibitors would be dismantling their booths and packing up their spangled costumes, loading up their wagons and setting off for the next fair.

And the fencers? An "itinerant swordsman," Philippe had called himself. Would he, too, be traveling on to the next fair, even finding some other young woman receptive to his attentions, only to leave her in three days' time with a wave and a kiss and an "I have nothing to offer you" on his lips?

My dear girl, I'm the biggest fraud of the lot…the biggest fraud…my dear girl…

"No," she spoke into the darkness, the single whispered word seeming as loud as a shout in the stillness before dawn. "I don't—I *won't* believe it!"

Suddenly she recalled that same voice saying something else, something very different.

No one can tell you your future…you must make it for yourself…

Without a single thought for the propriety of such a course of action, she flung back the counterpane and all but leapt from the bed. Moving quietly so as not to awaken the household, she dragged a gown and pelisse from the clothes-press. They were the same garments she'd worn on the trip to London some five months earlier, and although they had been the best clothes she'd owned at the time, they now paled in comparison to the wardrobe that had been made for her after her arrival in Town, in preparation for the brilliant Season that was to have ended in her betrothal and marriage. They made the perfect costume for her present errand, neither so dowdy nor so modish as to attract undue attention. She twisted her hair into a knot on the crown of her head and shoved a few pins in to hold it in place, then tied her plainest bonnet over this unfashionable coiffure.

Carrying her sturdy half-boots in her hand, she padded down the stairs in her stockinged feet, taking care to avoid the tread that always creaked beneath even so slight a weight as Benjy's; if she were to be discovered at this late stage in her clandestine escape, she feared she would be hard-pressed to concoct any excuse that would pass muster with Mama.

Having reached the ground floor without incident, she sank onto the nearest of the two straight chairs in the foyer and put on her half-boots, then opened the door very quietly, stepped out onto the portico, and carefully closed the door behind her.

The sky was somewhat lighter now, and in the pearly grey dawn Penelope could see the solitary figure of a maid sweeping the front stoop of a house some distance up the street. The sight triggered a sudden longing for Patsy's companionship—or, more specifically, the companionship of Patsy's beau, Jim. Her errand was, after all, highly unsuitable and perhaps even dangerous for an unaccompanied lady.

When she reached the corner where she, Patsy, and Jim had hailed a hackney, she found the street alive with activity. Two women with baskets over their arms conversed animatedly as they made their way to market on foot, determined to have their pick of the best and freshest produce while less diligent cooks and housekeepers were still abed. Occasionally she met or was passed by a wagon laden with wooden crates or burlap sacks, its driver shifting the reins of his huge draft horses to one hand in order to touch the brim of his hat to her. On the pavement opposite, a liveried footman, clearly dispatched on an errand of some importance, walked briskly up the street, to the obvious displeasure of the bespectacled clerk who was obliged to step aside for him.

Several of the younger men (and not a few of the older ones) cast admiring glances her way, but Penelope paid no heed to any of them. Not even the boldest of the lot made any attempt to approach her, daunted, perhaps, by the urgency of her bearing as she hurried down the street. She was keenly aware of the fact that she would be deemed "fast," should the news of her indiscretion be made public. Still, few of her *ton* acquaintances remained in London, and those who did were no doubt sound asleep, having sought their beds not so very long ago after a night spent engaged in those amusements still available in the Metropolis even after the Season was over. In any case, she reasoned, what good was a reputation as a biddable, pretty-behaved young lady if those qualities only served to doom one to a life of marital misery with a man one could not, could never, love?

Breathing a sigh of relief for having reached Smithfield without incident, she rounded the corner opening onto the "smooth field" that had given the northern suburb its name, and came to an abrupt halt. She gazed stupidly over the unoccupied ground spread before her, unable to believe the evidence of her own eyes. Here were no painted booths, no brilliantly colored tents, no strings of Japanese lanterns swaying overhead, only an open space that made a mockery of the street sign reading "Cloth Fair."

It's gone, she told herself, as if by repeating the thought she could eventually make sense of the concept. *The fair is already gone. He* is already gone.

Of their own volition, her feet propelled her slowly forward until she stood in the middle of the empty space that only a few hours ago had been the bustling fair. The smell of flat ale hung in the air, while on the ground at her feet, industrious ants hauled away crumbs of gingerbread. A flash of bright poppy-red caught her eye, and she moved toward it like an automaton. It was a ribbon of satin grosgrain, just like the ribbon she'd won from the unscrupulous Jack, except that this one was crushed and trampled.

Just like her hopes.

She wasn't quite sure what she had been hoping for. One thing, however, was clear: There was nothing left for her now, nothing but a loveless marriage to the next eligible suitor to ask for her hand.

The ribbon slipped through her fingers and landed in the dust at her feet as she turned and began the long walk back to Upper Gower Street.

* * *

The first light of dawn found Smithfield a hive of activity, albeit of a very different kind than that which had predominated a scant six hours earlier. The music and laughter were gone now, replaced by the ripping sounds of crowbars tearing the nails from the boards that had held the booths together, and the whack of wood upon wood as those same boards, now separated, were stacked up and loaded onto the wagons that would convey them northward from Smithfield to Barnet. Here they would set up for a few days at the beginning of September before repeating the process all over again at the Stourbridge Fair in Cambridge, then working their way northwestward until they reached Leicestershire.

Having torn down their booth, rolled up the posters, and carefully wrapped the rapiers in a shroud of somewhat threadbare velvet, Philip and Andrew (for now that the fair was concluded, they had reverted to the more mundane English forms of their names) climbed onto the driver's box. Andrew took up the reins, and soon they had taken their place in the line of similar vehicles rumbling down Cowcross Street.

"Penny for your thoughts," Andrew said, when they reached the far end of the street without having exchanged a word.

"I dare not open my mouth for fear of finding it full of dust." Philip made a waving motion with his hand for emphasis, as if he could sweep away the cloud of dust rising from the wheels of the wagon several feet in front of their own.

"Well, that's a relief," Andrew said, eyeing his companion suspiciously. "Here I was, thinking you were pining after that girl."

"What girl?" asked Philip, all innocence.

Andrew's eyebrows rose. "Do I look stupid to you?"

Philip's brow cleared, as if he had just that moment remembered her. "Oh, *that* girl. A brief amusement, no more." He darted a mischievous glance at his companion. "Surely you won't begrudge me that, not after the ginger-haired charmer you picked up in Scarborough."

It was a false comparison, and he knew it. Andrew's pert redhead had known the rules of the game, and had apparently played it to perfection. His own inamorata had been a lady of birth and breeding. Had she not introduced the other young woman, Patsy, as her maid? He was certain she had, for he had goaded her with the suggestion that it was she who indulged her servant's whims, instead of the other way 'round. In any case, Patsy's manner toward her had certainly been deferential, and several times she had referred to her as "miss." Yes, "Miss Fair" had come to the fair without parental permission—he'd known that even without her confession—although her fears of discovery, and of being forced into an unwelcome marriage, had seemed to be centered on her mother. He could not recall any mention of her father at all. Was the man dead, or was he perhaps ruled by his wife?

He frowned. "I do wish she'd told me her name."

"I thought she had."

Philip had not realized he'd spoken aloud until Andrew

answered. Now he gave a snort of derision. "She called herself 'Miss Fair.' If I'd asked her father's name, I daresay she would have said it was Bartholomew."

Andrew regarded his passenger through the corner of his eye. "A mystery lady, in fact,"

Philip inclined his head in acknowledgment. "Just so. Now, do watch your driving, and mind you don't tip us into the ditch."

11

Autumn at Markham Grange was truly a sight to behold. Most of the trees in the South Lawn (many of them strategically planted more than a century ago by the renowned landscaper Capability Brown) had by this time lost their leaves, leaving a latticework of bare limbs to frame the deer that sometimes ventured out of the shelter of the Home Wood to sample the cool, clear waters of the ornamental lake fed by the River Mar. To anyone fortunate enough to glimpse this view from the windows of one of the Grange's many south-facing rooms, the early morning mist off the water blurred the scene, giving it an ethereal, otherworldly quality that had made more than one resident catch his breath, and inspired more than one visitor to declare impulsively that the Barons Markham must be the most fortunate family in all of Leicestershire, possibly in all of England.

Beyond the house and its grounds, the trees of the Home Wood, more densely forested and therefore more protected against the chill of the autumn nights, were ablaze with color. Just south of the Home Wood lay the neat rows of the fields, where the baron's tenants labored to bring in the late corn and barley, while to the north, the picturesque village of Markham straddled the river, its two halves joined by a humpbacked bridge of local grey stone, the northern end of which was presided over by an ancient half-timbered inn called the Huntsman's Horn. Early that morning, a solitary figure had set out from this edifice, crossed the humpbacked bridge on foot, and turned his leisurely steps in the direction of the Grange. It was no longer morning, however, and midafternoon found that same figure now trudging up the raked-gravel drive toward the house. This was more than two miles in length, and cut through the Home Wood, opening upon the South Lawn at precisely the angle at which the full glory of the ornamental lake and its accompanying trees most effectively burst upon the sight of the new and, presumably, unsuspecting arrival. It did not fail in its effect now. The solitary figure stopped at the edge of the Home Wood, the breath catching in his throat at the vista that lay before him.

He had thought he would not remember it. He had not laid eyes on the house since he had been—what? Five years old? Six? Certainly no more than seven, for he had been seven when—

But he would not think of that. Dwelling on what was long past could serve no purpose now.

No, he had not forgotten the Grange, but he had never realized it was so beautiful, so breathtakingly beautiful. He'd been a child, and children took familiar things for granted. To his childish mind, it had simply been "home"—no more and no less.

Now, seeing it again after more than twenty years, and this

time through the eyes of an adult, he was gripped with a sense of possessiveness and love so strong that his knees were momentarily weak. At the same time, he acknowledged with a sinking heart that anyone already in possession of such a place would be unlikely to surrender it without a fight. *And so,* he reasoned, *it is perhaps fortunate that I have never been known to back down from one.* Steeling himself for the task at hand, he squared his shoulders and started up the remaining quarter-mile of raked gravel.

His steps slowed at the point where the drive skirted the ornamental lake, and he paused for a moment and looked down into the water. The willows along this end of the lake trailed their long fronds in the water, as if bowing their heads in deference to the young man reflected in the blue-grey depths. He was not a very impressive-looking young man for all that. His clothes were plain, his height was no more than the average, and his straight black hair fell forward over his brow, rather badly in need of a trim.

He dismissed this apparition with a shrug, and continued on his way. He did not approach the front door—or doors, rather, for there were two of them, made of carved oak and flanked by sidelights of leaded glass—but made his way around the near end of the house and thence to the service entrance. He should, of course, have taken the road from the village that would have delivered him straight to this more utilitarian entrance at the rear of the house, but he could not regret that first, overwhelming view, any more than he could have denied himself the opportunity to savor that view in privacy before making his presence known.

And so he strode up to the service door and rapped smartly on the plain wooden panel. It was opened a moment later by a young woman in a starched apron and a mobcap.

"Good afternoon, sir," she said, subjecting the visitor to an appraising gaze. "How may I help you?"

"I should like to see the butler, if I may," he said pleasantly, in a carefully neutral voice that held no trace of a French accent and gave no hint as to his identity or social status, nor any clue as to the nature of his business.

The housemaid, finding no way of indirectly ascertaining the information she sought, tried the direct route. "Who shall I say is calling, if you please?"

He had anticipated this question, of course, and was prepared for it.

"My name is Charles."

And so it is, he added mentally. *Right there in the church register, amongst the baptisms. It's just that one has to read through a few more names before getting to the Charles bit.*

She paused for one uncertain moment, as if awaiting another name, or at least some indication whether Charles should have a surname following it or a "Mr." preceding it. Finding no further information forthcoming, only the visitor regarding her with an expression of patient expectation, she bobbed a rather flustered curtsy.

"One moment, sir." She gently closed the door, and returned shortly with the information that Mr. Crumley could give him a few minutes, but no more. "On account of we're all at sixes and sevens, getting ready for the grand party his lordship is giving," she added apologetically.

Crumley, he thought, following her past the kitchen and through the servants' hall. *Crumley. Who'd have ever guessed old Crumley would still be here?*

In fact, the familiar name had set him back on his heels a bit. He wasn't quite certain whether the butler's unexpected presence would prove a blessing or a curse. His memories of the man were vague—no surprise there, given that he'd been no more than seven years old the last time they'd met—but he retained disquieting recollections of a man who had seemed to his younger self to be, if not quite omniscient, then something alarmingly close. Crumley had always seemed to know instinctively when one had been filching raisins or chestnuts from the larder. On the other hand, Crumley had never, to his knowledge, betrayed these juvenile larcenies to Lord Markham. If the butler recognized him—and this was by no means a certainty, after an absence of twenty years—might he perhaps enlist the man's aid? Or would it be better to play a lone hand?

He had still not arrived at a satisfactory answer to this question when his escort reached the butler's pantry.

"Mr. Charles, sir." The maid had apparently settled on the surname, or perhaps decided that should she guess incorrectly, this form of address would be the lesser infraction. Having made this judgment call, she bobbed another curtsy and took herself off, seemingly eager to make her escape before any error could be brought to her attention.

With her departure, the visitor was left alone with the butler, and the past twenty years seemed to melt away. Crumley's thinning hair was now more salt than pepper, and the butler was not so tall as he had expected (no surprise, he supposed, since he himself was considerably taller than he had been on those earlier occasions) but the keen blue eyes set in the thin face, the lean frame, and the fastidiousness of the man's neat dark suit beneath his workaday apron—yes, he would have known Crumley anywhere.

"Charles," echoed the butler, subjecting his visitor to an appraising look. "Is that your surname, or your Christian name?"

"Does it matter?" the caller asked with a shrug. "It is my understanding that the most junior footman in this house is always called Charles. An eccentricity of the fourth baron, I believe, who disliked having to learn new names every time there was a change in the household staff."

Crumley's eyebrows drew together over his long, thin nose. "You appear to be familiar with the inner workings of this establishment," he observed, by no means pleased.

The visitor gave him a surprisingly sweet smile. "It's a wise man who takes the trouble to learn something of the household in which he hopes to find a place."

"So you have come in search of employment. Tell me, who is your informant?"

"What?" asked the visitor, momentarily taken aback by the question. "Oh, I see. You want to know who told me about the junior footman being called Charles. I'm afraid I really couldn't say. It was so long ago that I no longer remember."

"Hmph." Crumley clearly doubted this claim, but did not press the matter. "You've worked in a nobleman's house before?"

"I have been a member of noble households here in England as well as on the Continent."

Crumley unbent somewhat and said, albeit not without sympathy, "I'm afraid there are no permanent positions open at present. As it happens, however, Lord Markham is preparing to host a hunting-party in a few weeks, a large affair that will bring in guests from across the country, and which will culminate in a formal dinner and ball. It may be that I can offer you employment for the duration of the hunting-party, at least, if that would be agreeable to you."

"Very agreeable indeed," the visitor said. "I would be very much obliged to you."

"Still, I can't let this matter of a name go. If I am to inquire into your references, I must be able to tell them the name of the man I am considering for the post." Again the stern, keen gaze, so long forgotten, so readily recalled. "You do have references, I trust?"

The visitor assured him on this head.

"Your name, then," commanded Crumley, in the very same voice that had once ordered a small thief to surrender the slightly squished raisins clutched behind his back in plump, sticky hands.

Coming to a decision, the visitor looked the butler squarely in the eye, and burned his boats.

"Markham."

Crumley's eyes first widened and then narrowed, as if he were studying every detail of his visitor's face and measuring it against a once-familiar countenance buried deep in his memory. Then, to that visitor's patent astonishment, the butler seized his hand and, covering it with kisses, fell to his knees.

"Master Philip, Master Philip! Never did I expect to—we thought you were all dead!"

"As you can see, I am very much alive," Philip said soothingly, gently extracting his hand so that he might slip it beneath the butler's elbow and ease the older man to his feet.

"And your father?" asked Crumley, rising with the assistance of the young master he had thought never to see again. "Your mother?"

"I am convinced that my father must have fallen victim to the guillotine, for nothing but death would have kept him from my mother."

"And her ladyship?" Having gained control of his tears, the butler withdrew a handkerchief from his pocket and began mopping at his wet cheeks.

"She died only recently, after living very quietly in Bristol."

"Bristol?" echoed the butler. But why did she not come home, or at least write?"

A reminiscent smile touched Philip's lips. The staff of Markham Grange considered this estate to be the family's true home, while the servants at *La Maison de Sainte-Marguerite*, if they were still alive, would swear that *monsieur le duc* and *madame la duchesse* really belonged to them, the family's English surname notwithstanding. Still, to answer the question required some delicacy, so he took a moment to consider how best to frame his answer.

"Mama was much affected by the Terror," he said at last. "We contrived to escape Paris in a wagon, hidden beneath a load of cabbages and onions—I was apparently quite vocal on the subject of these last, if Andrew is to be believed—"

"Andrew? Never say Andrew Walker is with you!"

Philip shook his head. "Not just at present. He dared not

come with me lest someone see us and quite literally put two and two together, where I alone might go unrecognized after so many years. But he is very much alive, and usually travels with me."

Crumley, it appeared, had lost none of his keenness. "Travels where, pray?"

"Here, there—anywhere." Philip's shrug betrayed the Gallic ancestry that comprised half his heritage. "Since Mama died, I have followed the fairs as a swordsman, earning my bread and—not coincidentally—sharpening my skills while at the same time working my way toward the Grange."

"Aye, where you come begging to serve as junior footman in the house where you ought by rights to be master!" Crumley said bitterly.

"Which brings us back to Mama," Philip continued, ignoring this interruption. "We reached England safely, but as time passed, it became more and more obvious that Papa would not be joining us as he'd planned. Andrew traveled incognito to Leicestershire to see how matters stood, and reported back that my uncle Robert, barely of age at the time, had offered the College of Arms sufficient proofs of our deaths—my father's and my own—that he was allowed to assume the title."

Crumley cast a furtive glance in the direction of the ceiling, as if fearful that the current baron might somehow be eavesdropping on their conversation.

"Just so," Philip drawled, envisioning his uncle, now a man of middle age, lying on the floor of the room directly above with his ear pressed to the carpet. "Mama became convinced that Papa was not simply one more *aristo* sent to the guillotine for the crime of possessing a title and riches. She thought there had been some plot afoot, that my uncle had conspired with radical Jacobins, perhaps even with Robespierre himself, to disclose my father's whereabouts in Paris. Thus, the Jacobins would have three more heads for their beastly apparatus, and my uncle could succeed to the title—the title of Lord Markham, anyway. He has no claim to the *duché de Sainte-Marguerite*, as it passes through my mother's line, if it still exists at all. God only knows what's happened to the *château* by now. What?"

Crumley had listened to this account with rapt attention, but at the suggestion of a plot, something in the butler's face had changed ever so slightly.

"It's nothing, Master Philip. That is," he amended hastily, "it might be nothing, and then again, it might not. It's just that— well, sir, people will talk, and your father being so well-liked, there were bound to be rumors..." His voice trailed away uncomfortably, and he made a great show of folding his damp handkerchief and returning it to his coat pocket.

Philip considered the implications of this statement thoughtfully. "So there's a chance Mama may have been right? Is that it?" The butler merely stammered something about idle gossip, so Philip picked up his narrative where he'd left off. "In any case, Mama became convinced that if my uncle knew that I, the rightful heir, had escaped, he would not rest until he hunted me down and, er, solidified his claim. She made me promise not to make any attempt to claim the title during her lifetime." He grimaced at the memory. "She would have preferred that I never pressed my claim at all, but I made it clear to her that upon her death, I would consider myself no longer bound by that promise.

That much, at least, I owe to my father, even if I can do nothing else to avenge his murder by fiends drunk on human blood. Still, instead of a public homecoming, I thought it might be wise to plant myself in the household as a servant for a time and see what I could discover."

"It wouldn't be right, Master Philip, you taking orders from me!" protested the butler, much shocked by this upheaval of the natural order.

"But no one would know who I was—unless you chose to tell them. I shall be called Charles, just as any junior footman. If any servants remain from those days when my father was Lord Markham of Markham Grange, they are unlikely to remember that Charles is one of my names, and I know I can trust you to say nothing that might remind them."

Crumley declared that he would cut out his own tongue before he would commit so heinous a sin against the young master who had returned, as it were, from the grave.

"I knew you wouldn't disappoint me," Philip said, flashing the smile that had won him forgiveness for more than one raid on the pantry. He seized the butler's hand and shook it warmly. "I won't forget this, Crumley, I promise. If—no, *when* I succeed to my father's honors, you will have your reward."

"Seeing you in your rightful place will be reward enough, my lord," declared Crumley, seeking recourse to his handkerchief once more.

"'My lord,'" echoed Philip with a shaky laugh. "I suppose I am 'my lord,' or soon shall be, God willing. But remember, I am 'Charles,' at least for the nonce, so let us have no 'my lords' or 'Master Philips,' if you please."

The butler placed a hand over his heart. "I shall do everything in my power to obey your first instructions as master of the house, my—er, Charles."

"There, now! That wasn't so bad, was it?" asked Philip, grinning.

Crumley failed to take the bait, however, for a new thought had occurred to him. "If you will pardon my impertinence, er, Charles, you must be twenty-five years old, at the least reckoning—"

"Twenty-seven."

"Twenty-seven." He shook his head in disbelief. "How time flies! Still, it occurs to me that having reached, let us say, a susceptible age—in short, my, er, Charles, has the Grange a new mistress as well?"

Philip stiffened. "Have I taken a wife, you mean."

"Just so, sir." Receiving no answer, the butler put in hastily, "Pray forgive me if I've spoken out of turn—"

"Not at all." Philip assured him with perhaps less than perfect truth. "No, Crumley, I have no wife. How could I ask any lady to marry me, when I have nothing to offer her?"

He had asked himself that question again and again over the past few weeks, and was no closer now than he had been when the question had first presented itself. So there was no point, no point at all, in thinking of a starry-eyed girl in poppy-red ribbons who by this time must be well on her way to the altar.

12

Whatever her disappointment at reaching the fairground too late, Penelope was not allowed to dwell on it, for upon her return to Upper Gower Street, she was plunged into a whirlwind of preparations for the hunting-party at Markham Grange. Ironically, it was to this dreaded event that she owed her deliverance, for she arrived back home to find her mother in alt, having received a notice from the dressmaker announcing that the latest winter fabrics were now in stock. So determined was Mrs. Fayre to steal a march on her daughter's wealthier rivals that she scarcely noticed Penelope's look of bleak despair or the fact that the hem of her pelisse was fully two inches deep in dust. In any case, her mother said little beyond scolding Penelope for appearing publicly in the oldest garments she owned, followed by commanding her to change her clothes at once, lest they be late to the dressmaker. Although Mrs. Fayre could not have known it, this course of action was a stroke of genius, for it would be a very odd young lady indeed who was not at least a bit cheered by the sight of rich velvets and fine, soft wools, to say nothing of enormous fur muffs and trimmings of swansdown.

Over the weeks that followed, Penelope's days were filled with fittings at the dressmaker's shop or visits to the most fashionable milliner in London for hats and bonnets, Mrs. Fayre indulging the hope that the exodus from Town of her wealthier clientele might inspire that canny businesswoman to lower her prices.

Benjy's Cummings grandparents arrived to collect him, for Lord Markham's invitation had quite naturally made no mention of small boys. The child would stay with his paternal grandparents until Penelope and her mother returned to London, but until their departure, and apart from Caroline's weekly half-day, it fell to Mrs. Fayre and her younger daughter to extend to Mr. and Mrs. Cummings the hospitality of the house.

With so much to distract her, it was perhaps inevitable that her adventures at the fair began gradually to fade from Penelope's memory.

Patsy married her Jim at last, and left the Fayre ladies' service to live with her new husband in furnished rooms above his father's shop. Without the maid to confide in, Penelope had no one with whom to share recollections of those magical days in late August, and eventually the whole affair took on the sense of a particularly vivid dream, a single ribbon of poppy-red grosgrain offering the only concrete evidence that it had ever taken place at all.

Finally, there came a day when she discovered she could no longer recall Philippe's face to mind. She could remember him in pieces—she knew his hair was straight and black, and that it had a tendency to fall over his forehead. His eyes were black, as well. She remembered, too, that he was of no more than medium height, and that although he was slender and his movements were graceful, he possessed a wiry strength that cautioned would-be fencers to challenge him at their peril. A wealth of detail, one might have thought, and yet when she tried to blend all these characteristics into a unified whole, he utterly eluded her.

Such was the state of affairs when, at last, the day came for Penelope and her mother to board the mail coach that would convey them to Leicestershire, and the hunting-party that would decide her fate.

* * *

"The first of his lordship's guests will be arriving tomorrow, very likely in the early afternoon," Crumley announced to the assembled male staff, and if he flinched slightly at being obliged to refer to his employer as "his lordship," this involuntary gesture was so subtle that it was very likely overlooked by all the servants except one. "I should like for each of you to familiarize yourself with the room assignments of all the guests in advance, to avoid any delays in conveying their bags to the proper chambers."

A similar conversation was taking place in the house-keeper's sitting room, where she issued orders to the female staff, while some distance away in the stables, the groom gave instructions to his underlings as to the care of not only the various phaetons and curricles in which the guests would be traveling and the teams of high-stepping horses pulling these vehicles, but also of those guests' hunters, a few of which had been sent ahead so as to allow these sensitive animals time to acclimate themselves to their new surroundings prior to the hunt.

"Of course," Crumley continued, "Mrs. Overton has her list, but I'm sure I need not tell you that she will have quite enough of her own work to do without your adding to her burden by interrupting her labors to ask where to leave Mr. Edmondson's newly polished boots, or whether it is Mrs. Fayre or her daughter who occupies the Rose Bedroom."

Something flared in the dark eyes of the Grange's newest footman, but if the butler noticed this spontaneous reaction, he gave no indication of it. It was not until fully fifteen minutes later, when he dismissed his staff to attend to their regular duties, that he said, "A moment, Charles, if you please."

A knowing look passed between the other footmen, as if they were hardly surprised that this newest addition to their ranks should be singled out for the butler's displeasure. They had not forgotten Charles's first week in the household, when the fellow couldn't seem to complete the simplest tasks without one or the other of them on hand to set him straight. It was unlikely that he was about to be given the sack, not with a houseful of guests set to descend upon the Grange the very next day for an extended stay, but poor Charles had best step lively if he didn't want to be expelled from the house on the heels of the last visitor's departure.

Once they were alone, however, the butler showed no inclination to scold the unsatisfactory footman, much less threaten him with dismissal. "What is the matter, Master Phi— er, Charles? If you fear exposure by Mr. Edmondson, I'm sure you need not. His father might have known yours well enough to recognize Lord Markham's son, but that gentleman died some five years ago. *This* Mr. Edmondson would have been in the schoolroom when your father met his sad fate."

Philip dismissed the unknown Mr. Edmondson with an impatient shake of his head. "This woman in the Rose Bedroom. Mrs.—Fair, did you say? Is she a real person, or did you merely invent a name as an example?" But Mr. Edmondson had been real enough, and in that case…

"Aye, she's a widowed lady. Mrs. Cordelia Fayre, F-A-Y-R-E."

"And she really has a daughter?"

Crumley cast a pitying look upon the young man who was his master in all but name. "You have been kept in the dark, and no mistake! Miss Fayre was apparently the Toast of this past Season."

"Then she really was Miss Fayre," Philip murmured to himself.

"I beg your pardon?"

"Never mind. You were saying about Miss Fayre?"

"The young lady is said to be a great beauty, with her pick of gentlemen, but as I understand it, she wouldn't have any of them."

Then she isn't married yet. Thank God for that, anyway, Philip thought, although he kept this observation to himself.

"I haven't seen her, mind you," the butler continued, "and even if I had, it wouldn't be my place to pass judgment on the lady's charms, but there are those who believe the real purpose of this hunting-party is to allow your uncle to fix his interest with

Miss Fayre."

"Are there, by Jove?" breathed Philip, his brain still reeling. She'd said she was Miss Fayre, but since they'd met at Bartholomew Fair, he'd assumed the more modern spelling and thought she'd made it up in order to preserve her incognito. And now she was coming here, still unmarried and unbetrothed, in order for Uncle Robert to court her at his leisure…

Crumley, unaware of his inner turmoil, saw nothing to wonder at in his young master's sudden interest in the lady. "Aye, so if you'll not object to a word of advice, I would tread warily around Miss Fayre, if I were you. She just might be Lady Markham someday."

"She will be, Crumley," pronounced Philip, setting his jaw. "Of that, my old friend, you may be certain."

* * *

For those without the means to keep a carriage, a team of horses to pull it, and a coachman to drive it, the fastest way to travel from one point to another was to procure a seat on the Royal Mail, provided one's destination lay upon its route. The village of Markham, though its thatch-roofed cottages and hump-backed bridges over the River Mar were certainly quaint, was too small and insignificant to merit this distinction.

Space for passengers was limited on the distinctive maroon-and-black vehicles whose primary purpose was, after all, the transportation of letters and parcels, and since the demand for these coveted seats often exceeded the supply, travel on the Mail was considerably more expensive than a comparable seat on the slower but undeniably cheaper stagecoach, which possessed the further advantage of a regularly scheduled stop in the Markham High Street.

Still, Mrs. Fayre had no intention of cutting so poor a figure as to arrive practically on Lord Markham's doorstep by means of the common stage. And so the Fayre ladies betook themselves to the Bull and Mouth very early on the morning of their departure and, after seeing their not inconsiderable baggage securely tied to the boot, boarded the Mail coach and took their places on its rear-facing seat, as this was the only vacant spot remaining in the crowded vehicle. However, one look at Miss Fayre was sufficient to inspire one of their fellow passengers to insist that the ladies take his forward-facing seat and allow him to sit facing the rear.

"That way, you can pass the time by taking in the scenery," he explained to Penelope. "I believe the views along some stretches of the route are quite picturesque."

Mrs. Fayre was profuse in her thanks, and the change was made, although Penelope suppressed a sigh at the realization that she herself was to be the "view" with which her admirer whiled away the time. She soon had cause to be grateful to her gallant, however, for she did find it amusing, as they drove through smaller villages where the Mail did not stop, to watch through the window as the Mail Guard on the roof of the coach threw down the incoming sacks of mail to the Postmaster and snatched the outgoing sacks from his hand, all without the coach ever slackening its pace.

Even this amusement eventually began to pall, however, and by the end of the day both she and her mother were more than ready to disembark from the vehicle and procure a hot meal and a room for the night, fortifying themselves for another day of travel with the assurance that this should see their arrival at Markham Grange.

"And not a moment too soon," Penelope sighed blissfully after a second morning of travel, stretching her aching limbs as she descended from the carriage into the yard of a Leicester coaching inn.

Mrs. Fayre made no reply, for she watched with a keen eye as a hostler hurried forward to cut their bags loose from the boot and hand then down, her gaze scarcely less critical than that of the Mail Guard who no doubt knew who would be held responsible should anything go amiss with either the mail itself or the passengers who accompanied it.

After the briefest of stops, during which the horses were changed and the bolder (or more desperate) passengers disembarked to answer nature's call or provide themselves with sustenance for the next leg of the journey, well aware that the Mail would not wait for them if they dawdled, the Fayre ladies bided their time until the Mail was once more on its way before Mrs. Fayre addressed herself to the hostler, who had taken charge of the spent and sweating horses and was now leading them toward the stables.

"Excuse me," she began, bearing down upon this industrious individual, "can you tell me where I may hire a post-chaise?"

The hostler paused in his labors, scratched a spot behind his ear, then made his pronouncement. "Can't. Not here, anyway."

"Can't?" echoed Mrs. Fayre incredulously. "*Can't?*"

"'Fraid not." He glanced at the young lady standing some

little distance behind her, and belatedly added, "Beggin' your pardon, ma'am."

Mrs. Fayre regarded him through shrewdly narrowed eyes, wishing she had not given him quite so generous a gratuity upon taking possession of her bags. "Are you saying you can't, or you won't?"

"Can't, ma'am," he said again, albeit apologetically this time. "His lordship's giving a big party over t'Markham way." He jerked his thumb, presumably indicating the direction in which Markham Grange lay.

"Yes, I know," Mrs. Fayre said impatiently. "That's where we—my daughter and I—are going."

"Not all of his lordship's guests are driving their own rigs," the hostler continued as if she had not spoken. "Come to that, not all of 'em *have* their own rigs. Drop their blunt on hunters and hacks, they do, and hire a yellow bounder for aught further afield."

Having been for many years on the friendliest of terms with her brother, Penelope had a much greater store of slang at her disposal than her mother had any reason to suspect; even Caroline's late and bitterly lamented husband had added one or two unobjectionable terms to her vocabulary. Given these masculine influences, she had no difficulty in understanding that several of Lord Markham's guests were being conveyed to Markham Grange by the same post-chaises from whose number she and her mother were now trying unsuccessfully to procure one for themselves.

"If they set out for the Grange this morning," she began thoughtfully, wishing she knew the precise location of Lord

Markham's estate and its distance from their present position, and weighing her best guess against a sky that still promised several hours of daylight remaining, "might not at least a few post-chaises be returning today?"

"Aye, there's the ticket," pronounced the hostler, bestowing a gap-toothed grin upon the prettiest young lady he had seen in many a long day. "First bounder what comes in, I'll have those boys of mine put a fresh team to harness, and we'll have you back on the road before you can say Bob's your uncle."

"Very well," said Mrs. Fayre, unbending somewhat.

Penelope felt a little thrill of satisfaction in having been the one to effect a resolution to their dilemma—a very gratifying feeling that, alas, proved to be short-lived.

"I expect it won't be more'n four or five hours," the hostler predicted cheerfully, apparently laboring under the delusion that the two ladies would be pleased with this revelation.

"*Four or five hours?*" mother and daughter echoed in chorus, and the hostler might have found their dismay comical, had he not received a second premonition, this one concerning the rapidly dwindling sum of the vails he had fully expected them to bestow upon him as he handed them tenderly into the promised vehicle.

It was perhaps fortunate that the door to the inn opened at that moment and a fashionably dressed young gentleman in a caped driving coat stepped into the yard. Sizing up at a glance the defensive posture of the hostler as well as the two ladies and the rather forlorn-looking bags lying on the ground at their feet, he adjusted his curly brimmed beaver to a jaunty angle and strode gamely into their midst.

"Hullo, is there a problem?" he asked, addressing himself to Mrs. Fayre. "Perhaps I may be of some assistance. The name is Markham—Freddie Markham, ma'am, yours to command."

Mrs. Fayre, by this time well accustomed to strange gentlemen looking for some pretext upon which to strike up an acquaintance with her daughter, would have sent this latest specimen about his business, and that right speedily, had he not supplied his name at the crucial juncture.

"Mr. Markham." She offered a gloved hand, but regarded him through narrowed eyes, as if searching his good-humored albeit somewhat vacuous countenance for some indication of dishonorable intent. "Are you by any chance related to Lord Markham of Markham Grange?"

He inclined his head—an unfortunate gesture, as it allowed his hat to escape its moorings. "His lordship is my uncle," he explained, setting his wayward headgear to rights. "In fact, I'm on my way to the Grange now. Dare I hope to see you at his hunting-party?"

Although this hopeful question was certainly directed at Penelope, it was her mother who answered somewhat tartly, "I suppose that will depend upon when this fellow has a post-chaise we may hire."

Mr. Markham turned to the hostler in mock horror. "Come, come, man, this will never do!"

"I only told 'em—" began the hostler, but he was ignored as the gentleman addressed himself once more to the ladies.

"I was obliged to break my journey here for fresh horses, but I would be honored if you would accept a seat in my carriage for the rest of the way."

Although this invitation was directed to Mrs. Fayre, that lady did not flatter herself that it was for the pleasure of her company that it had been issued. She could not quite like the irregularity of the situation—besides, it was clear that Mr. Markham was the scion of some cadet branch of the family, and heaven only knew where he stood in relation to the succession. Still, as the only alternative appeared to be a four- or five-hour wait, the outcome was never really in doubt.

To his credit, Mr. Markham was a genial traveling companion, and the miles passed with surprising swiftness, to the accompaniment of a steady flow of amusing and often self-effacing anecdotes concerning past parties hosted by his uncle at Markham Grange and his own less than illustrious exploits on the hunting field.

Mrs. Fayre listened with mixed feelings to her daughter's peals of laughter. There was no denying the fact that Mr. Markham's well-sprung carriage was far more comfortable than even the most well-made post-chaise would have been, but she told herself she would be a very unnatural mother were she to value her own comfort over her daughter's marriage prospects. Still, what was done was done. She would at least have the satisfaction of knowing that Penelope would descend upon Markham Grange in her best looks, for there were roses in her cheeks and a sparkle in her eyes that had not been there in quite some time.

Looking back, it occurred to her that Penelope was *herself* again, in a way she had not been for several weeks. Indeed, she had been obliged to send for the doctor during the first week of September, so uncharacteristically quiet and biddable had the girl become. He had been unable to find anything wrong with her, only claiming she was worn down from the demands of the Season, and, when told of their upcoming departure for a hunting-party in Leicestershire, opining that the fresh air would no doubt be good for her, and jovially cautioning his patient not to rush her fences, either literally or figuratively.

If young Mr. Markham's conversation had the happy effect of restoring to Penelope the glow that had made her the belle of the Season, then surely a few hours in his company were time well spent. Besides, that pragmatic lady told herself, sometimes the threat of a rival was exactly what was needed to bring a more eligible *parti* up to scratch.

* * *

Forewarned is forearmed, Philip told himself, not for the first time.

It had been a very busy morning, not least because he, along with the rest of the household staff, had been obliged to abandon his chores every time a vehicle was sighted coming up the long avenue of oaks. They would form two parallel lines, footmen in one and housemaids in the other, through which the new arrivals would make their way to the portico, where the nominal Lord Markham stood waiting to welcome them to what his lordship, with a not entirely successful attempt at modesty, termed his "humble abode." Since this was an elegant Palladian structure with more than twenty bedrooms, set in grounds comprising almost four thousand acres, Philip had to wonder what his uncle would consider a stately abode.

Still, as he watched his uncle greet each new arrival, Philip had to wonder. Was it possible that this smiling, urbane man, scarcely more than a boy at the time, was capable of arranging for the murder of his own brother, as well as that brother's wife and child? Surely not. He did not doubt his mother's sincerity, or her very real fears for his own safety, but she must have been mistaken. The death of her husband, along with the fact that her native country now considered her and her small son enemies of the state, had affected her wits. And who could wonder at it?

He was jerked from his reverie by the glint of sunlight on glass in the distance, heralding the arrival of yet another vehicle, and steeled himself for a meeting for which he felt ill-prepared.

Forewarned is forearmed.

He had known, of course, that Miss Fayre was a lady, in spite of the fact that she had been, for all practical purposes, unchaperoned in the midst of the hubbub that was Bartholomew Fair. He had known, too, that her family was in what was euphemistically called "straitened circumstances," hence her need, real or imagined, to make an advantageous marriage.

Given these facts, he thought it very likely that she and her mother would arrive in a hired post-chaise, not having sufficient funds to keep their own stables. Every time one of the familiar "yellow bounders" hove into view, he reminded himself of what was by this time a litany. *Forewarned is forearmed.* As the vehicle drew nearer, he realized that this was no post-chaise, but a private vehicle. He let out a long breath, not quite certain whether to be sorry or glad.

She probably won't even recognize me, he assured himself. Indeed, he hardly recognized himself in the reflection he occasionally glimpsed in the mirror. Charles the footman, with his black and gold livery and his powdered hair, bore little resemblance to Philippe Valois, the Blade of Paris, who had taken on all comers at Bartholomew Fair.

For that matter, he wasn't sure he would recognize her, either. It seemed unlikely that anyone could be as beautiful as he'd imagined her to be, and, well, the effects upon a young man of even a passably pretty girl in the moonlight were well-documented.

And so the occupants of Mr. Markham's carriage, disembarking before the portico, took him completely by surprise.

13

"Freddie! Well met, nevvy," exclaimed Lord Markham, looking up from bowing over the hand of a modishly dressed lady of middle age.

Freddie? With an effort, Philip kept his countenance impassive, betraying no hint of his surprise. *This* was Freddie Markham? He'd last seen his cousin Freddie as a chubby, curly haired five-year-old with a penchant for following him about like a Tantony pig. He could only hope the intervening years had rendered himself equally unrecognizable.

But still greater surprises were in store, for Freddie had turned back to the carriage and handed out a second lady—a young lady clad in a pelisse of crimson wool with a collar of sable fur. Her hands were tucked into a large muff of the same dark fur, and she withdrew one gloved hand and placed it in Freddie's.

Suddenly she lost her footing, and Philip instinctively started, as if to catch her. He need not have bothered. She fell against Freddie's chest, and his arms were quick to enfold her. She smiled shyly up at him and said something Philip could not hear.

Over the past weeks, he'd almost convinced himself that she had been more than half a figment of his imagination, but he'd been wrong. She was every bit as beautiful as he remembered. Now she was here, at Markham Grange, the ancestral seat where he'd dreamed of bringing her to live as its mistress.

And she'd made the journey in the company of his cousin.

* * *

She thought she had forgotten his face.

She was wrong.

The carriage had rolled to a stop before the impressive pedimented portico of Markham Grange, and as soon as the door had been opened, Mr. Markham had leapt down to lower the step and assist Penelope's mother to alight. As soon as Mrs. Fayre's feet had safely reached *terra firma*, he had turned his attention to Penelope.

Ducking her head so as not to knock her modish new hat askew on the low roof of the vehicle, she had leaned out the door of the carriage, placed her kid-gloved hand in his—and caught a glimpse of the footman over his shoulder. Upon the instant, she was once again at Bartholomew Fair, gazing up in distress at a young man.

My dear girl, I'm the biggest fraud of the lot…

The memory was so vivid, and the sight of that same young man—or another with an uncanny resemblance to him—here, standing in a line of household servants, was so disconcerting that she missed the carriage step and would no doubt have landed in a heap on the ground, had not Mr. Markham been there to halt her descent.

"How—How clumsy of me!" Resisting an overwhelming urge to steal another glance at the eerily familiar footman, she turned her attention to her rescuer with a shaky laugh. "I'm very much obliged to you, Mr. Markham."

"Freddie! Well met, nevvy," exclaimed Lord Markham, bowing over her mother's hand. "But I see you've stolen a march on the rest of us. The hunt doesn't begin until tomorrow, and here you've already captured the most desirable prey."

"What can I say?" Taking the portico's shallow steps two at a time, Freddie Markham strode up to shake his lordship's hand. "I was fortunate enough to be stopped at the Huntsman's Horn for a change of horses when the Royal Mail dropped these 'Fayre' ladies practically into my lap."

"Some people have all the luck," complained his lordship, pulling a wry face for the ladies' benefit. "I shall forgive you only because you have brought us such a delightful surprise. Mrs. Fayre, Miss Fayre, welcome to Markham Grange. You honor my humble abode with your presence. If anything is lacking for your comfort, you have only to ask for it."

He continued for some time in this vein, tucking Mrs. Fayre's hand into the curve of his arm and leading her into the house while addressing his remarks over his shoulder to include Penelope in his conversation.

He might have saved himself the trouble. She heard not a word of his gallant pleasantries, for her brain was awhirl. Philippe, here! Her first, joyous thought—that he had come for her, to rescue her from the brilliant marriage she dreaded—was very quickly dismissed, for he could not have known that he would find her here. What, then, was he doing at Markham Grange? It had been her impression that he had enjoyed, indeed, had reveled in the freedom inherent in following the fairs from one city to the next. Why would he give up such an adventuresome existence for the tedium of servanthood?

She was given little opportunity to ponder these questions, for after leading them into the house, Lord Markham turned Penelope and her mother over to the housekeeper, Mrs. Overton, who ushered them upstairs and showed them both into their adjoining rooms. Mama, it soon transpired, was given a corner apartment called the Wedgwood Suite, for it was decorated in the same blue-and-cream color scheme as the famous stoneware for which it was named.

Penelope's own room must of necessity have suffered in comparison to the classical splendor of her mother's suite. Still, only the most demanding of guests could find any fault in the sunny chamber of rose pink that had been assigned to her, its windows overlooking the same grounds that had so moved its rightful owner upon his return to his ancestral home.

It was while Mrs. Overton was drawing back the curtains in order to point out this view that Penelope, hearing someone enter the room behind them, turned and saw the footman bearing her portmanteau on his shoulder.

Please leave, she silently begged the housekeeper. *Please, please leave us alone. If I can't speak privately with him soon, I shall burst!*

Mrs. Overton, however, showed no sign of having heard this silent communication. "I'll send Betty up to unpack your bag," she said, then indicated the bell pull hanging from the wall beside the bed. "You can ring for her to help you dress for dinner. We keep Town hours when his lordship is in residence, so we'll dine promptly at nine o'clock."

She turned and left the room, presumably to be ready for the next guests to arrive. The footman placed the valise on the floor beside the clothes-press, then turned to follow in Mrs. Overton's wake.

She might never have a better chance.

"Philippe!"

The footman paused in the doorway and turned back. "Beg pardon, miss?"

His voice held no trace of a French accent, and there was no spark of recognition in the familiar black eyes.

"Philippe?" she said again, with considerably less confidence. "Do you not remember me?"

"I'm afraid you have mistaken me for someone else, miss," he said in the wooden tones of the well-trained servant. "I am called Charles."

He turned and left the room, leaving Penelope alone, hurt, and bewildered.

* * *

Like most of the other guests, Penelope and her mother spent the rest of the afternoon in their respective bedchambers, recovering from the rigors of the journey and washing the dusty residue of the road from their persons before dressing for dinner later that evening.

"Wear your new white gown," Mrs. Fayre instructed her daughter. "White always looks lovely in candlelight, and I'm sure I need not tell you that first impressions are everything."

Penelope might have pointed out that Lord Markham's

first impression of her had no doubt been formed six months earlier, when Lady Jersey had introduced his lordship to them upon Penelope's first visit to Almack's. Still, she was determined to be a biddable daughter, so she merely acceded to her mother's directions and rang for Mrs. Overton's Betty to assist her into this garment and dress her hair. Upon her completion of these tasks, the plump, smiling Betty ventured the opinion that "Miss looks very fine," and then took herself off, presumably to lend her services to another of the female guests.

Penelope gave herself a long, appraising look in the cheval glass, noting with satisfaction that no one would suspect that the beadwork adorning this creation had been sewn on by the Fayre ladies themselves, in order to curb costs sufficiently to allow for a narrow border of swansdown at the low neckline and another two at the hem, this trimming having become all the rage since the heiress Miss Tilney-Long had worn it on her wedding day two years earlier. She wondered if Philippe, or his double, would be waiting at table. If he was, would her impression be as strong as it had been at that first meeting, or would she see such a difference that she would think her earlier reaction more than a little foolish?

One thing, at least, was certain: She would find no answers so long as she lingered in her room. She pulled a face at her reflection, then rapped on the door connecting her bedchamber to her mother's suite. Mrs. Fayre was already smartly dressed in a gown of purple-bloom trimmed with black lace, and so, after she had subjected her daughter to a thorough inspection and pronounced Penelope acceptable, the two ladies set off together for the drawing room where the company was to assemble before dinner.

Since they had arrived in the afternoon, the staircase leading from the entrance hall to the upper floors had been cast in shadow. Now that evening had fallen, a fine crystal chandelier suspended over the half-landing cast a warm glow over the stairs, not only providing light for their steps, but also illuminating the enormous painting that would have greeted them as the housekeeper led them up the stairs, had the lighting at the time been better. Now Penelope paused on the half-landing for a closer look.

It was a portrait, and was so large that its subjects were very nearly life-sized. It depicted a family dressed in the styles that had prevailed in the latter half of the previous century. The man wore a coat of crimson brocade, the turned-back cuffs of his sleeves fully six inches wide. Although the front of his coat as well as its cuffs were adorned with large mother-of-pearl buttons, their function was presumably ornamental, for the coat was worn open to reveal the long, beautifully embroidered waistcoat underneath. The man's grey eyes gleamed with what looked to Penelope like amusement, and one side of his mouth was ever so slightly tipped up in a half-smile, as if he possessed a secret to which neither the long-ago artist nor the present-day viewer was privy. His age appeared to be somewhere in the mid-forties, although to Penelope, accustomed as she was to men who wore their hair more naturally dressed, the white wigs so popular in previous generations merely made their wearers look old.

The man's lady wife, seated on a stool at her husband's side, must have agreed with Penelope's sentiments, for her own hair, dressed high on her head with one long ringlet caressing her shoulder, was the glossy black of a raven's wing—a trait she had passed on to her small son, a black-haired, black-eyed child who leaned against his mother's wide skirts of cerulean blue satin. Her hand rested on the boy's shoulder, calling the viewer's attention to the fall of lace foaming at her elbow as well as the sapphire gleaming on her finger.

For reasons she could not explain, the portrait held Penelope's attention. Who was this family? Presumably they were in some way connected with Lord Markham. And yet his lordship must surely be older than this child would be today, assuming that the boy was still alive. Nor could he be the man in the portrait, for this gentleman must have been at the time he was painted very nearly the same age that Lord Markham was now.

"Come along, Penelope, my dear," chided Mrs. Fayre, who was halfway down the last flight of stairs before realizing she'd left her daughter behind. "We don't want to be late, certainly not on the very first night. We mustn't have his lordship thinking you one of those tiresome ladies who think they must make an 'entrance' to be interesting."

"Yes, Mama," Penelope said meekly, gathering her skirts and following her mother down the remaining stairs. But still she found her eyes straying back to the family in the portrait, finding them strangely mesmerizing in some way she could not understand.

14

It was at the dinner table that the entire company was assembled for the first time, the local gentry who would be participating in the hunt as well as those visitors from farther afield who would be staying at the Grange for the next two weeks. Penelope discovered with some chagrin that she had been given the place of honor at Lord Markham's right hand. He could not have made his intentions any plainer had he gone down on one knee in the middle of the fish course.

Glancing around a table gleaming with gold plate and sparkling crystal, she realized that if she were truly to accept the next eligible offer she received, her choices were limited indeed. Aside from Lord Markham and his nephew Mr. Freddie Markham, who appeared to be his lordship's heir presumptive, most of the men present were accompanied by their wives, and the few who were single were either decades older than her own nineteen years, or very nearly her own age and thus too young to be thinking seriously of matrimony—young men recently emancipated from Oxford or Cambridge, such as the squire's hunting-mad son and the vicar's bookish one.

Given the dearth of prospective suitors, it seemed likely that she would become Lady Markham by default. While Mama would no doubt consider this an excellent outcome, Penelope found her thoughts straying back to Bartholomew Fair, and an itinerant swordsman who had taken her chin in his hand and tipped it up ever so slowly for his kiss…and who bore such a disturbing resemblance to the footman even now bending over her shoulder to refill her wineglass…

"Do you, Miss Fayre?"

To her dismay, Penelope realized that everyone at the table was looking at her, awaiting her answer to the vicar's query—and that she had no idea what she had just been asked.

"I—I—"

She cast her gaze wildly about the table for some hint, and found it in a lean man with disheveled white hair and kindly light-blue eyes framed by wire-rimmed spectacles. His gaze met hers, and he gave her a sympathetic smile.

"If you dislike hunting, you need not fear owning it before your present company." He cast a fond glance at the tall, angular woman who had been introduced to Penelope as Mrs. Hatton, the vicar's wife. "My wife and I have amicably disagreed on the subject for more than thirty years."

"Of course, it helps that my marriage portion was sufficient for me to maintain a modest stable without requiring Mr. Hatton to compromise his principles," the vicar's wife put in, with a mischievous twinkle at her spouse that utterly transformed her plain countenance. Penelope breathed a sigh of relief at being no longer the cynosure of all eyes, and wondered if that had been the kindly couple's intent.

"Mrs. Hatton overstates her case, Miss Fayre. I have no real objection to the sport on moral grounds, although I confess to feeling a certain sympathy for the fox. Still, I enjoy my daily poached egg too much to allow the creatures unchecked access to the henhouse."

"I've never hunted before, so I can't say whether I would enjoy it or not," Penelope said, having seen a way to justify her inattention even as her face grew warm at the thought of her *faux pas*. "But I used to enjoy riding very much, and whenever the subject of horses comes up, I find myself thinking of my old mare, Daisy. When Papa died, Mama was obliged to sell her. I was at school, you see, so there was no one to exercise her." This last was for the edification of anyone who might suspect the liquidation of the Fayre stables had been a matter of financial necessity—which was, in fact, the truth.

"Aye, mares indeed," chuckled the stout, red-faced squire from the opposite end of the table, giving her a knowing wink. "Never seen the mare yet that would make a girl blush like a rose. Depend upon it, she's got some handsome young fellow on her mind."

If Penelope's cheeks had been pink before, they were now crimson with mortification—all the more so because the squire's supposition was entirely correct.

"Now look, Tom, you've gone and embarrassed her," chided his wife, a large woman whose loud, boisterous laugh was a study in cheerful vulgarity. "Daresay she thought she'd got away from that sort of thing when the Season was over. And who can blame her? Better to ride a brood mare than become one."

The company was momentarily silenced by this earthy metaphor until Mrs. Fayre, speaking in failing accents, gave it as her opinion that, while she certainly had no objection to females riding, she considered hunting far too dangerous a pastime for gently bred ladies.

"That's dished you, Mama," young Mr. Edward Hatton laughingly chided his mother. "Either you're not gently bred, or else you're no lady."

"I'm sure I never—" faltered Mrs. Fayre.

"Why, Edward Hatton, how wicked of you!" Lady Eleanor Bartlesby, still unattached after three Seasons, simpered at the vicar's son over the rim of her wineglass.

Mrs. Hatton bent a gimlet eye on her firstborn that promised retribution at no very late date. "You've certainly given Mrs. Fayre to suppose that you are no gentleman." In conciliating tones, she addressed the mortified widow. "I know of many others, male and female, who share your opinion, ma'am. And it is true that jumping while riding sidesaddle presents challenges to us ladies that sporting gentlemen are spared."

"I've never tried to jump," Penelope confessed, eager to further any conversation of which she was not the unwilling subject. "Are ladies more likely to fall off, Mrs. Hatton? Is that what you mean by the challenges of jumping sidesaddle?"

"I should say the greater danger is in their *not* falling off," the vicar's wife said, clearly in her element. "That is, a lady may be unseated, but because her foot is caught in the stirrup, she may be dragged for some considerable distance."

"Ugh," Penelope murmured, grimacing at the image

conjured by Mrs. Hatton's words.

"To be sure, hunting is not for any lady who is a new rider, nor even an experienced one who cannot maintain complete control of her mount," Mrs. Hatton continued, "but one might say the same of gentlemen, for that matter. No, the challenge for a lady is that she must know how to fall. Before she braces for the jump, she must be sure that she can kick her foot free of the stirrup, should she not land cleanly, and her horse must be trained to take in his stride—no pun intended—any small adjustments she might make to ensure this. Then, too, any rider, male or female, must roll away from the horse as quickly as possible in order to prevent being trampled."

"You terrify me, ma'am," Penelope said, only half in jest.

Lord Markham laid his hand over hers for the merest fraction of a second. "Have no fear, Miss Fayre. No one will be pressured to participate in the hunt who does not wish to do so. I daresay you may count on Mrs. Hatton to more than adequately represent your sex. In the meantime, I hope you and the other ladies"—his glance took in all the women seated around the table—"will join us when we assemble in the field for breakfast, and will ride over to meet us at the Huntsman's Horn afterward. While I'm sure no horse could take the place of your Daisy, I trust that my stables can offer some mount that will meet with your approval."

"I hope I am not so hard to please as all that, my lord," protested Penelope.

"On the contrary," he replied. "Rumor credits you with having the most exacting of standards."

The gleam in his eye gave her to understand that he was no

longer discussing horseflesh, but making an oblique reference to the numerous marriage proposals she had rebuffed. She was not quite certain how to answer.

"I don't—I think—That is, until a lady can be sure of her own heart, my lord—"

"And now I have put you to the blush," he said, filled with self-reproach. "Although you do it so charmingly that I cannot be sorry. Caddish of me, I know, but there it is. In any case, I hope your accommodations meet with your approval."

"Oh, yes!" Relieved to be back on solid ground, her answer was perhaps more enthusiastic than it otherwise might have been. "It's a beautiful house, my lord. I can't imagine anyone *not* approving of it."

"You relieve my mind, Miss Fayre."

The warm look that accompanied his words might have thrown Penelope into further confusion, had not the turn of the conversation provided her with the opening to ask a question she had made up her mind to put to him at the first opportunity.

"My lord, I could not help noticing a portrait on the half-landing," she began.

He nodded sagely. "If it is the one I have in mind, it would be hard *not* to notice it, Miss Fayre."

"It is very large, certainly, but who is it? The lady, I mean, and the man and the little boy."

His warm smile faded, and he gazed down at his plate as if searching for answers in the filet of sole. "The lady was the *Duchesse de Sainte-Marguerite*. Through some quirk in French inheritance laws which I don't pretend to understand, her husband held the title of *Duc de Sainte-Marguerite*, even though he was English and the title devolved upon him through his wife. Their son, portrayed at the age of six, was the *Vicomte de Valois*."

Some wisp of memory tickled Penelope's brain, but vanished when Lady Eleanor, determined not to be left out, put in her own query.

"Was," she echoed, noting their host's use of the past tense. "Why not 'is,' my lord? Are they all dead?"

"The gentleman is dead; the lady and the boy"—his shrug was the helpless gesture of a man who has pondered for too long a question for which there seemed to be no answer—"who can say?"

Penelope thought of the intriguing half-smile on the duke's face, the painted countenance so lifelike that she had almost expected it to speak. It was strange to think that he no longer existed except on the enormous canvas. "What happened to them?"

"He met his fate on a Parisian guillotine during the Terror of '94. His wife and son apparently escaped, but were never heard from again."

"Forgive me, my lord, if this is a subject that pains you, but why do you display their portrait so prominently?"

"Because—where is that footman?"

He interrupted himself to gesture for a footman to refill his glass, and the footman called Charles answered the impatient summons. He refilled Lord Markham's glass (which was still half full) and returned to his station against the wall, all without casting so much as a glance in Penelope's direction.

"I have told you the gentleman was an Englishman," Lord Markham said, picking up his tale where he'd left off. "What I did not tell you was that he also held a title of his own."

"Oh?"

In fact, it took Penelope a moment to recall exactly what "gentleman" he was talking about, so distracted was she by her awareness of "Charles" standing practically at her elbow. She had known, of course, that the footmen were positioned against the wall at her back, but she had not noticed Philippe, or his double, amongst them. Clearly, his five feet nine inches had been rendered inconspicuous by the six-foot specimens flanking him.

"Yes, the gentleman was also"—his lordship drank deeply from his glass— "my elder brother, the eighth Baron Markham."

Her eyes grew wide as comprehension dawned. "But that means—"

"Precisely. I am the ninth baron to hold the title. If he or his son had survived, then one of them would be Lord Markham, and I"—he flicked a glance down the length of the table at Mr. Markham, flirting animatedly with a lady whose name Penelope could not recall— "I would occupy the same ambiguous position now held by my nephew."

"How odd it must seem, to know you hold a lofty position only through another's tragedy," Penelope observed.

"On the contrary," said his lordship, "unless it is a new creation, every title in the kingdom is held by a man who inherited it after his predecessor's death. One can only try not to dwell on such matters—that, and, in my own case, ensure the succession without delay so that my nephew has no cause to hope for my own misfortune."

Penelope gave an uncomfortable laugh, although she could

not have said whether it was the flippant manner in which he'd spoken of the tragedy, or the hint of what might be his intentions toward herself that had so disconcerted her.

"Speaking of paintings," put in Mrs. Fayre, "am I correct in thinking I detect the hand of George Romney in that portrait?"

Lord Markham inclined his head in her direction. "You have a keen eye, Mrs. Fayre. It is indeed a Romney. It was done in 1793, scarcely a year before my poor brother's death. Did you notice the Grecian folly in the background? It is the same one you can see at the far end of the lake." He looked down at Penelope and added, with a caress in his voice, "I hope I may take you to see it, if weather permits."

Penelope, however, was not quite ready to give up the subjects of the painting in favor of its background. "But you said the bodies of his wife and child were never found," she reminded him. "Is it not possible that they made their escape and are alive somewhere today?"

He gave her an indulgent smile such as one might bestow on a precocious child. "I am fond of the occasional Gothic novel myself, Miss Fayre, but we must not confuse our reading with real life. What chance would a woman and a small child have, traveling alone in a country grown drunk on blood? Even if they were able to escape Paris, where could they go? By '94, every town of even middling size had its guillotine."

"Perhaps if they had reached the coast, they might have fled to England, or Rotterdam, or the Peninsula—"

Lord Markham shook his head. "I'm sure your tender heart does you credit, Miss Fayre. But consider, it has been twenty years. Is it not reasonable to think they must have made some attempt to claim the boy's birthright in all that time?"

Penelope might have pressed her point, had not a quelling look from her mother silenced her. Still, as she followed her mother up the stairs shortly after dinner (Lord Markham having suggested they all forgo a late tea and seek their beds early, in order to be well-rested for the hunt's early start on the morrow) she found her gaze drawn once more to the portrait and its three tragic figures. She had thought the gentleman's half-smile had hinted at a secret, but it appeared that she'd been wrong. The secret belonged to the lady and her small son—their fates a mystery, their whereabouts unknown.

What happened to you? she silently asked the painted likenesses. *Where are you now?*

The mother and child naturally made no reply, so she dismissed them with a shake of her head, wishing she could banish the portrait's haunting history as easily. If she were to marry Lord Markham, she decided, continuing up the stairs in her mother's wake, the first thing she would do as mistress of Markham Grange would be to turn the disturbing portrait's face to the wall.

15

The day of the hunt dawned cool and slightly overcast, with a light fog over the lake that gave the scene a dreamlike quality. Penelope, admiring the view from her window as so many other guests to the Grange had done, thought any lady who would pass up the chance to be mistress of such a place must have rats in her upper story—especially if the lady in question had only recently considered the prospect of traveling the country from one fair to the next in a painted wagon a preferable fate.

A movement in the distance caught her eye, and a moment later, a red deer emerged from the woods and picked its way to the water's edge, its head held high to better display its impressive set of antlers. Clearly, his lordship was not the only resident of Markham Grange on the hunt for a mate. But unlike the buck, Lord Markham was obliged to limit his choice to one, and that one was permanent—"'til death do us part," as the lines from the Book of Common Prayer made clear.

A lady could do a great deal worse, she scolded herself. True, there was more than twenty years' difference in their ages, but this in itself was not unusual; she could think of several couples with as many or more years between them, and they seemed happy enough to all appearances. And even though he must be well into his forties, Lord Markham was a remarkably handsome man; Mama had not been wrong about that. Perhaps more to the point, he was wealthy enough that neither she nor Mama need lack for anything, and his lordship's connections might well open all the right doors for Oliver's nascent diplomatic career. And although it was true that Caroline had never expressed a desire for remarriage, she herself, as Lady Markham, would be able to put her sister in the way of meeting just the sort of gentleman who might persuade her to change her mind.

Why, then, was it so difficult to reconcile herself to the prospect of marriage with him?

The answer was not far to seek. Last night, she'd decided her first act as mistress of Markham Grange would be to banish the family portrait from the half-landing, but in the pale light of dawn, she decided this was of only secondary importance. Her first move would be to give the sack to the footman who bore such a disturbing resemblance to the fencer of Bartholomew Fair. She had not been able to study him at dinner as she'd wished, for his duties had required him to stand, silent and self-effacing, against the wall. Indeed, so discreet had he been that she hadn't even been aware of his presence until Lord Markham had summoned him. Granted, the staff was not expected to fraternize with the guests—in fact, any attempt by a servant to do so would almost certainly result in immediate dismissal—but surely no footman had ever avoided her gaze so determinedly as

"Charles" had.

This unproductive train of thought was interrupted by a light scratching at the door, followed by the maid Betty's entrance with a pitcher of water, the faint curl of steam rising from it especially inviting in the cool of an October morning.

"Up already, miss?" she asked cheerfully, placing her burden on the washstand. "I thought you might want your bathing water early, what with the hunt and all."

"Yes, indeed," Penelope said, turning away from the window and wishing she might put aside her troubled thoughts so easily. "Thank you, Betty."

"'Tis no trouble, miss. Only let me see to Mrs. Fayre, and I'll be back to help you dress."

Betty was as good as her word, and soon Penelope, clad in a new riding habit of bottle-green wool with a modish toque hat set at a jaunty angle, joined the other guests making their way to the stables. There was no sign of the footman "Charles," and she hardly knew whether to be sorry or glad; to be sure, it was disturbing to endure the presence of one so very like the itinerant swordsman to whom she had lost her heart, and yet at the same time, she knew her riding habit was particularly becoming, its almost masculine trimming of gold braid *à la militaire* somehow emphasizing her femininity instead of concealing it. Since she had been obliged to wear her oldest and plainest gowns to the fair so as not to attract attention, she felt it was a great pity that Philippe—if the footman was indeed Philippe—was not on hand to see her looking her best.

Philippe's loss, however, was certainly Lord Markham's gain. He lost no time in excusing himself to the squire and his wife, and attached himself at once to Penelope.

"For shame, Miss Fayre!" he exclaimed in a scolding tone. "How do you expect us to concentrate on the fox when you offer us a far more tempting quarry? It is too bad of you!"

Penelope could not help smiling at this sally, which was admittedly far more clever a tribute than the compliments she usually received from those gentlemen nearer her own age.

I can offer you no compliment that you have not heard, and despised, a hundred times before…

Thrusting the memory resolutely to the back of her mind, she accepted Lord Markham's proffered arm and allowed him to lead her into the stables and past the rows of stalls until they reached a beautiful sorrel mare with a flaxen mane and tail.

"Her name is Juno," his lordship said, as Penelope stroked the horse's velvety nose. "I bought her four years ago for my late wife. I would consider it an honor if you would consent to ride her today. She is quite gentle, and is good with strangers, so you need have no fears on that head."

"The honor will be all mine, my lord," Penelope said, and meant it. From the time the hunting-party invitation had arrived in Upper Gower Street, she had regarded the event as a very different kind of hunt, with herself as the quarry; she hadn't realized until that moment how much she missed riding.

"I shall leave you two to become better acquainted, then." Excusing himself with a slight bow, he turned his attention back to his other guests.

Penelope had known, of course, that the group would assemble for breakfast at the place selected the previous morning as offering the best sport, and she had fully expected to eat a cold collation while seated on a blanket spread on the ground. Great was her surprise, then, when they arrived at the designated place and discovered a large tent erected some little distance away, under which stood a table set with crystal and silver only slightly less fine than that upon which they had dined the night before. She no longer wondered at the absence that morning of the footman her heart could not think of as Charles; along with what appeared to be half the household staff, he was bustling about, now offering cups of steaming coffee with which the hunters and huntresses could ward off the chill, now filling their plates with food still hot from half a dozen chafing dishes, all under the watchful eye of Lord Markham's butler, Crumley.

She was still marveling at this unexpected touch of elegance—and wondering if the unorthodox setting might provide her an opportunity to speak to "Charles" alone—when Lord Markham rode up to her on his large bay gelding and swung himself out of the saddle.

"You and Juno appear to be on the most agreeable of terms," he observed, reaching up to help her alight from her own mount.

"Who could not be, with such a well-mannered lady?" She patted the mare's neck below her neatly braided mane, then leaned down, bracing herself for the descent with her hands on his lordship's shoulders.

When she'd ridden while her father was still alive, it had been Papa to lift her down from the saddle, or else the grizzled old groom who had taught all three Fayre siblings to ride. She had never thought of this purely utilitarian act as being particularly sensual. Now, however, she found herself in disturbingly close proximity to Lord Markham, so close that she could feel the warmth of his hands on her waist through the fabric of her riding habit, the pressure of his thumbs digging into the flesh covering her ribs. Even the tender smile Lord Markham bent upon her seemed a bit knowing, as if he were fully aware of her thoughts and enjoyed her discomfiture.

She would have taken a hasty step backwards, had not Juno, the traitress, blocked her way. "I—I must go and find Mama," she stammered, and pushed past him—only to discover Charles the footman regarding them with an inscrutable expression on his oh-so-familiar countenance. For one brief moment his eyes met hers, and something flashed in their obsidian depths.

"Philippe?" she asked breathlessly, Lord Markham's animal magnetism entirely forgotten.

"I am called 'Charles,' miss," he said woodenly, and turned away.

But Penelope was not deceived. She'd seen that look in his eye, and knew it for what it was.

Recognition.

16

He knew her. There was no longer any doubt in her mind. But why was he so determined to ignore her? Presumably because he was afraid she would tell everyone—or someone in particular—that only a few weeks ago, he'd been duelling for his bread at Bartholomew Fair. She might have told him that these fears were unfounded; he must realize that she could hardly betray his secret without also betraying her own.

Of one thing, however, she was absolutely certain: Any attempt on her part to question him on the subject would yield no response beyond a wooden expression and an assertion that his name was Charles, and that she had mistaken him for someone else. Surely, she thought with rising indignation, it was not unreasonable to expect some explanation, after all that had passed between them during those two glorious days at the fair.

She soon discovered that the informality of the dining arrangements left her seated between the squire's son on the one hand and Mr. Freddie Markham, his lordship's heir presumptive, on the other, those enterprising young men having cut out their elders for the privilege. As both were fully engaged in recounting for her edification earlier hunts during which they had shown to particular advantage, the conversation required no greater effort on her part than making suitably admiring noises whenever her dining partners paused for breath, leaving her free to consider possible solutions to her dilemma.

But when at last the hunt-master gave the signal for the hunters to assemble, she was no nearer an answer as to how she might force a *tête-à-tête*. Plates and coffee cups were abandoned as the participants left the breakfast tent and made their way to the stand of beeches where some horses were tied while others were solicitously walked by those grooms whose employers held more exacting opinions as to the wisdom of allowing their horses to stand. Penelope cast a brief, regretful look at Philippe, busily clearing away the detritus left behind by more than a dozen diners. She had no doubt that he, along with the other footmen as well as the butler, would soon be returning to the house, bearing with them crates of dirty dishes, coffee cups, and flatware, to say nothing of coffee pots, decanters, and chafing dishes. And once again within the confines of the house, she would find it practically impossible to catch him alone, or to speak to him without being overheard. No, the hunt breakfast had been her best chance—and she had lost it.

"We'll move out in three flights," announced the squire in his role of master of the hunt, raising his voice to be heard. "The first will be the truly neck-or-nothing riders: Lord Markham; young Mr. Hatton; my son, Thomas; Mrs. Hatton—"

"I should hardly describe myself as a neck-or-nothing rider, Squire," protested the vicar's wife, laughing, although clearly pleased by what she must consider a compliment of no small magnitude.

"Nevertheless, ma'am, you're the only female I'd feel comfortable including in the first flight," he replied, sketching a courtly little bow in her direction. "The other ladies prefer going around fences, rather than over them."

Someone made an amusing response and everyone laughed, but Penelope paid no heed, for her thoughts were elsewhere. The squire's tribute to Mrs. Hatton's skill in the saddle recalled to her mind something that lady had said at dinner the previous night. If Philippe was determined to snub her at every turn, then maybe, just maybe, his defenses might be breached through more indirect means…

The first flight of hunters was soon off in a cacophony of baying hounds and blaring horns. Penelope could not help noticing the skill with which Mrs. Hatton fearlessly urged her mount into the *mêlée*, the crop in her right hand guiding the horse in place of her right leg, which lay across the horse's back, demurely covered by the long skirts of her Prussian-blue riding habit.

She certainly looks *like someone who knows what she's about*, Penelope reasoned. *At least, I hope she does.*

Once the more bruising riders were well on their way, the second flight assembled. This group included all of the younger women and several of the older ones, mostly mothers of the young bruisers in the first flight. Penelope took her place in this second flight, maneuvering her borrowed mare into a position toward the rear. When the signal was given, she set off with every appearance of eagerness, but held Juno to a canter until she could be certain no rider would be coming up from behind.

Murmuring soothingly to the mare, she worked her foot free of the sidesaddle stirrup—a movement concealed by the heavy folds of her riding habit—then took a deep breath and launched herself sideways off the horse's back.

She had not meant to scream, but the entirely spontaneous little shriek that accompanied her fall no doubt gave an air of verisimilitude to the act. Then she hit the ground with sufficient force to knock the breath from her body, rendering her temporarily incapable of speech. A pounding in her head resolved itself into running footsteps, and a moment later a footman in black and gold livery fell to his knees beside her.

"Miss Fayre! My dear girl, are you all right? No, don't try to get up."

In fact, Penelope had not been attempting to stand. She'd been gingerly moving each arm and leg in turn, and was relieved to discover that, although she would no doubt be black and blue by morning, Mrs. Hatton's advice had been essentially sound, for nothing appeared to be broken. At the footman's urging, however, every discomfort seemed to disappear. For he had spoken to her with the same French accent he'd affected as Philippe Valois, the Blade of Paris.

"It *is* you!" she exclaimed, raising glowing eyes to his. "I *knew* I could not be mistaken!"

Under different circumstances, the change in his expression from concern to mortification might have been comical. He had no time to deny the charge, however, for Mrs. Fayre was even now flying to her daughter's aid, followed by the vicar and, at a more sedate pace, Crumley, the butler.

"Penelope!" Mrs. Fayre seized her daughter's hands and

began to chafe them. "Are you injured? What happened, pray?"

Penelope uttered disjointed excuses about the difficulties inherent in riding an unfamiliar horse, while Juno, who upon finding herself riderless had circled back, regarded Penelope with a look of equine contempt.

"Never mind, poor child. What has happened to your hat? Ah, here it is."

Mrs. Fayre retrieved the hat from the turf where it had fallen, then brushed the dirt from its crown and attempted without much success to straighten the feather that now hung at a drunken angle.

Penelope had not noticed the absence of her hat until her mother mentioned it, although in retrospect she recognized the unlikelihood of its surviving such an ordeal unscathed. Now that the sad state of her headgear was brought to her attention, she realized that her coiffeur must be no better, for a lock of her hair had come loose from its moorings and now hung over her shoulder. While her fond parent exclaimed over her "accident," Penelope tried to tuck the lock back into place, and only succeeded in bringing still more hair down to join it before her mother's words drove such trivial matters from her mind.

"—Back to the house, where you can wash and change clothes," her mother was saying, then added, "How I wish Lord Markham had not ridden off with the first flight! Crumley, do you suppose his lordship would have any objection to our taking the carriage back to the house? I realize it must wreak havoc with his plans for the remainder of his guests, but if the groom returns with it as soon as may be, I daresay the other ladies will not be so very late in joining the hunters."

Did she only imagine it, Penelope wondered, or did some unspoken communication pass between Philippe and the butler? For she was certain that the butler's gaze had fallen for the briefest instance, shifting from her mother to something—or someone—nearer the ground before returning to Mama.

"If you will pardon my presumption, ma'am," Crumley said, "I feel sure his lordship would not wish you to miss the luncheon party. I fear the grooms are all out with the hunt, but I shall send Charles to accompany Miss Fayre back to the house."

"I'm not at all certain she will be safe on horseback," Mrs. Fayre fretted, looking from her disheveled daughter to the mare, who regarded the company with an air of detached boredom, as if the affairs of humans were of the utmost indifference to her.

"It wasn't Juno's fault," Penelope objected, with perfect truth. "Besides, she must be got back to the house somehow, and there is no one left to ride her. The other hunters in the second flight have their own mounts, and no one in the carriage party is dressed for riding."

The butler nodded. "Very true, miss."

"Nevertheless—" began Mrs. Fayre, unconvinced.

Penelope heard very little of the discussion that followed, for she was too occupied in fervent prayers that Crumley would triumph in the end. She never knew exactly what arguments the butler had employed, but he had obviously prevailed, for by the time she concluded her heavenly entreaties with a silent "Amen," the squire's wife had joined the group and taken charge of Juno's reins.

"Much ado about nothing, if you ask me," she said briskly,

the kindly smile she bestowed upon Penelope robbing the words of any callousness. "Best thing you can do after taking a tumble is to get back in the saddle. No time to dwell on it that way."

"I'm sure you're right," Penelope said warmly, and the grateful smile that accompanied these words was sufficient to make the squire's good lady confide to her husband, some hours later, that she was glad their impressionable young son had not been present to witness it.

The matter having been settled to everyone's satisfaction, "Charles" the footman approached the mare, going down on one knee and lacing his fingers to make a stirrup of his hands.

"If you please, Miss Fayre?" His tone was impersonal, inviting her to place her booted foot into this improvised mounting block, but conveying nothing that might be interpreted as a more intimate communication.

Holding the voluminous skirts of her riding habit over one arm, she put her other hand on his shoulder to steady herself, then looked uncertainly into his eyes as she placed her foot into his clasped hands.

"Later," he breathed, so softly that she might have thought she imagined it, had the single word not been accompanied by the slight twitch of his right eyelid in a wink. Then his hands closed about her foot and he tossed her into the saddle.

Nothing else was said, save for Mrs. Fayre's admonitions to her daughter to be careful, and Penelope's assurances on this point. The silence between them stretched out, broken only by the occasional whicker from Juno or the baying of the hounds in the distance. Once they had crested the rising ground and descended on the other side, however, Penelope darted a quick glance over her shoulder to ascertain whether they were out of sight of the remaining hunters. Once assured on this point, she bent an accusing glare upon her escort.

"So it *is* you, after all! I *knew* it was! Only—Philippe, what does it all mean? What are you doing here—and as a footman, no less? And why were you so beastly to me when I recognized you?" Belatedly recollecting one possible reason for his repeated denials, she gave a disdainful sniff. "If you feared I was going to badger you into picking up where we left off at the fair, let me set your mind at ease, for nothing could be further from the truth!"

The effect of this speech was considerably diminished by the fact that he appeared not to have heard it.

"Look here," he said, "do you think you could walk if you leaned upon my arm? It's not so very far if we cut across the fields, and I can't talk to you like this." As if to demonstrate his dilemma, he raised one hand and began to massage the back of his neck.

Penelope was in complete agreement with this plan as opposed to the present arrangement. She was painfully aware of having betrayed too much, however, so she gave no response beyond a regal nod and a cool "Very well."

Still, it appeared that even this rather tepid encouragement was enough. "My dearest girl," he said warmly, and reached up to receive her.

All her pride seemed to melt away. She kicked her foot free of the stirrup and slid off the saddle and into his arms. Their kiss at the fair and been slow and infinitely tender; this one was deep and almost frantic, the desperate reconciliation of two people who had each believed the other lost forever.

"I beg your pardon," he said somewhat breathlessly, when at last they drew apart. "This is exactly what I'd most hoped to avoid."

"Avoid?" she echoed, as he took her hand and drew it through his arm. "But why? Philippe, I thought I would never see you again, and then when I stepped out of Mr. Markham's carriage and saw you—it was like a miracle!"

He gave a snort of derision, but his fingers tightened over hers nonetheless. "Some miracle! Crumley told me you were on the guest list—and that your name was 'Miss Fayre,' just as you'd said. And then to see you arriving with my cousin Freddie, just as if you were one of the family—well, I won't say your 'miracle' was the worst moment of my life, but it was near enough! Look here, am I walking too fast for you?"

"Oh, no," she assured him dreamily. She was indeed leaning on his proffered arm, but far from feeling any pain, she was conscious only of the rich blue of the October sky, the crunch of the gold and scarlet leaves beneath her feet, and most of all, the latent strength of the lean, muscular arm beneath her fingers. "I'll admit, it hurt a bit more than I expected, but I'm not seriously injured."

But he heard nothing of the latter part of this speech, for he'd stopped in his tracks and now held her by the shoulders. "*More than you expected?*" he repeated sharply. "Do you mean to tell me that performance was *on purpose?*"

Penelope plummeted sharply back to earth. "I had to do *something* to shake you out of your horrid indifference!"

"You might have killed yourself!"

"Nonsense! You heard Mrs. Hatton at dinner last night; she told me just how it should be done." As he struggled for words with which to bring her to some sense of her own recklessness, she pressed her advantage. "What would you have done if I hadn't forced the issue—ignored me until the hunting-party is over and I return to London, betrothed to Lord Markham, if Mama has anything to say to the matter?"

His jaw tightened, but he said only, "You do understand, don't you, that it is imperative you say nothing of our earlier acquaintance? In fact, it would be better by far if you ignore me entirely."

Penelope regarded him steadily, recalling their time at the fair and trying in vain to make it fit with their present circumstances. "That night at the fair, you told me you were a fraud," she said at last. "Does this—you being here, I mean—does it have anything to do with that?"

"It has *everything* to do with it! That is why you must not do or say anything that might betray me. Do you understand?"

"No," she said candidly. "How can I, unless you tell me?"

"Very well, then." He took her hand and drew it back through his arm. "What do you want to know?"

Penelope hardly knew where to start. Arranging her disordered thoughts with an effort, she considered and rejected at least a dozen possible lines of inquiry before deciding to begin, as it were, at the beginning. "Who are you? What is your real name?"

He gave a bitter little laugh. "What would you say," he asked, answering her question with one of his own, "if I were to tell you I am Lord Markham?"

17

Yᵒᵘ are Lord Markham?" Penelope echoed incredulously. She made a vague gesture in the general direction of the baying hounds. "But what about—?"

She broke off, suddenly seeing in her mind's eye the portrait of a family clothed in the fashions of a generation ago: a gentleman and his lady wife and, leaning against his mother's skirts, a black-eyed boy about six years old, a lock of straight black hair falling over his forehead…

"It's you," she said, staring up into those same black eyes set in a face some twenty years older than its painted representation. "That painting—the one on the half-landing— the *vicomte de Valois*—no wonder your title sounded so familiar! The boy in the portrait is you!"

He sketched an ironic little bow. "At your service."

"But Lord Markham—the man recognized as Lord Markham, I mean—he said the people in the portrait were dead!"

"He was partially correct. My father—besides being Lord Markham, he was the *Duc de Sainte-Marguerite*—he died in Paris during the Reign of Terror. My mother followed him only six months ago. She went to her grave convinced that my father's younger brother, my uncle Robert, conspired with French revolutionaries to kill him."

"That would mean his lordship—the host of the hunting-party, I mean—is a murderer," said Penelope, struggling to take it in.

"Exactly." Philippe's lip curled in a contemptuous expression that betrayed his Continental ancestry. "Your host, and my employer."

"Does he know?"

"That the true heir is toiling below stairs as a footman? No—at least, not yet." He regarded her keenly, and when he spoke again, it was in a voice from which all traces of irony had vanished. "So you see, do you not, why you must not appear to notice me in any way?"

"I can see why you don't want him to recognize you," she said slowly, "but I don't quite see why you're here. I daresay you wish to claim your rightful place, although how you can do that while playing at being a footman quite escapes me."

He laughed at that, banishing the earlier bitterness from his countenance. "Anyone who thinks Crumley allows the footmen to 'play' has a very odd notion of life below stairs!"

"Does Crumley know who you are?"

"He does now, although he didn't recognize me at first. It went sorely against the grain with him to allow me to work as a servant in the house that ought by rights to be mine."

"But when do you intend to declare yourself? What are you waiting for?"

"Proof," he said simply. "Mama was convinced that my uncle was conspiring with someone in France. Even before war was declared between the two countries, travel between England and France was both difficult and dangerous, especially for those French *aristos* trying to escape *la guillotine*, but letters could still get through with relative ease. My father had been in communication with his brother while he laid his plans for escaping with Mama and me. Who is to say Uncle Robert was not in communication with someone else in France as well, someone who might have helped him step into my father's English shoes in exchange for information regarding Papa's whereabouts in Paris?"

"I see how such a thing can be easily imagined," Penelope said thoughtfully, "but even if there were such an exchange of letters, surely they must have been destroyed. What man would keep letters that had the power to hang him for murder?"

"A man who did not entirely trust his co-conspirator." Philippe's answer came so readily that she realized he had wrestled with these same questions many times before. "A man who feared that his French contact, having helped him to a fortune, might one day require a part of it in exchange for his silence. I daresay the French contact holds similar letters from my uncle, and for the same purpose. There is, as they say, no honor among thieves."

"And still less among murderers, I should think."

"Just so. It is my intention to search the house for any such letters, or any other evidence that might confirm my mother's suspicions."

"And as a footman," Penelope deduced, "you have the run

of the house, especially since Crumley will support you in any claim that you were sent into the muniments room or some such place on an errand."

He nodded. "Yes, within reason. The presence of a houseful of guests helps matters in that his lordship's duties as host give him little time to notice, much less wonder at, my movements. Unfortunately," he added with a grimace, "those same guests make it more challenging to conduct my search uninterrupted. Take the library, for instance. In my father's day, many estate papers were kept there, as well as books. Only think how awkward it would be if a guest were to come to the library in search of a book to read, only to discover me rifling the drawers of his lordship's desk. And then there is my uncle's bedchamber. How the devil am I to search that? What possible excuse could I offer for my presence if he should discover me there?"

Penelope's eyes grew wider as an idea occurred to her, and her hand tightened impulsively on his arm. "Perhaps I could help you!"

He froze where he stood, regarding her with a look of almost comical dismay. "My dear girl, your presence in Uncle's bedchamber would be even more objectionable than mine would be!"

"I didn't mean that," she said impatiently, too caught up with the notion to register embarrassment at the implication, much less blush. "But, as you say, one of Lord Markham's guests—yes, I believe you are the real Lord Markham, but I don't know what else to call him!— as you say, one of his guests might be unable to sleep, and might go downstairs to the library in search of a book to read, so why should that guest not be me? I could—" she broke off abruptly, seeing him shake his head emphatically in the negative.

"Don't think I'm not grateful for the offer, but no. I will not permit you to put yourself in danger."

"What danger? What could he do to me?"

"Other than dismiss you from the house in disgrace, you mean?"

"Because I had difficulty falling asleep in a strange house? Stuff and nonsense!"

They were still engaged in lively debate when they reached a copse of beech trees. As if by mutual consent, they fell silent as they entered the shelter of the trees, their steps becoming slower until at last he came to a stop at the edge of the wood, taking hold of her sleeve to detain her. "Once we emerge from the wood, we'll be in full view of the house, so while we still have some degree of privacy, let me say this: I told you at the fair that I had nothing to offer a woman. I still have nothing; this much has not changed. I will not offer for you unless and until I can offer you a better life than following the fairs from town to town as a mountebank's wife. The moment I take possession of my father's honors, I fully intend to lay them, along with my heart, at your feet. Still, I don't know how long that may take—or if I will ever find the proof I need at all. If you should grow tired of waiting—if you should meet someone else—"

In answer, she seized the lapels of his black and gold livery and leaned toward him with chin lifted, eyes closed, and lips puckered. He did not avail himself of this invitation, however, but held her firmly at arm's length.

"No," he said in a voice that brooked no argument. "I will not kiss you until I've earned the right."

She rocked back on her heels, deflated. "Your sentiments have certainly changed in the last fifteen minutes!"

He gave a rather exasperated sigh. "A temporary madness. Such was not my intention, I assure you."

"And when you kissed me at the fair?"

His lip curled in a rather cynical smile. "The fair is a world unto itself. The ordinary rules don't apply there."

"I wish we were still there," she said wistfully. "I wish we'd never had to leave it."

He made no reply, but took her hand and, against his better judgment, pressed it to his lips. Then he once again made a stirrup of his hands and tossed her into the saddle. A few minutes later, they emerged from the shelter of the beech wood into the real world.

* * *

"My dear Miss Fayre! I was never more shocked!" exclaimed Lord Markham, hurrying forward to take her hands in his. The hunting party had just returned, and it was clear that the tale of Penelope's tumble had lost nothing in the telling. "And here I thought Juno so gentle a mount! I shall never forgive myself for so egregious an error in judgment."

"Nor is there the slightest need for you to do so," Penelope insisted, allowing but not returning the pressure of his fingers on hers. She suppressed a shudder at the thought that, were she to look down at them, she might see blood on his hands. "Neither you nor Juno did anything wrong. It was entirely my own fault, I assure you."

Lord Markham looked as if he might argue this point, but since both the squire's and the vicar's families were preparing to say their goodbyes and return to their own homes, he was obliged to accept their thanks for the invitation and assure them that the pleasure had been all his. By the time he had fulfilled these duties, those members of the hunting-party who were staying at the Grange had gone upstairs to their respective bed-chambers in order to recruit their strength from the exertions of the morning with a nap before assembling for dinner that evening.

Since Penelope's "accident" had precluded her wearing herself out in the hunt, she found herself untroubled by somnolence. And so, having immediately upon her return set her hair to rights and changed her riding habit for a gown better suited for an afternoon spent indoors, she picked up the book she'd been reading and went downstairs to the drawing room.

Alas, it soon transpired that there was one other of the Grange's inhabitants still at large. Lord Markham was there before her, standing before the fire and staring abstractedly down into the flames, one hand propped against the mantel and one foot resting on the gleaming brass fender.

My mother went to her grave convinced that my father's brother Robert conspired with French revolutionaries to kill him...

Philippe's words rose unbidden to her mind. He had made it sound so very convincing, and yet, seeing the warmth of his lordship's smile as he looked up at her entrance, it scarcely seemed possible. In any case, courtesy prevented her from beating a hasty retreat, so it behooved her to withhold judgment, at least for the nonce.

"It appears the others have abandoned us to our own devices, Miss Fayre," his lordship said, turning away from the fire. "Until Morpheus releases them, I suppose we must pass the time as best we can. May I show you the garden? It is not at its best so late in the year, of course, but I daresay we can find something there to interest us."

With this suggestion for her entertainment, Penelope found herself on the horns of a dilemma. Having previously declared herself to be in no need of rest, she could hardly offer weariness as a rationale for crying off, and she could think of no other excuse that sounded in the least degree plausible. In the end, she was compelled to take his proffered arm and allow him to lead her out of the house and into the elegant formal garden at the back of the residence.

She soon discovered they were not alone there, for as they strolled down the pebbled path, they came upon a gardener engaged in preparing some of the plantings for the coming winter. He looked up at their approach and, upon recognizing the master of the house with one of his guests, gave a tug to his forelock with one grimy hand, then made himself scarce so quickly that she wondered if Lord Markham had given him some signal to take himself off.

A few minutes later, she was sure of it.

"I suppose you know," his lordship began, breaking off one of the last of the Michaelmas daisies and presenting it to her with a flourish, "why I have invited you here."

Penelope's hackles rose, but she chose to be obtuse, exclaiming brightly, "Oh, yes! The hunting in this part of the country is known to be excellent. I only regret that I was unseated before I had a chance to experience it for myself." Realizing too late that this comment might be interpreted as a hint for a second invitation, she added in a rush, "Mama has had nothing but praise for the luncheon at the Huntsman's Horn."

"I am pleased to hear it, for I have every hope that I may soon require his services in another capacity."

"Oh?" Penelope had been unconsciously stripping off the purple petals one by one, but at this oblique reference to the vicar, she instinctively took a step backwards, only to find her retreat blocked by the brittle and leafless stems of what in milder weather had been the herbaceous border, now catching at her skirts like skeletal hands. I believe Mr. Hatton must have done very well as surrogate host, for he appears to have taken very good care of the ladies who chose to meet the hunters there rather than ride to hounds themselves.

"Come now, Miss Fayre, no false modesty," chided his lordship, closing the distance between them. "Surely you, who have received so many proposals of marriage, cannot have failed to recognize when another is in the offing."

"But how could I?" she was moved to protest. "You never showed any particular interest in me during the Season."

He chuckled. "And that rankles, does it?"

In fact, nothing could have been further from the truth. Far from hoping to attract his attention, Penelope had scarcely noticed him at all. To be sure, he had been pointed out to her, and Lady Jersey had introduced him to her at Almack's, but if she'd formed any impression of him, it had been to observe that he, in his forties, was rather old to be seeking a wife amongst the debutantes. Since she could hardly make him a gift of this information, it was a relief to discover that the question he'd posed had been purely rhetorical.

"Let us say," he continued, "that mine was the superior strategy, for while your other admirers have been obliged to retire, crushed, from the lists, I now have you all to myself. I confess, my vanity will not allow me to consider either the squire's or the vicar's progeny as serious rivals."

What a pity you cannot say the same for your footman, Penelope thought, wishing his lordship would not stand quite so close.

"But you have given me no answer," he admonished her, capturing her hands with his. "Having seen my home, can you picture yourself making me the happiest of men by living here as its mistress?"

He had spoken no words of love, or even of admiration. She hardly knew whether to feel relieved at not being obliged to fend off his advances, or indignant that he apparently thought her so mercenary that she had only to see a rich estate to fall into the arms of its master. And so she might have done, she conceded, had her discovery of the Bartholomew Fair swordsman's true identity not suggested a way for her to keep the pledge she'd made to herself and still make the love match her heart craved.

But Philippe had not made her an offer. In fact, he'd gone out of his way not to make her an offer, at least not yet. Then, too, she had not promised to wait for him, not in so many words. Was she still bound, then, by her resolution to accept the next eligible offer she received? To be sure, she owed her mother no less, and of course, Mama had no way of knowing that their genial host stood on the edge of a precipice.

On the other hand, if she declined his lordship's offer, she and her mother would have no choice but to pack their bags and return to London the very next morning, if not sooner. One could, after all, hardly continue to enjoy a gentleman's hospitality after having rejected his proposal of marriage. The other guests would never be told the reason for their hasty departure, although the more astute could probably hazard a very good guess, for Lord Markham had certainly made no secret of his intentions. She would almost certainly be labeled an arrant flirt, but that was nothing new. Perhaps more to the point, she would be powerless to help Philippe search for the letter that would prove his claim, if such proof existed at all.

All things considered, there was only one answer she could make.

"I can think of no greater honor," she said with a secretive little smile, "than to be Lady Markham."

18

So pleased was Penelope with this dissemblance that she was quite unprepared for its aftermath. Lord Markham abruptly released her hands, and the next moment she was in his arms.

"Then let us seal the bargain, shall we?"

His voice was husky, and she, realizing what he was about, contrived to turn her head away just in time for his kiss to land somewhere in the vicinity of her ear.

"Not—Not yet, my lord!" she protested, trying to sound merely timid rather than repulsed.

Far from being offended, his lordship chuckled softly, a low, rumbling sound that stirred the hair at her ear and raised gooseflesh on her arms.

A man of passion and danger...

Where had she heard those words before, and to whom had they referred?

"Little prude," said her affianced husband. "Maidenly modesty and shy blushes are all very charming in their way, but be warned, my pet: I want no cringing mouse in my bed. Once we are married, I shall expect my wife's complete submission."

Submission, she wondered, *or subjugation?* The former was offered freely; the latter was demanded by force. Without warning, Penelope heard once again her sister's discourse on the marital act. She'd told Caroline it sounded disgusting, but until that moment, feeling his lordship's hot breath and hearing his voice low and vaguely threatening in her ear, she'd never thought of it as particularly frightening. Then she saw the glint in his eye, and it suddenly occurred to her that he *knew* he'd frightened her—and he was pleased by the notion.

The discovery emboldened her as nothing else could. For the first time, she could picture his lordship not as a genial host or even a solicitous suitor, but a man ruthless enough to arrange for the murder of three people, one of them only a child, for his own gain. Very well, then, she decided. If he had no desire for a timid wife, he would soon discover that his betrothed was a great deal bolder than he'd bargained for.

She looked down at the flower in her hand—she was surprised to discover that she'd stripped it down to a bare stem —and tried to assume the manner of a young woman overcome with her own good fortune and slightly in awe of her affianced husband. "I'm sure you must be aware that my birth is no more than respectable, and my dowry so small as to be almost non-existent. So tell me, my lord, why do you wish to marry me?"

He cocked one eyebrow. "Fishing for compliments, Miss Fayre?"

"N-no," she said, settling more comfortably into the role she'd chosen, "I only thought—it seems to me that you might have chosen someone more sophisticated." Without raising her chin, she peeped up at him through her lashes, an affectation that her siblings would have recognized as a sure sign that she was plotting some mischief. "A dashing young widow, perhaps, or a lady of independent means."

"I'm sure you do yourself an injustice." He took the denuded stem from her hand and tossed it into what remained of the herbaceous border, then drew her hand through his arm as they resumed their walk down the garden path. "Still, since you ask, I shall be honest with you. I am almost forty-five years old, and I have need of an heir."

"But surely Mr. Markham—"

"Freddie Markham is, as you suggest, my heir presumptive," he said, readily conceding the point. "But a man wants a son of his own loins to succeed him. I had such a son once. Both the boy and his mother—my late wife—were taken from me over the course of one cruel winter. I was spared the malady that carried them off, but I learned my lesson well. Illnesses or accidents may strike at any time—how well I know it!—and so I made up my mind to marry a young woman, one with many childbearing years ahead of her. Never again will I put all my eggs, so to speak, in one basket."

Rather like a brood mare, Penelope thought, recalling the squire's wife's earthy observation on this subject, and resisting the temptation to repeat it aloud.

She found herself thinking of that other Markham son, the black-eyed child in the portrait with his mother and father. Did it prey on Lord Markham's mind, the knowledge that the boy's body had never been identified? Did he ever wonder if, somehow, somewhere, that boy had managed to survive and was now grown to manhood, and might someday come to claim his rightful inheritance?

Oh, I hope so. I very much hope so.

What poetic justice it would be, for his lordship to be trapped in a hell of his own making while the true heir was beneath his own roof at this very moment, searching for the evidence that would bring his uncle's misdeeds to light.

Lord Markham noted her long silence, and drew his own entirely erroneous conclusions. "I daresay you are thinking there are many other young ladies I might have taken to wife. To that I would say, look about you." The sweep of his arm encompassed everything from the stately home at their backs to the distant lake and the autumnal splendor of the Home Wood beyond. "So beautiful a setting demands a jewel of comparable beauty to adorn it."

The metaphor was so typical of the heavy-handed praise that had been lavished upon her throughout her London Season that she was obliged to turn away lest her contempt be evident in her expression. First his lordship had called her his "pet"—as if she were a poodle, or perhaps a pug—and now it seemed she was a jewel: an inanimate object, incapable of thought or feeling, whose only value lay in its appearance and, perhaps, how avidly others might covet it.

Over the course of the Season, she had become so adept at fielding such exaggerated gallantries that she responded to his lordship as if by rote, all the while gazing across the expanse of lawn and the sheet of grey-blue water beyond it and wondering if Philippe as a child had ever got grass stains on his breeches or fallen into the lake.

His lordship, all unsuspecting, led her back into the house

a short time later, congratulating himself on a most satisfactory afternoon's work.

* * *

"My dearest girl!"

Upon entering the house, Penelope had adjourned to her bedchamber in the hope of a few quiet minutes in which to consider how and when she might free herself from what she firmly intended to be a temporary betrothal. She was foiled in this quest, however, by the appearance of her mother, wreathed in smiles, entering the room through the connecting door. Penelope had a sinking feeling that only one thing could account for such a degree of maternal happiness—a feeling confirmed a moment later, when Mrs. Fayre enveloped her daughter in a fond embrace.

"To think of my own child as Lady Markham! I vow, I was never so pleased by anything!"

Penelope was not surprised by her mother's reaction to the news—in fact, she would have expected nothing less—but she was seized by the notion that, matters having been set into motion, they were now moving a great deal too quickly and spinning out of her control. "H-Has his lordship already spoken to you, then?"

"Indeed he has! Of course, if we were still in London, he should have applied to Oliver for permission, your brother being the head of the family, but he said he was too impatient to wait, so eager as he was to make you his own. Was that not prettily said?"

Ignoring this question, Penelope asked one of her own. "Does anyone else know?"

Mrs. Fayre's face fell. "No. That is, they don't *know*, for they haven't been told, but I daresay some may have *guessed*, for such secretive looks passed between his lordship and me as you never saw!" She giggled like a schoolgirl at the memory.

"Must we—that is, may we wait a while before making an announcement?"

Mrs. Fayre gave Penelope's cheek an affectionate pinch. "I'm sure your modesty does you credit, what with you not wanting to puff off your good fortune in front of poor Lady Eleanor Bartlesby, who hasn't had an offer in three Seasons, and with her having an earl for a papa and ten thousand pounds per annum beside! But nor must there be anything furtive about the match, for to be secretive is as bad as being boastful—perhaps even worse, for it hints at something scandalous, and that would never do. So Lord Markham and I have fixed it between us that the betrothal will be announced at the hunt ball on the last night of the party. Will that be agreeable to you?"

"Most agreeable, Mama," Penelope said warmly, and meant it.

For with almost two full weeks before the hunting-party came to an end, she and Philippe must surely find the evidence he sought. Then—and only then—would she be able to break her engagement to the false Lord Markham, and become betrothed to the real one.

19

The tinny chimes of the long-case clock sounded two. Penelope's bedchamber was some distance removed from this imposing timepiece, but her ear was attuned to the sound, for she had been waiting to hear it for quite some time. Now that the moment had come, she slipped quietly from her bed, pulled her dressing-gown over her nightrail, and lit the bedside candle with hands that were not entirely steady. Then, picking up the candle in its brass holder, she stole silently from the room, pulling the door closed behind her lest some other late-night prowler should pass by and discover her empty bed.

She lingered just outside the door for a long moment, straining her ears for any sound. Hearing none, she padded down the corridor to the stairs, then, picking up her skirts with one hand and holding the candle in the other, she began to descend. As always, her gaze was drawn to the large portrait hanging above the half-landing.

The flame of her candle dipped and bobbed with every step she took, and the shifting light flickering over the canvas gave the painted figures a sense of movement, so much so that

Penelope half-expected the duchess to turn and inspect the young lady who aspired to marriage with her son.

"You can't fool me," Penelope informed the little family in a whisper. "I know your secret now. And I have one or two secrets of my own."

None of them disputed this claim, so she continued her descent. Still, she could almost feel the painted gazes on her back, and it was with an odd sense of abandonment that she moved away from the staircase and made her way to the library.

She had not been in this room before, but it had been pointed out to her on the day she'd first arrived at the Grange, so she went unerringly to the door. She pushed it open, relieved to find that the well-oiled hinges made no protest, then stole inside and closed it behind her. She held her candle high, illuminating an empty room.

"Philippe?"

Her whisper was hardly more than a breath, but it was enough.

"And about time, too!"

The disembodied voice held a hint of amusement, and a moment later Philippe crawled out of the knee hole beneath the heavy desk positioned before the window.

"I'd begun to wonder if you weren't coming," he said, clambering to his feet.

"I promised to help, didn't I?"

"Still, it wouldn't be entirely surprising if you'd overslept. Or," he added diffidently, "if you'd judged it more practical to marry the current holder of the title."

"That is a beastly thing to say!" she cried a bit too

vehemently, wondering what he might already have heard about her betrothal. She supposed she ought to tell him—it was her understanding that nothing remained a secret in the servants' hall for long—but their stolen moments together were so rare that she was extremely reluctant to let his lordship intrude even more than he had already.

Philippe's thoughts must have been running along similar lines, for he did not press the issue, but only sighed. "It was rather beastly, wasn't it? Pray forgive me. It isn't easy, you know, to watch that murderous blackguard making love to you while my hands"—he spread them wide in a gesture of helpless frustration— "are tied."

"They won't be for long," she declared, setting her jaw. "They can't be."

"They will if we don't get to work. Crumley gave me the key to the desk—I thought it best not to ask how he'd come by it—so I'll search through the drawers while you examine the books."

At first she thought he'd meant the estate's accounting books, and was about to protest that she hadn't the expertise to decipher the records of a large estate, especially one that belonged to a stranger. Then she realized he'd meant the words quite literally. The library, unsurprisingly, was filled with books collected by generations of Markhams, any one of which might have incriminating papers tucked between its pages or sandwiched between it and its nearest neighbor.

It was a daunting task. Abandoning with a sigh any thoughts she might have entertained of a romantic tryst by moonlight, she positioned her candle for optimal illumination and set to work.

The bookshelves, she soon discovered, held a disorganized collection of volumes ranging from scholarly treatises on Greek and Roman history to scientific discourses on subjects ranging from astronomy to zoology. Volumes of poetry by Shakespeare and Spenser stood cheek by jowl with well-worn novels that had been popular in the previous century. Penelope's interest was piqued by these latter. She remembered the lady in the painting, and wondered if it had been Philippe's mother who had read and re-read them.

Alas, she hadn't the luxury of dwelling on this interesting possibility. Time was scarce, so she made mental note of a few titles to take to her room later, then turned her attention to the task at hand. One by one, she removed each volume from the shelf, flipped through its pages, and even peered down its spine in search of any paper that might have been hidden there. She could hear Philippe at work on the desk behind her, opening each drawer in turn and rifling through its contents before sliding it closed and moving on to the next. They worked on in companionable silence for some quarter of an hour, until Penelope reached up to remove a neglected volume from the top shelf and unwittingly dislodged a fine layer of dust. The cloud tickled her nostrils, and she sneezed.

Instantly the room grew darker, casting her shadow into strong relief. At first she thought her sneeze had extinguished her candle, but its bobbing flame, along with a scrabbling sound at her back, gave her to understand that it was Philippe who had snuffed his candle, and who now sought hasty recourse to his hidey-hole. Even as she opened her mouth to question this curious behavior, the door opened to reveal Lord Markham, resplendent in a burgundy-colored banyan of quilted satin.

"Miss Fayre? Penelope, my pet, what are you doing here at this time of night?"

At any other time, she might have taken exception to his making free with her given name, their "betrothal" notwithstanding, to say nothing of the nickname she found demeaning. At the moment, however, she was all too keenly aware of the precariousness of her position—and more keenly still of the presence of Philippe, curled tightly into the kneehole of his lordship's desk.

"I—I couldn't sleep," she stammered, thinking even as she said the words what a feeble excuse they sounded.

"Could you not, indeed? I wonder what might be keeping you awake. Something preying upon your mind, perhaps?"

The shadows cast by the candlelight over his deep-set eyes gave him an appearance so saturnine as to be almost demonic, and it required no playacting on her part to turn her face away from him.

"I remembered being shown the library, so I thought I should come down and choose a book to take upstairs with me."

Lord Markham made no reply, but removed the book from her unresisting hands, then beat the dust from its covers and turned it over to inspect the spine.

"Fordyce's *Sermons to Young Women*," he read aloud. "Hardly the sort of reading material I might have expected from the belle of the Season."

"I'm sure we could all benefit from moral instruction," she said primly, with an inward grimace at the words coming out of her own mouth. Even well-behaved Caroline, the epitome of the country vicar's wife, would have rolled her eyes at so pedantic a claim. She sighed and said, with what she hoped was disarming sheepishness, "Truth to tell, I found *The Romance of the Forest* a thrilling book by day, but a bit too frightening for reading just before bed. I feared it might give me bad dreams, so I thought to find something a bit more restful."

But Lord Markham did not appear to be listening. Instead, his gaze had drifted past her, and was now fixed upon some point beyond and to her right. Fearing the worst, she turned and saw what had attracted his lordship's attention: One of the tails of Philippe's liveried coat protruded from the kneehole of the mahogany desk.

"Never mind, Charles," she said hastily, addressing herself to the telltale fold of gold-braided black wool. "I'm sure my earring will turn up eventually."

"Yes, miss," came a voice from beneath the desk.

"What's this?" asked Lord Markham, his frowning gaze shifting from his affianced bride to the footman who was even now backing out from under the desk, his face averted. "An earring, you say?"

Silently willing Philippe not to say anything to contradict her, Penelope plunged into explanation. "I must have lost it sometime yesterday, or perhaps earlier today, for now that I think of it, I was wearing the same pair at dinner."

His lordship's left eyebrow arched quizzically toward his hairline. "These earrings must be valuable indeed, to compel you to search for them in the middle of the night. But I thought you said you'd come down to the library because you couldn't sleep."

"Yes, for I kept thinking about my earring and wondering where I might have lost it," agreed Penelope, deriving considerable satisfaction from disabusing his lordship of any notion that it had been thoughts of him which had kept her from slumber. "So I tried Mrs. Radcliffe's novel, and when that gave me gooseflesh, I came downstairs to find another book. Then it occurred to me that I might have lost it here, for I did spend a good deal of time in the library after my—my tumble compelled me to return to the house. And I thought since I was already in the library, and wide awake, I might as well search for my earring while I was here."

"Allow me to set your mind at ease, my pet. If you wore these earrings at dinner, at which time the pair was presumably intact, you could not have lost one of them earlier in the day, while recovering from your unfortunate accident."

She opened her eyes wide, and set out to disarm him with flattery. "How very clever you are! You make me feel quite ashamed. I fear I wasn't thinking clearly. As you say, it is very late—"

"Far too late to rouse the servants from their beds in such a cause, surely." He returned the volume of sermons to its place on the shelf, and although there was nothing in Lord Markham's voice to suggest a reproof, Penelope found herself flushing nonetheless.

"Begging your pardon, my lord," put in Philippe in a voice that was perhaps not quite as servile as it should have been, "but Miss Fayre did not ring for me, or trouble any of the servants at all. In fact, I was acting on Mr. Crumley's instructions, making sure the house was locked up for the night when I saw a light under the library door. I came to see what it was about, thinking to bank the fire or extinguish any candles that might have been left burning, and discovered Miss Fayre."

"And stayed to join in the search for the lost earring," drawled his lordship, acknowledging the footman with an impersonal nod. "Very obliging of you, to be sure."

"Thank you, my lord," murmured Philippe, sketching a little bow without the least hint of irony.

"Still"—Lord Markham turned back to his betrothed—"you must agree that such an enterprise would be better carried out by day. Pray allow me to conduct you back upstairs to your bedchamber before you catch your death of cold. Then in the morning, I shall order a proper search."

His fingers curled about her arm, and she knew that to object would be both useless and undignified. And so, without daring so much as a backward glance at Philippe, she allowed Lord Markham to lead her from the room.

You needn't look at me like that, she silently chided the lady in the portrait as they started up the stairs. *This wasn't* my *idea*.

* * *

True to his word, Lord Markham ordered a thorough search the following morning, with the result that Penelope's earring was eventually discovered just beneath the edge of an elegantly bowed bombe table at the top of the landing, where she'd had the forethought to drop it on her way down to breakfast. In fact, she'd lain awake for a considerable time trying to decide where she might leave the earring that would not be too difficult for the household staff to discover it, while at the same time not being so obvious as to make her look like a scatterbrained ninny for not finding it herself. In any case, this mental exercise had served to keep her from dwelling on the memory of the goodnight kiss Lord Markham had insisted upon giving her after escorting her to the door of her bedchamber.

For her fears of being disbelieved had soon given way to more immediate concerns. Upon reaching her bedroom door, Penelope had begun to thank his lordship very prettily for his quite unnecessary concern, but her words were cut off half-spoken as he pulled her roughly into his arms.

"God, but you're beautiful," he said, his voice husky with desire. He raked his fingers through her cascading curls, and she gave a startled cry as his hand closed in a sharp tug that forced her head back until her face was scant inches from his. Even as she steeled herself to meet his kiss without flinching, he dipped his head lower and pressed his mouth to her throat. "It's very late, and everyone is asleep," he murmured against her racing pulse. "No one will know if we anticipate the marriage vows by a few weeks."

She squirmed to free herself from hands that were becoming rather too bold in their explorations, and was shocked to feel something hot and wet in her ear that could only be his tongue. "*I* would know. And I am persuaded you would not want a—a 'soiled bride,' my lord, even if you yourself had done the soiling."

"On the contrary: Were I to bear you to the altar with my heir in your belly, I would have at least confirmed your fittedness for the duty I shall require of you."

Penelope took a step backwards, and although he made no attempt to recapture her in his embrace, he didn't have to: She was brought up short by her own bedroom door at her back. "I don't think Mama would approve of your speaking to me in that way, my lord," she said frostily.

He gave a rather ugly little laugh. "My dear girl, your mother is so eager for the match that I could take you on the half-landing in full view of my assembled guests, and she wouldn't utter a word of protest."

"You are offensive, my lord," she said with all the dignity she could muster. "I think you must have drunk too much wine at dinner, for no gentleman would speak so to a lady, and certainly not to the lady he wished to marry. Let us both hope you will be returned to sobriety by morning."

She had been more than half afraid that he would attempt to follow her into her room, but to her infinite relief, he made no move to do so. She closed the door and turned the key in the lock, then sagged against the gilded panel. Caroline had never said anything about this! It was horrid, it was hateful, it was frightening—and yet, under different circumstances—with a different person, for instance—might it not have been just a bit…intriguing?

Suddenly, everything about the night's adventure—the furtive search, the unexpected appearance of Lord Markham in the library, and, finally, his lordship's disturbing assault on her senses—it was all too much. She wanted only to fall into bed and sleep until morning. First, though, there was something else she must do. She made straight for the washstand and poured what remained of the water Betty had brought up the previous morning from the ewer into the big porcelain bowl. It had long since grown cold, but she didn't care. She plunged a cloth into the water and wrung it out, then scrubbed her face, her neck, and, most of all, her ears.

Now, much as she would have liked to avoid him altogether, she was forced into a *tête-à-tête* with Lord Markham for which she had only herself, and her concocted story of a lost earring, to blame. For after the earring was "found," nothing would do but that his lordship must return the bauble to her personally. And she, unwilling to set up his back at such a juncture, had no choice but to meet him with what civility she could muster.

"I am obliged to you," she said coolly, wishing someone—anyone—would enter the drawing room, putting an end to private conversation.

"But not pleased with me, I think." He took her hand and turned it over, then dropped into the palm a single pearl depending from a curved gold wire. He closed her fingers over it, then raised the resulting fist to his lips. "I fear I have offended you."

She bristled. "Why, whatever gave you that idea? Just because you spoke to me in a way that most gentlemen would not speak to a barmaid—"

"Only because I am more honest than they. Depend upon it, I have said nothing to you that every other gentleman of the *ton* has not thought."

"Really, my lord, you are giving me the oddest notion of your sex."

He gave a low, rumbling laugh. "I think you do not know much about men, my pet. It will be my pleasure to teach you." His hooded gaze raked her from her face to her bosom and still lower, as if he were seeing her in her thin muslin nightrail—or, worse, out of it. "Would that I might begin the lesson at once."

Face flaming, she pulled away from him, and this time he let her go. The reason for his sudden capitulation became clear as Crumley, clearing his throat, announced the arrival of the squire and his son, the pair having arrived for a day of pheasant-shooting with Lord Markham and the gentlemen of his party.

Penelope greeted the news of this outing with relief, as she had been wondering how best to avoid her betrothed, or at least avoid being alone with him, for the long day ahead. And it promised to be a very long day indeed. There was no hunt, either on the field by day or in the library by night, as both horses and riders were given a day to rest after their exertions on the hunting field, and the sedentary amusements offered as an alternative made it unlikely that anyone would sleep as deeply as they had the previous night, when even the hardiest souls had been glad to seek their beds by ten o'clock.

With no possibility of aiding Philippe's cause, Penelope found that time hung heavy on her hands. In fact, there was very little to do but engage in desultory conversation with the other ladies of the party over needlework (during which she was obliged to turn aside several coy inquiries as to her marital ambitions) and take a turn about the dormant gardens with Lady Eleanor Bartlesby, who had apparently been marked down as her bosom-bow by virtue of the fact that they were the only unmarried ladies present. She found her gaze turning to Philippe whenever his duties brought him into view, and searching his face for some look, some hint of silent communication—anything, really, that might confirm that he still considered her to be his partner in the quest to restore him to his rightful place.

She had her reward that afternoon when, on her way to dress for dinner, she encountered him on the stairs. "I hope you will be pleased to know that the lost earring was recovered," she said, her tone carefully impersonal.

"Yes, miss, so I was told," he said woodenly.

"I regret that you were put to so much inconvenience on my behalf."

"It was my pleasure, miss," he responded, then in the same expressionless tone, asked, "Begging your pardon, miss, but will you be riding out with the hunt tomorrow morning?"

"That is certainly my intention." She grimaced at the memory of her earlier foray. "Unless I have given Juno so great a disgust of me that she makes it her mission to unseat me, I daresay I shall not require your escort again."

She could not quite suppress the wistful note that crept into her voice, but if Philippe was aware of it, he gave no outward sign.

"Very good, miss," he said, inclining his head in acknowledgement. Then, with the slightest twitch of an eyelid that might or might not have been a wink, he added, "I trust miss will not be quite weary of hunting by the time she returns to the house."

"Oh, no." Penelope assured him, permitting herself a mischievous smile. "I'm sure I won't be."

20

The second day of hunting passed without incident, although Penelope was hard-pressed to dissuade her mother from asking Lord Markham to exchange Juno for a "nice, safe horse" for her daughter, by which Penelope greatly feared her mother meant a slug capable of no gait beyond a lazy shuffle. In any case, she had no trouble at all remaining in the saddle, and returned to the Grange that afternoon pleasantly tired and becomingly flushed. Mrs. Fayre was somewhat surprised at the ease with which she convinced her daughter to lie down and rest a bit before dinner, but beyond telling herself, quite erroneously, that Penelope had always been a good, biddable girl, she had no reason to suspect that this suggestion fitted exactly with Penelope's own plans for the evening.

And so it went. After each day spent in the field, Penelope met Philippe in the library, secure in the knowledge that the day's exertions would guarantee an excellent night's sleep for her fellow guests and an hour or two in which they could search uninterrupted. At times they would converse lightly as they worked, voices pitched low so as not to be overheard as Philippe shared some interesting albeit irrelevant item found in a desk drawer or Penelope read aloud some amusing tidbit discovered within the pages of an old book.

On one subject, however, they remained silent: Philippe never asked Penelope if she were being pressured to marry his uncle, and she never confessed that she was in fact betrothed to him. She had no idea what, if anything, he'd heard, and she dared not ask. It was, she thought, as if they were both trying to return to those glorious days at Bartholomew Fair, when such concerns could be left for some vague but distant future date, for the present was filled with infinite possibilities and newly discovered love.

And yet, their present happiness was as illusory as a soap-bubble, whose swirling colors only signified its imminent collapse. For as the end of the hunting-party drew inexorably nearer, a sense of urgency intruded upon their time together like a distant drumbeat, faint at first but growing daily more difficult to ignore. All too soon, Penelope's return to London was less than forty-eight hours away. There could be no search on that last night, for the party was to end with a brilliant ball to which all the surrounding gentry would be invited, and at which her betrothal to Lord Markham would be announced. The local gentry would not leave until the moon was high enough to provide sufficient light for the drive home, and those guests staying at the Grange would not seek their beds until the wee hours of the morning.

If she was to help Philippe find some proof of his uncle's perfidy, then, it must be tonight. Her ear had by this time become attuned to the chime of the long-case clock in the hall below, so when it tolled the two o'clock hour, she rose from her bed, shrugged on her dressing-gown, and lit her bedside candle. She was sorely tempted to make her way down the stairs without it, and light her own candle from Philippe's once she'd reached the library; they had not been interrupted by Lord Markham again, and she was extremely disinclined to alert him to their nocturnal activities by showing a light. Only the possibility of inadvertently creating an even more obvious alarum in the dark—by running into a wall, perhaps, or tumbling down the stairs—compelled her to make use of the flint.

When she joined Philippe in the library, Penelope found that he, too, must have been keenly aware of the passage of time, for he gave her only the most perfunctory of greetings before resuming his search. He had finished perusing the contents of the desk drawers during their most recent meeting—a task made longer by the necessity of leaving the papers in as near as possible to the same condition in which he had found them— and had now joined her in examining the books on the shelves, beginning on the opposite end of the room and working his way toward her, the idea being that they would eventually meet in the center.

There was no conversation as they worked, but even the quality of their silence had changed, for a tension hung in the air that had not been there before. The wordless companionship of their earlier assignations had given way to a sense of urgency and an almost frenzied need to make the most of the time remaining. At last, Penelope could bear it no longer.

"Philippe"—she didn't look up at him, although they were by now no more than three feet apart—"what will you do if we—you—don't find anything?" She kept her gaze fixed firmly on the book in her hands, suddenly afraid of what she might see in his eyes. Despair over the death of his hopes? Eagerness as he formulated some new plan in which she would have no part? She wasn't quite sure which would be worse.

He shrugged. "I daresay I can find a fair somewhere in need of a swordsman," he said flippantly. Seeing she was not reassured, he added, on a more serious note, "I won't stop searching. There must be some proof, and I won't quit looking until I find it. The library might have seemed the most likely place, but the Grange is a big house, with many other rooms where one might hide letters, or records of travel between the two countries, or some such thing—the muniments room, perhaps, or even my uncle's bedchamber. I won't give up until I've searched the entire house from attics to—"

He suddenly froze, looking up from the open book in his hands.

"Listen!" he hissed sharply.

Penelope obeyed, but heard nothing.

"What?" she whispered at last, her voice scarcely more than a breath.

He shook his head. "I thought I heard something—a creaking stair, or some such thing. I daresay it was only a mouse in the wainscoting."

"Perhaps the house is haunted," suggested Penelope, only half in jest.

"What a pity it isn't," Philippe said dryly. "His lordship might have taken fright and fled years ago, without any effort on my part."

She could summon no response to this sally beyond a rather halfhearted smile, and they lapsed once more into silence. All too soon, the clock in the great hall tolled three, and once again, they had nothing to show for their efforts. Still, they dared not linger, even on this last night, for the servants would be stirring in another hour or two, making preparations for the ball that would seal her own fate.

"Philippe," she said thoughtfully, "you said the proof, whatever it is, might be hidden in your uncle's bedchamber…"

"Yes." He took the dusty old volume from her hands and returned it to its place on the shelf. "What of it?"

"I was just thinking—" She was suddenly very conscious of his nearness, and wished she'd waited until after he'd snuffed the candles before broaching the subject. Having committed this tactical error, however, she was obliged to continue. "It just occurred to me that if I were to marry your uncle, I would have unfettered access to his—"

"No!" He had spoken softly enough, but the single word carried all the force of a gunshot. "Do you think I would want the Grange at such a price? I would give up a dozen, a hundred estates before I would ask such a thing of you!"

"You didn't ask; I offered." She put up a hand to forestall any further protest. "No, wait! Hear me out. After that first day's hunt, Lord Markham made me an offer of marriage, and I was obliged to accept. I'd made myself a promise, you remember, as a condition of slipping away to Bartholomew Fair, and besides, Mama—but that's neither here nor there. Our betrothal—his lordship's and mine, that is—will be announced tonight at the ball. I'd hoped we would discover something that would allow me to cry off, but since that hasn't happened—at least, not yet—I was thinking perhaps I ought to marry his lordship and use my position as mistress of the house to help you continue the search." Ignoring the sick feeling in the pit of her stomach at the thought of Lord Markham's groping hands and greedy kisses, she added, "It would only be for a short time, you know, just until we find the proof and his lordship is hanged for your father's murder."

"And if we don't find proof? You might find yourself tied to my uncle for years! In the meantime, what if he were to discover what you were about? He already has my father's blood on his hands; what do you think he would do to a wife who betrayed him?"

She knew she ought to make some brave retort, but no words would come. Instead, she felt again his brutal hands in her hair, his hot breath at her throat…no, he would not tolerate any disloyalty on the part of his wife, and he would know just how to punish the woman who committed so foolhardy an act, either by killing her outright or else by using her in such a way as to make her wish for death.

From somewhere in the dark and silent house came the faint sound of a bell as some wakeful guest rang for a servant. Philippe muttered a French oath.

"We can't talk now, not with others awake and moving about the house," he whispered impatiently. "Having come this far, I'll see the thing through, although it may take longer than I'd anticipated. Only promise me you won't do anything reckless in the meantime."

"Anything reckless?" she echoed sweetly. "Like taking a

position as servant to a man who would gladly murder you?"

The ghost of a lop-sided grin briefly lightened his countenance. "Just so." Lowering his voice, he said in a more serious vein, "Don't think I'm not grateful. I'm well aware of the risks you've taken for my sake, and of how much I'm indebted to you. Indeed, I shall never forget it."

And so saying, he pinched out the flame of first his own candle and then hers, plunging the room into darkness.

* * *

Penelope dragged herself up the stairs, feeling suddenly very tired. The moon rose later now, and its pale, silver light streamed through the tall windows at the front of the house, picking out the details of the portrait on the half-landing in shades of grey.

As she drew nearer to it with every step, it occurred to her to wonder why Lord Markham had kept it hanging at all, especially in so visible a place. She would have thought this man's countenance was the last one his lordship would wish to see day in and day out for the rest of his life. Did he feel any twinge of guilt when he looked at it, or merely a sense of satisfaction at having removed the only impediment standing between himself and a title and fortune?

Yes, Penelope decided, she could readily imagine Lord Markham savoring such a triumph. In fact, the painting might serve as a memento, the proof that he'd done what he'd set out to do.

Yes…

Of its own volition, her hand stretched out toward the painted canvas, and she knelt before it as if to pay homage.

Yes…

Before she was fully aware of her own actions, she slipped her hand beneath the bottom of the heavy frame, lifting it slightly away from the wall. Her fingers groped against the back of the canvas until they found what she sought: a folded paper, limp and creased with age. She scissored her fingers, finally catching one corner of the paper between her middle and index fingers, and carefully drew it toward the outer edge of the frame…

"What are you doing, Miss Fayre?"

There had been no movement, no sound to betray Lord Markham's presence, so his low voice in the darkness might as well have been a shout. Her hand jerked convulsively, losing her grip on the paper and allowing the heavy frame to fall back into place with a muffled *thud.*

"L-Lord Markham!" she stammered, searching frantically for some explanation that might allay his suspicions. "H-How you startled me!"

"Did I? But no more, surely, than you startled me. Dare I ask what brings you downstairs in the middle of the night this time?"

This time. Clearly, he had not been so readily accepting of her excuse on that earlier occasion as she'd thought—or, perhaps, as he'd wanted her to believe.

A man of passion, perhaps even danger…

The phrase once again echoed in her mind, and now she remembered exactly where she had heard it before. It had been spoken by an old Romany woman in a silk-draped tent, describing the all-powerful Magician depicted on a card, his arms outstretched and his fingers splayed. What else had the woman said? Something about secrets, her own and someone else's…

But there would be time to think about that later. Now she had to put his lordship off his guard, at least long enough to allow her to slip back downstairs after he'd gone and remove the paper from its hidey-hole. To that end, she accepted the hand he held down to her and allowed him to pull her to her feet, giving her brain a few precious seconds to put her tumultuous thoughts in order before she was compelled to give him an answer.

Had he been aware of their doings all along, and only chosen to reveal himself now, when it appeared she might have made an important discovery? It was maddening to think she had come so close only to be, as Oliver might have said, pipped at the post.

"It—the painting—it was crooked," she said, hoping against hope that he would not require an explanation as to why she had deemed it imperative to make this correction at an hour when any reasonable person would have been asleep in bed. "I only hope it was not I who knocked it askew in the first place—which I fear I may have done, for you know how much I admire it." She wished the laugh that accompanied this confession had not held a note of something akin to hysteria. In any case, it won no answering merriment from his lordship.

"My dear girl, you might have fallen down the stairs in the dark and done yourself a serious injury!"

Until that moment, Penelope had not given a thought to the unlit taper in its brass candlestick standing beside her on the half-landing, where she had placed it in order to free her hands. "I—the candle—it—"

But Lord Markham was all solicitousness as he tenderly drew her hand through his arm and steered her away from the portrait and up the remaining stairs. Powerless to resist, Penelope submitted meekly to this show of concern, but inside, her brain was awhirl. How much had he seen—or guessed? Of course, the paper might be perfectly innocent—a bill of sale from the framer, or instructions to the artist from the one who commissioned the portrait, most likely Philippe's father. One thing was certain: She could not rest until she knew for sure.

And so, after reaching the door of her bedchamber and parting from his lordship with expressions of gratitude that were very far from her real sentiments, she did not go to sleep, but lay in bed listening to the ticking of the clock on the mantel and wondering if it were safe to steal back down the stairs and retrieve her prize, if prize it were. There had been no more talk of anticipating the marriage vows, or any of the passionate lovemaking that had so disconcerted her before. In fact, his parting kiss had been almost perfunctory—a fact that should have been reassuring but was not, suggesting as it did that his lordship was impatient for his own opportunity to steal back down the stairs and remove any incriminating evidence.

Finally, when the patch of sky visible through her window had lightened from the blackest pitch to charcoal grey, she dared not wait longer. Throwing back the counterpane, she once again shrugged her dressing-gown on over her nightrail and padded her way up the corridor and down the stairs, feeling her way in the dark lest she fall as his lordship had predicted, not only doing herself the prophesied injury, but rousing the household into the bargain.

The familiar trek down the stairs to the half-landing seemed to take hours instead of minutes, but at last, having reached her goal, she knelt on the carpet and slipped her hand beneath the lower edge of the heavy picture frame. Her questing fingers groped from one lower corner of the frame to the other, but felt nothing but tightly stretched canvas over a rough infrastructure of unfinished wood.

The paper, and whatever secrets it might have contained, was gone.

21

Hssst! Crumley!" Receiving no response from the old family retainer, Philip put his hand on the butler's shoulder and gave him a shake. "Crumley, wake up!"

"Who—? What—?" Recognizing his nocturnal visitor, Crumley sat up in bed, all vestiges of sleep flown. "Master Philip, sir! What—?"

"*I'm* the one who's supposed to call *you* 'sir,' remember? But never mind that." Grinning mischievously, Philip took Crumley's hand and turned it up, then dropped a single key onto the palm and closed the butler's gnarled fingers about it. "I just wanted to return this. I won't be needing it again, at least not for some time."

Even in the dark, Crumley realized at once what his loosely clasped fist concealed, and the significance of its return. "Never say you've found something!"

"Actually, it was Miss Fayre who found it."

"In the desk drawer?" asked the butler, placing the key on the small table beside his bed.

"Not at all. It was tucked behind the portrait on the stairs.

I wonder what gave her the idea to look there? Ah well, perhaps I shall ask her one day."

"And—forgive me, Master Philip, but you are quite certain? It leaves no doubt?"

"Oh, it's certain enough."

He picked up the flint resting beside the candle on the bedside table and lit the taper. Once the flame took hold, he removed a folded paper, now yellowed with age, from his pocket and handed it to the butler. After an inquiring look at his young master, Crumley carefully opened the single sheet, then groped on the night table for his wire-rimmed spectacles, affixed them to his nose, and began to read the crossed lines.

My dear Lord Markham—the title was underscored, as if for emphasis—*permit me to remind you that your brother and predecessor, the man known in my own country as* le Duc de Sainte-Marguerite, *had his assignation with* Madame la Guillotine, *as per our agreement, on 29 June 1794. I even sent you several proofs of his demise at considerable risk to myself, including a lock of hair stained with his blood as well as an account of his death in the esteemed Revolutionary newspaper* L'Ami de la Liberté. *As I recall, you said these proofs were needed in order to spare you the necessity of waiting seven years before having him declared legally dead and asserting your own claim to his English title, and to that end I was happy to oblige; the question of an English barony is a matter of indifference to me, except so far as it concerned your ability to pay the agreed-upon price for my efforts. At no time during our negotiations was any mention made of the brat, nor even of* madame la duchesse. *If you perceived any threat from that quarter, you should have stated it at the outset; I would have arranged for its elimination, and adjusted my fee accordingly.*

In short, mon ami, *I have no intention of returning any part of the payment you made to me. If, as I suspect, your most recent correspondence suggests a willingness on your part to seek redress through a lawsuit for breach of contract, allow me to point out that I hold more than one letter written in your own hand that would make it abundantly clear to any magistrate worthy of the name exactly what were those "services rendered" for which you seek recompense. If, under these circumstances, you choose to proceed, then by all means do so. If, on the other hand, you decide to let sleeping dogs lie (much the wiser course, in my humble opinion), you may console yourself with the knowledge that it would be practically impossible for a woman and child traveling alone to reach the coast unmolested, to say nothing of procuring safe passage across* la Manche *to England. Your brother's wife and her brat have very likely been dead these many weeks.*

It was signed, ludicrously, *A Friend.*

Crumley transferred his gaze from the letter he held in his shaking hands to his young master. "This is it, then? What you've been looking for?"

Philippe shrugged. "I would have preferred to find that earlier letter, the one where my cousin and his 'friend' first struck their bargain. Still, I should think this one is sufficiently damning. What I need from you now, Crumley, is an excuse to be gone for most of the day tomorrow. I must away to Leicester to fetch Andrew."

The butler refolded the letter and returned it to his young master. "Andrew, my lord?"

"You mustn't call me that, not just yet. We can't risk being overheard at this late stage of the game. Yes, Andrew. I shall need him to act as my second."

"Surely you don't intend to challenge his lordship to a duel! Why, the magistrate—"

"I must, Crumley." Philip's voice was gentle, but there was something in his tone that suggested the butler would protest in vain. "The College of Arms won't take a title away from a man who has held it for twenty years and give it to an upstart, even if the upstart can prove that the possessor of that title acceded to his honors by murdering his predecessor. No, Crumley. His lordship must die, so that I may inherit it from him. Ironic, is it not?"

The butler squared his shoulders. "If you are determined on this course, Master Philip," he said resolutely, "then I would consider it an honor if you would allow me to serve as your second."

Visibly moved, Philip put his hand on the old man's shoulder and gave it a squeeze. "It is I who am honored by your devotion, Crumley, but you must see that it won't do. You must remain neutral, or at least give his lordship no reason to question your loyalty. That way, if anything goes wrong, you will still have your position and, eventually, the pension you are due."

"By 'anything,' you mean if his lordship kills you."

The butler's tone was slightly accusatory, but Philip said nothing to deny the charge, or even soften the blow. "Just so."

"And—begging your pardon, Master Philip, but the young lady?"

Philip gave a careless shrug, but his face grew warm and his cheeks reddened. "What about her?"

"There are those who believe her betrothal to his lordship

will be announced at the ball."

"I shall be back in time to prevent any such announcement," Philip predicted confidently. "All I need is an excuse for a prolonged absence from the house on a day when there is enough work to keep an army of servants busy. Can you think of one?"

Crumley considered the matter for a long moment. "I suppose I could send you to Leicester to alert the ostler at the posting house that some of our guests will require transportation on the morning after the ball," he said at last. "Will that suffice?"

"Most excellent of butlers! That will do splendidly!" exclaimed Philip, clapping him on the back. "I've a good feeling about this!"

And with this bold prediction, he left Crumley to resume his interrupted slumber.

"That makes one of us," the butler grumbled, collapsing onto his pillow and pulling the counterpane over his head.

* * *

Penelope awoke heavy-eyed the next morning, with a sense of lingering dread somewhere in the pit of her stomach. Something about Philippe…yes, and his lordship, too…

Then the fog began to lift, and it all came back to her: herself, kneeling on the half-landing before the portrait of the previous baron while the man currently claiming the title stood over her, the flickering light of his candle illuminating his face from below and casting his features into sharp relief, giving him the appearance of a demon king from one of the horrid novels so much in vogue.

She covered her face with her hands and groaned. She'd

found the proof Philippe had needed—she was as certain as if she'd actually held the paper in her hands and read it herself. And so she might have done, if only she'd had one more minute, or perhaps two, before being caught out by his lordship.

And now she had to tell Philippe of how close she'd come, and how the proof he had needed—perhaps the only such proof to exist—was now lost beyond recall. For any man of sense would surely have consigned it to the flames at the first opportunity, and even his lordship's worst enemies could not deny that he had sense, even if it was yoked to the service of cunning self-interest.

One thing, at least, was certain: Nothing would be gained by delay, however great the temptation. She threw back the counterpane and rolled out of bed, then rang for hot water. While she waited for it to arrive, she sat down at the writing desk beneath the window and, availing herself of the writing paper provided for the convenience of guests, dipped the quill into the inkpot and scribbled a hasty note, then folded her handiwork into a tight square.

"Good heavens!" exclaimed Mrs. Fayre a short time later, when Penelope joined her mother in her adjacent bedroom. "My dear, you look positively hag-ridden! What is the matter with you, child?"

"I—I didn't sleep well last night," Penelope confessed with perfect, if incomplete, truth.

Mrs. Fayre was instantly wreathed in smiles. "Well, I'm sure I shouldn't be surprised. It isn't every day a young lady announces her betrothal."

The uneasy feeling in the pit of her stomach hardened into

a knot. How could she have forgotten, even for a moment, that this last night of the hunting-party would end with the ball during which her coming marriage to his lordship would be announced?

"Mama," she began tentatively, "is it so very important that the betrothal be announced tonight?"

"Penelope Fayre!" Her mother's eyes narrowed, and she spoke with rising indignation. "Don't tell me you intend to whistle *another* eligible match down the wind!"

Penelope hastened to reassure her upon this head. "I fully intend to marry Lord Markham, Mama," she said. "Only might I have a little time to—to grow accustomed to my approaching nuptials before returning to Town? For when all the guests depart for their homes tomorrow, you may be sure they will be eager to be the first to spread the news to their friends that the finicking Miss Fayre is to be married at last."

Mrs. Fayre's reaction to the prospect of her daughter's coming notoriety was not precisely what that young lady might have hoped for. "Indeed, yes! And it will certainly be one in the eye for those who said you were a great deal too nice in your requirements. Granted, Lord Markham's rank is not so very high—only a baron, when you might easily have had an earl or even a duke for the asking—but he is said to be enormously wealthy, and Markham Grange is acknowledged to be one of the handsomest houses in the country."

Mrs. Fayre quacked happily on in this strain, and Penelope heaved a sigh of resignation, abandoning, at least for the nonce, any effort to curb her mother's enthusiasm. In fact, all her hopes were pinned on breakfast. She knew she was unlikely to have the opportunity of private speech with Philippe—he would be fully occupied in replenishing the chafing dishes of bacon and buttered eggs or refilling the pot with fresh coffee—but if she could contrive to drop her note somewhere he might see it and pick it up, he surely must find a way to see her alone.

Great, therefore, was her disappointment when she sat down to breakfast only to discover that Philippe was not in evidence at all.

He's gone down to the kitchen to fetch something, she assured herself, and tried hard to believe it.

Penelope spent the meal in an agony of impatience, jumping every time a servant entered the breakfast room only to suffer fresh agonies when the servant proved not to be the one she most wanted to see. She was a resourceful young lady, however, and by the time breakfast came to an end, she had conceived an alternate, albeit inferior, plan.

She withdrew her handkerchief from the long sleeve of her morning gown and removed the folded note she'd tucked inside it. She returned the note to her sleeve, but held her handkerchief at the ready. When Mrs. Fayre rose from the table, Penelope did likewise, but as she turned to follow her mother from the breakfast room, she allowed the handkerchief to slip from her fingers to the Aubusson carpet.

The Fayre ladies had scarcely reached the drawing room when Penelope exclaimed, "Oh, dear! I seem to have left my handkerchief in the breakfast room. Pray go on without me, Mama, and I shall return in a trice."

Suiting the word to the deed, she turned away before her mother could object, and quickly retraced her steps to the breakfast room. She had hardly reached the door when she saw the butler, Crumley, approaching her, a wooden expression on his face and a neatly folded square of fine white cambric in his hands.

"Miss Fayre," he said, sketching a slight bow. "Have you perhaps come to reclaim your lost property? I discovered this on the floor and, recollecting how the guests were seated, I thought it must belong to you."

"Yes, indeed. Thank you." Having achieved her purpose, Penelope accepted the handkerchief he offered, but made no move to return to the drawing room.

"Will there be anything else, miss?" asked Crumley, far too well-trained to turn his back on a guest.

She squared her shoulders and said somewhat breathlessly, "I noticed one of the footmen—I believe his name is Charles— he was not at breakfast this morning." She could feel her face growing warm, but Crumley did not appear to be at all surprised by her sudden interest in a footman, and she wondered how much the butler already knew. "I was hoping to have a word with him. Can you tell him, please, that Miss Fayre wishes to speak to him?"

He regarded her with an expression she found impossible to interpret. Understanding, perhaps? How embarrassing, if that were so! Pity? That would be even worse.

"I'm afraid Charles is not here just at present."

"Oh." Penelope was rather nonplussed by this revelation. "Well, in that case, will you tell him as soon as he returns that I wish to see him on a matter of—of some urgency?"

Crumley inclined his head. "Certainly, miss. However, I

feel I must warn you that I have no idea of when he may return."

"Surely he will be back before the ball!" Recognizing a note of panic in her voice, she carefully schooled it into a more indifferent tone. "I should think such an entertainment would entail work enough for the entire household."

The butler readily agreed. "That and more, miss, which is why I have hired extra help from the village, with his lordship's permission."

"Oh," Penelope said again, in a very small voice.

"Still, you may be assured that I shall deliver your message as soon as Charles returns, miss."

Penelope nodded, but in truth, she hardly heard Crumley's words at all. She was struggling to grasp the revelation that Philippe was gone. She could think of only one explanation: Lord Markham—the usurper Lord Markham—had penetrated "Charles's" disguise, perhaps had even confronted him with the knowledge of his true identity. Philippe would doubtless have been obliged to flee in peril of his life; to be sure, now that his lordship knew the true heir was alive, he would not rest until he'd killed Philippe just as he had the previous baron.

All of which meant she could count on no one to rescue her. If she were to avoid first a public betrothal and then a marriage to a man she could never, ever love, she must save herself.

And Mama would never forgive her for it.

22

Andrew, fast asleep in the attic room of a Leicestershire inn, was roused from slumber by the rapping of knuckles upon the door of his temporary domicile.

"Go 'way," he grumbled, rolling over in bed and pressing the pillow to his ears.

The tattoo was repeated, more emphatically this time, and Andrew, recognizing its source, threw back the counterpane, crossed the room in two strides, and flung open the door.

"Philip!"

The visitor did not wait for an invitation, but entered the room and closed it swiftly behind him. "I can't stay," he said without preamble as he shot the bolt home. "I've a lot to do today, even without—this." He removed the folded paper from the inside pocket of his coat and offered it to Andrew with a flourish.

Andrew gave him a speaking look, but took the proffered paper without comment. He strode to the window, where the light was better, then spread open the folds and scrutinized the lines of faded ink, his eyes growing wider as the meaning of the words became clear.

"You found it!"

"Actually," Philip confessed cheerfully, "it was Miss Fayre who found it."

"Miss Fayre?"

"Surely you remember her? She has a face not easily forgotten."

At this rather glib reminder, Andrew gave his friend and business partner a reproachful look. "Oh, I remember her right enough, but as to what your 'Miss Fair' should be doing at Markham Grange, though—months after Bartholomew Fair, and miles away from Smithfield—I'll admit I'm at a loss."

"As it happens, her name really is Fayre. F-A-Y-R-E. She and her mother are guests of my uncle. In fact"—he retrieved the letter from Andrew's slackened grasp and returned it to his coat pocket—"her betrothal to Lord Markham is to be announced at the Hunt Ball this very night. Obliging of Uncle Robert, is it not? Not only does he tend to my estate during my absence, he even procures for me the hand of my chosen bride."

"And now that you've come back from the dead, I daresay he'll just hand both the girl and the Grange over to you, meek as a lamb," observed Andrew, the lift of one eyebrow indicating his skepticism of this happy prospect.

"Not a bit of it!" Spying the tools of his trade propped against the wall in one corner of the room, Philip strode past his co-conspirator, then seized the hilt of his favorite rapier and tested the weight of the familiar weapon in his hand with the easy affection of one becoming reacquainted with an old friend. "That's why I'm here. I need you to come back to the Grange with me and act as my second."

"D'you mean to tell me you've challenged the fellow to a duel?" demanded Andrew, dodging the sweep of Philip's blade as he made a couple of test passes through the air.

"No," Philip said regretfully, then added, "at least, not yet."

"Don't tell me you intend to turn this dance into a donnybrook!"

"The Donnybrook Ball," Philip said, trying the sound of it on his tongue. "It's a tempting prospect, is it not? By next Season, every hostess in London would be trying to imitate it. But alas, no. Much as I would relish the opportunity to denounce my uncle publicly, I don't know how many of those present—guests or servants—would support his claim over my own. A fine thing it would be, if I were to kill his lordship only to find the entire county allied against me."

"Or something even worse," Andrew grumbled under his breath.

"You think I couldn't hold my own against dear Uncle Robert?" Philip demanded, bristling at the very suggestion of such an outcome.

"On the contrary, I think you could very likely do the thing blindfolded." With a sigh of resignation, Andrew yielded to the inevitable. "Very well, I'll come back to the Grange with you, but I'll not act as your second."

"Not—?"

"No, for I'll be waiting in the stable with two swift horses ready to take you to the coast, and the first available ship to the Low Countries!"

* * *

Like the other ladies of the party, Penelope had repaired to her bedchamber shortly after tea in order to recruit her strength for the evening's festivities. Sleep had eluded her, however, and she had abandoned her bed in favor of the winged armchair before the fire, where she had stared blindly at the pages of *The Romance of the Forest* and listened in vain for the tread of footsteps in the corridor that would herald Philippe's return. At last she had fallen into an uneasy slumber troubled by dreams in which she stood pale and trembling beside Lord Markham as he announced their betrothal.

"I will never marry this man!" she cried, addressing herself to the assembled crowd. "He is a usurper who arranged for the murder of the previous baron!"

A shocked silence fell over the multitude (a crowd far larger than might have been expected to attend a mere country ball), and then, horribly, they began to laugh. Louder and louder their laughter grew—and the one laughing the loudest of all was a wiry young man clad in the black and gold livery of the Markham servants.

"Philippe," she whispered, staring at the footman who was by now doubled over with mirth, to the point that the silver tray in his hands slipped from his grasp and fell to the floor with a crash.

The noise jerked Penelope awake, and she realized the sound had been nothing more than her neglected book slipping from her slackened grip and landing with a *thud* on the carpet.

It was a dream, she thought stupidly. *It was only a dream.*

"Miss Fayre?"

A light scratching on the door banished the last vestiges of slumber, and she hurried to admit Betty, the maid whose services she and her mother shared.

"Mrs. Fayre said I was to see to your toilette first tonight," she said, giving Penelope a knowing smile. "This being a special occasion and all."

Penelope returned some noncommittal answer, then sat down at the dressing-table and submitted her head to Betty's ministrations. Listening only half-heartedly to the maid's chatter, Penelope found her mind drifting back to her interrupted dream. What would really happen, she wondered, if she were to denounce Lord Markham as a usurper and a murderer before the assembled guests? Granted, it was unlikely that everyone would laugh, but it was equally unlikely that they would believe her claims—at least, not without proof. And that proof, she had no doubt, was by this time burned to ash or, at the very least, concealed somewhere neither she nor Philippe would ever find it.

If Philippe was ever coming back.

Long after Betty had finished and taken herself off, Penelope sat before the dressing-table, staring blindly at her reflection in the mirror mounted above it. Instead of crimping her hair in one of the fashionable new styles dependent upon the lavish use of curling tongs, the maid had pulled the dark mass tightly back from Penelope's face and pinned it into a topknot at the crown of her head. The severity of this style should have been unbecoming in the extreme, for it gave no quarter to any flaws of feature or expression; instead, it served to call attention to her excellent bone structure and large brown eyes framed by long lashes. Economy had necessitated the alteration of an existing gown rather than the order of a new one, so the skirt of the gown she'd worn to Almack's a few months earlier—a blush-pink silk taffeta of so pale a hue that it appeared almost white—had been fitted with a new bodice. In an effort to further contain costs, Penelope herself had worked the embroidered border of red, orange, and purple flowers adorning the short puffed sleeves and the edge of the low-cut neckline. The narrow silhouette of the gown was as flattering to her figure as the severe coiffure was to her face, and most young ladies would have been delighted with the image that looked back at them.

Penelope's thoughts, however, ran on very different lines. *Admit it,* her reflection commanded accusingly. *You're still hoping he will return before your betrothal to Lord Markham is announced.*

"I have to tell him about that letter," she insisted in her own defense. "He needs to know that I found it—"

Yes, and that you lost it. Why else would you be so eager to impart bad news, unless you were also counting on him to save you from Lord Markham by marrying you himself? Your London Season has made you so puffed up in your own conceit that you think every man you meet has a burning desire to marry you.

"No, I don't," she said, but the words lacked conviction even to her own ears. In truth, most of the young men she'd met over the course of those spring and summer months *had* professed a burning desire to marry her, although she suspected most of these declarations had been inspired by no deeper emotion than a desire to follow the prevailing fashion for dangling after her. By next spring, they would have set their sights on someone else.

And she?

She'd been so sure Philippe had felt it, too, the thrill of attraction that had accompanied every word, every touch they'd exchanged. And yet once the fair had closed, he'd left London without a backward glance, not even lingering long enough to see if she would slip away to say goodbye. The fact that they had found one another again had been the merest chance, and even then, he had resolutely refused to acknowledge her until she had tricked him into lowering his guard.

This much she admitted, albeit reluctantly, but her brain shied away from the thought that, his incognito having been discovered, he might have encouraged her affections in order to ensure her silence, perhaps even to enlist her help in reclaiming his heritage, only to leave her in the lurch once it became clear that their efforts were fruitless. No, however bleak her situation, she could not believe him capable of such perfidy.

Her gaze fell from the likeness in the looking-glass to the top of the dressing table, its polished surface littered with the usual accoutrements to feminine beauty. Almost without conscious thought, her hand went to the narrow strip of coquelicot-colored silk, and she began (not for the first time) to wind it idly about her forefinger, recalling once more the circumstances that had brought it into her possession.

She'd bartered her future for two glorious days at Bartholomew Fair. *And it was worth it,* she reminded herself fiercely. She had experienced the glories of the fair, and had even found love there, however briefly. Now it was time to uphold her end of the bargain, and if she could not do so eagerly, she would at least fulfill her obligation without complaint. At least, she thought wistfully, her position as Lady Markham would give her access to her husband's bedchamber, where she might yet discover the letter she'd lost, or some other proof. Then his lordship would hang for his crime, and Philippe, filled with gratitude, would take her hand and say—

"Penelope?" called her mother, rapping impatiently on the door. "Aren't you ready yet?"

"Coming," she said with a sigh, unwinding the ribbon from her finger and letting it fall.

You never give up, do you? her reflection chided mockingly.

She made a face at the image looking back at her, and had almost reached the door when a sudden impulse called her back to the mirror. Reaching behind her, she unclasped the single strand of pearls about her neck and returned it to her sparsely-filled jewel case, then picked up the length of ribbon and tied it in a small bow knot at her throat, the ends so recently wrapped around her finger now hanging in loose spirals over the bare flesh of her *décolletage*, a fashion which the duchess of the portrait and her contemporaries would have instantly recognized.

Having made what preparation she could, she took a deep breath and opened the door to her mother's knock, ready to face whatever the evening might bring.

23

Are you still vexed with me for cheating you of your discovery?" Lord Markham asked coaxingly as the figures of the dance brought them together. He gave a low chuckle. "You would have been disappointed in it, I fear. Nothing but a note to the housekeeper concerning the bedsheets in the room which family tradition calls the Queen's Bedchamber. I daresay she tucked it behind the portrait to keep the frame from bumping against the wall. The housekeeper, that is, not the queen."

"Imagine that." Penelope gave him a brittle smile, then turned away to take the squire's hand in accordance with the next movement of the dance. So this was what the rest of her life was to be like: His lordship baiting her with knowing remarks to which she could not respond in kind without putting Philippe's life, and possibly her own, in danger.

She forced herself to smile at the squire, and to answer his playful compliments with a sally of her own. At least the gentlemen in the adjacent pairs—the squire partnering Mrs. Hatton on one side and Philippe's cousin, Mr. Freddie Markham, with Lady

Eleanor on the other—gave her a brief respite from his lordship's barbs.

She had known, of course, that she would not be able to avoid him all the evening. To be sure, she had been surprised (though undeniably relieved) when Mr. Markham had been before him in requesting the first dance, and she had taken considerable satisfaction in the annoyance that his lordship, despite his urbane manner, could not quite suppress when she had informed him of the fact. Still, there had been little point in delaying the inevitable, so she'd given him this dance, along with the supper dance to come later in the evening—at which time the betrothal would be announced, unless anything occurred to stop it. Preferably, she thought, something not too tall, but lean and wiry, with black eyes and straight black hair falling over his forehead…

But no such interruption came. She performed the cotillion before supper with Lord Markham, then went to the dining room on his arm, although she ate scarcely a bite of the lavish spread his lordship had arranged for his guests. All too soon, supper was over, and it was time to return to the ballroom for the announcement that would be made as soon as the last stragglers had left the dining room and joined them there.

"Are you ready, my dear?"

Lord Markham's voice was caressing, but his grip on her arm warned her to object at her peril. Moving like an automaton, she allowed him to lead her to the raised dais at one end of the room, where the musicians were set up.

"Friends and neighbors, ladies and gentlemen," his lordship began, assuming a humility that was wholly false, "it is hard to believe the fortnight has come to an end. I hope you have all derived some small amusement from my poor party."

Warm applause informed him that his hopes were not disappointed. Indeed, a few of the more avid riders to hounds added enthusiastic shouts of "Huzzah!"

"But I have one more surprise for you before you depart for your homes on the morrow. I am pleased to announce that Miss Fayre—"

Penelope, her face as pale as her dress, forced a smile. In the candlelight, the poppy-red ribbon at her throat resembled nothing so much as a slash of blood.

"—Has done me the honor of—"

"One moment, if you please."

A bewildered hush fell over the ballroom as a slender young man strolled toward the dais. He wore no coat or waistcoat, only a full white shirt, open at the throat and tucked loosely into the waistband of his breeches. A rapier hung from the scabbard at his hip, and one of his hands rested lightly on its hilt. In his other hand, he carried a similar, perhaps even an identical weapon. It seemed to Penelope that there was no sound in the room at all save for the ringing of his boot-heels on the waxed and polished boards of the ballroom floor and the mad pounding of her heart in rhythm with his footsteps.

He stepped up onto the dais, his gaze firmly fixed on the man at her side. She felt his lordship's hand tighten convulsively on her arm, and realized he had grown rigid with some tightly suppressed emotion. Anger, perhaps? Or fear?

"Who the devil are you?" he demanded.

The newcomer continued as if he had not spoken. "I must

confess, the land appears to be in excellent heart. But I must—no, I really *must* draw the line at your becoming betrothed to my intended bride."

The hush that had greeted his arrival now gave way to a buzz of whispered speculation. His lordship paid no heed.

"State your business or get out of my house," he hissed between clenched teeth. "Who are you, and what do you want?"

Philip stroked a forefinger almost lovingly along the smooth length of tempered steel in his hand. "I have been many people, and have had many names. Most recently, I have been Charles the footman, but before that, I was Philippe Valois, the Blade of Paris, and before that—" He shrugged as if dismissing the more distant past as a matter of no importance. "But you"—his eyes, black and glittering, lifted from the rapier in his hand to the baron, and his bared teeth had nothing in common with a smile—"you may call me 'Retribution.'"

"I've no idea what you're talking about. Crumley!" Lord Markham raised his voice to issue an order to the butler. "Summon a couple of footmen and get this fellow out of my house!"

But Crumley took no notice. His eyes, like everyone else's, were fixed on the young man who, until that moment, he had always believed to be the image of his French mother. But something about Philip Markham—the set of his jaw, perhaps, or the easy confidence of his stride—took the old butler back to the master he had not seen in twenty long years.

"'No idea'?" Philip echoed in surprise, advancing on his uncle by leisured steps. "Just as you had no idea who I was, or what was my business here. I hope you have seen a physician about these memory lapses; they are most distressing. Permit me to refresh your memory: Twenty years ago, you colluded with some person or persons unknown in France, divulging the location of the Parisian hovel in which my family was holed up, ensuring my father's death at the hands of *madame la guillotine* and, at the same time, your own accession to his English title."

"What balderdash!" Perhaps it was nothing more than the heat generated by the dozens of wax candles that illuminated the ballroom, but whatever the reason, his lordship's aristocratic brow bore a fine sheen of perspiration.

"It was a clever scheme," continued Philip, "but you made one rather crucial error. There was still one who stood between you and my father in the succession; you neglected to make sure that he was removed. He stands before you now." He made a little bow in his uncle's direction.

"*Cousin Philip?*" Freddie Markham exclaimed, putting up his quizzing-glass. "Never say it's you, Coz!"

"Later, Freddie," Philip said, his eyes never leaving his uncle's face. "I'm rather busy at the moment."

"*That's* my Cousin Philip." Freddie nodded sagely, addressing himself to anyone who would listen. "Never would let me in on his adventures."

"Lies! All lies!" bellowed his lordship, but beneath the ruddy glow he'd acquired on the hunting-field, his face had assumed an ashen hue. "You would call me a murderer before my friends and neighbors, before my affianced bride?"

Philip darted a quick glance at Penelope, wide-eyed and white-faced at his lordship's side. "As to that last bit, we won't quibble just at present, but as for the rest, yes, I would. I do."

Lord Markham's hand went to his hip, as if expecting to find a weapon there. "I demand satisfaction, sirrah!"

"Somehow I thought you might," Philip said placidly, drawing the rapier from its sheath and presenting the hilts of both weapons to his uncle. "See, I come prepared. I even allow you, the challenger, to choose the sword with which you will run me through."

With a noise like the growl of a wild beast, Lord Markham snatched one of the swords seemingly at random, grazing his thumb on the razor-sharp blade in the process. A ribbon of bright-red blood oozed from the shallow wound, but his lordship paid no heed.

Like many gentlemen of his generation, Robert Markham had frequented a fencing *salle* as a young man, even though the sword had already begun losing ground to the pistol as the weapon of choice for duelling. Although he had rarely had occasion to use this skill, he remembered enough to know that the satisfaction he now demanded went against every rule, written or not, regarding the procedure for such lethal engagements. Still, his blood was up, and he would not have drawn back even if his pride had permitted it. It was perhaps fortunate, then, that cooler heads—one cooler head, at least—intervened, as Freddie Markham pushed his way to the front of the crowd.

"I say, Uncle," protested Freddie, "can't kill Cousin Philip, doncher know! Deuced if I didn't think you was dead, Coz. Glad to see you ain't, even if you did shove me into the lake last time we met."

"Served you right for being a plaguey nuisance," said his

cousin, unrepentant. "It's nice to know that some things haven't changed."

"Still, not at all the thing to go skewering each other. Family, and all. Won't do."

"Perhaps you should have pointed that out to my uncle twenty years ago."

"Dash it, Coz!" exclaimed Freddie, filled with righteous indignation. "I was only five years old at the time!"

"Be quiet, you nodcock!" snapped Lord Markham, brandishing his sword in the direction of his hapless heir.

"Right-ho," Freddie said, quickly effacing himself. "Whatever you say. Only thought—well, never mind."

Having put one nephew in his place, Lord Markham turned his attention to the other. But even as he assumed the fencer's stance with feet apart and knees slightly bent, his right hand holding his sword at the ready and his left arched gracefully over his head, another voice was raised in protest.

"Gentlemen, gentlemen!" Mr. Hatton cried in a chiding tone rarely heard from him even in the pulpit. "This young man has made a shocking accusation, to be sure, but both of you must be well aware that this is neither the time nor the place to settle the matter."

"On the contrary," Philip said smoothly, "I have had an appointment with my uncle for these past twenty years. I should hate to keep him waiting any longer."

And so saying, he removed the bead covering the tip of his sword and tossed it into the assembly, just as he'd done at Bartholomew Fair. On that occasion, however, it had been his challenger's blade whose tip he had exposed while leaving his own covered, increasing the danger to himself but not his opponent.

The message was clear: This was no exhibition, such as those he had performed at the fair.

This was not even a contest of superior swordsmanship.

This was a fight to the death.

"Have you any proof of this extraordinary claim, young man?" the vicar persisted, trying in vain to make peace between two mortal enemies.

"As a matter of fact, I do. I have in my possession a letter, discovered in this very house—"

"*You* took it?" Penelope asked incredulously.

No one heard her. At the mention of the letter, Lord Markham made a guttural cry and lunged. Philip was hard-pressed to jump back and parry the thrust, but he was not caught unawares again. Still, the unexpected attack had not been without its effect: The sleeve of Philip's white shirt was slit from wrist to elbow, and blood seeped from a wound both deeper and longer than Lord Markham's self-inflicted one. Philip paid it no heed, but continued to parry his uncle's thrusts, gauging the level of his opponent's skill and allowing the man, his elder by more than fifteen years, to expend his energy on pent-up fury, while the blood ran down Philip's arm and dripped from his elbow onto the floor.

Penelope's eyes never strayed from the combatants as she left her place on the dais and moved to Freddie Markham's side. "Tell me, Mr. Markham,"—her words were scarcely audible beneath the ring of steel on steel—"who is the justice of the peace? Do you know?"

Freddie dipped his head in the direction of Lord Markham. "My uncle Robert."

Of course he was. She could have screamed with frustration. But since this would have served no useful purpose, she racked her brain for someone whose word might hold some weight with the two men, each of whom seemed determined to make an end of the other.

"What about the squire?" Penelope urged. "He must be somewhere nearby, for I saw him earlier."

"Daresay he's out on the terrace blowing a cloud or taking snuff. Saw him headed that way earlier."

She clutched at Freddie's sleeve, but still did not look at him, laboring under the wholly illogical conviction that the fixity of her gaze was the only thing standing between Philippe and certain death. "Will you go and fetch him? Tell him he must come at once, that it's urgent!"

Freddie gave a last, regretful look at the fight he was charged with breaking up, then, having been taught from his earliest youth that a gentleman of honor should never disoblige a lady, took himself off in search of the squire.

Meanwhile, the duel went on. Any student of the art would have given the advantage to Lord Markham despite the difference in their ages. In addition to his superior height and the longer reach it conferred, his lordship had once had lessons at Angelo Tremamondo's prestigious fencing academy in Old Bond Street under the tutelage of no less a personage than the master's own son.

Philip, half French, had begun his lessons at the age of six, taking instruction at one of the finest *salles* in Paris, but these had been sadly cut short by his flight from that city to his father's native country. With no money for such nonessentials, it had been left to Andrew, who had formerly been charged with delivering the boy to his lessons and fetching him home again afterwards, to keep his master's young heir in practice. This he had done to the best of his ability, eventually adding to Philip's repertoire what he could recall from the practice matches between the older pupils he had often watched while awaiting the end of the boy's lesson. Consequently, the older Philip had grown, the further removed his technique had become from that taught at any fencing school worthy of the name.

Perhaps more to the point, Philip had spent almost every day for the previous six months either developing additional maneuvers for what Andrew called his bag of tricks, or fighting a succession of challengers of varying ages, ranks, and skills. Thus, regardless of his superior technique, Lord Markham could not show his nephew anything that young man had not faced at some point, in some English city, town, or village over the previous six months. On the other hand, Philip's fencing was unlike anything his lordship had ever seen before, and he found his nephew's irregular moves impossible to anticipate. Having failed to penetrate his opponent's guard by ordinary means, Lord Markham resorted to taunts in an effort to discompose the young man.

"Tell me—if you can—what took you so long?" he asked, gasping for breath. "D'you think—I haven't felt you—out there somewhere—biding your time?—Looked for you—year you turned eighteen—and again—when—turned twenty-one."

"You flatter me," Philip replied, parrying another attack

from his uncle's blade. "I fear my mother is to blame for my tardiness. She was convinced that you would be eager to meet me again—we see now how right she was—so I delayed my return in deference to her wishes. I assure you, with every day I watched her working her fingers to the bone, plying her needle until the candle guttered in its socket, still hoping against hope that my father had contrived to escape and would someday be joining us, I looked forward all the more eagerly to our eventual meeting."

The two rapiers sang as Lord Markham swept Philip's blade aside with the edge of his own, then lunged before his nephew could gather himself for a fresh attack. This attempt was foiled, however, when his lordship stepped squarely on a patch of the blood that had been dripping steadily from Philip's injured arm. For one instant he slid, and it appeared he might fall.

"Have a care," the younger man chided. "That's my life's blood you're tramping about in."

His lordship managed to regain his balance, but at the expense of his weapon, for as he windmilled his arms in an effort to stay upright, the sword slipped from his sweaty hand. Withdrawing his own weapon, Philip pushed the rapier back to his opponent with the toe of his boot. "Pick it up," he commanded, panting. "I take no pleasure in defeating an unarmed man."

But despite his insouciance, Philip's arm was growing weary, and even the thin, lightweight blade seemed to grow heavier by the minute. His dilemma was not lost on Lord Markham, who, seeing the end in view, snatched up his rapier from off the floor and charged straight into a fresh assault. Philip yielded ground, clutching the hilt of his sword with both hands, and Lord Markham, sensing victory was at hand, bared his teeth in a feral grin. Great was his surprise when Philip let his injured right arm fall and fought with renewed vigor, the rapier now held in his left hand.

"I say!" exclaimed the squire's son, much impressed. "I wish he'd teach me to do that!"

"It will—do you—no good." Lord Markham's rasped words were scarcely more than a whisper, so labored was his breathing. "Even if you—kill me—you'll not enjoy—inheritance long—before you—hang for murder!"

"I know," replied Philip, rather breathless himself. "That's why I've a carriage and two swift horses awaiting me outside. I find it's best to always be prepared. That would make an excellent addition to the family crest, would it not? '*Semper paratus*.'"

"You appear—to have—everything—all worked out," retorted his lordship, trying to sound cynical but succeeding only in sounding thoroughly spent, as if fear, hatred, and a fine instinct for self-preservation were the only things keeping him on his feet.

"Not quite everything." Without looking away from his adversary, he called to Penelope, "Miss Fayre, it appears I shall be leaving very shortly for the coast, and from there sailing to the Low Countries on the next ship. Will you come with me?"

Vibrant color flooded her pallid countenance, and the radiance of her smile outshone the dozens of wax candles.

"With all my heart," she said simply.

"*Ohhhh*," Mrs. Fayre moaned, and slipped quietly into a swoon.

24

Wha—What happened?" Mrs. Fayre asked in faltering tones, awaking to find herself lying on a sofa in the drawing room with the squire's wife in attendance.

"Never you mind about that," advised that lady briskly, bathing her forehead with lavender water. "My husband has everything well in hand, and there's nothing for you to worry about. Lady Eleanor has gone to fetch some brandy—a good sort of girl, if just the tiniest bit insipid, and it seems to me that Freddie Markham would do well to fix his interest with her, now that it looks as if he's in a fair way to losing his place in the succession—so there's naught for you to do but lie here and rest."

In spite of this recommendation, Mrs. Fayre struggled to sit upright, then, discovering that the previously stationary room had begun to spin, thought better of it. "Penelope—" she began, only to be cut off.

"Oh, she's as merry as a grig, or would be, if it weren't for—ah, here's Lady Eleanor with the brandy. Thank you, child."

Having dismissed this young lady as readily as she had recruited her for this errand, she assisted Mrs. Fayre to rise and coaxed her into taking a few sips. "Drink it slowly, mind you. That's the way."

"What happened?" Mrs. Fayre asked again, once the room had ceased its gyrations. "His lordship—and—that young man—"

"As it happens, that young man *is* his lordship. Don't know why I didn't see it at once, for he was always the image of his mother."

"And his lordship—that is, *that man* really did arrange to have his brother murdered?"

The squire's wife gave an emphatic nod. "Most certainly."

"Will he hang? Penelope's betrothal—the scandal—"

"Oh, there'll be gossip aplenty, I don't doubt, but as for scandal, not a bit of it! In fact, I daresay she will be quite the romantic heroine, once his story leaks out. Now, if you're feeling better, may I let those two foolish children in? They are quite worried about you, you know."

Mrs. Fayre agreed, albeit rather feebly, and a moment later Penelope entered the room in a swirl of pale-pink skirts, followed at a more decorous pace by Philip, his injured arm bandaged and resting in a sling.

"Mama! Are you quite all right? It has been the most shocking affair! I could almost envy you for being well out of it."

"I'm quite all right, my dear, but what happened after I swooned?" Her gaze shifted from her daughter to the man standing protectively at her side. "I take it you are the new Lord Markham, young man, but pray, what has happened to the old one?"

Over her head, the young couple's eyes met in a look that conveyed more than words.

"He is—gone, Mama. The squire came in and broke up the fight, and Lord Markham—I daresay he recollected the carriage and two swift horses waiting in the stables, and thought to make his escape that way. But when he leapt out the window, he—he—" She broke off, shuddering.

Putting a comforting arm about Penelope's shoulders, Philip took up the tale. "He appears to have caught his toe on the window sill. In any case, he struck the pavement headfirst. He died instantly."

"I'm glad you didn't have to see it, Mama. I wish *I* hadn't had to see it, for it was quite horrible!"

She dashed a hand over her eyes as if to erase the memory, and Philip, Lord Markham and *Duc de Sainte-Marguerite*, judged it time to give the ladies' minds a happier direction.

"Madame," he said, addressing Mrs. Fayre, "to whom should I apply for permission to marry your daughter? Yourself, or your son, Mr. Oliver Fayre?"

"I'm sure no mother could have any objection to seeing her daughter so advantageously settled," she said, still a bit dazed by the sudden turn of events. "But how—forgive me, Duke—"

"Please," he protested, "call me Philip, or Philippe, as Penelope does."

"Philip, then—I'm afraid I don't quite understand how you and Penelope became acquainted with one another. I don't remember your being introduced to us during the Season."

Surprisingly, this simple question seemed to throw the self-possessed young man into confusion. "Well, er—um, actually, ma'am, it was like this—"

"It was my own fault, Mama." Penelope flung herself to her knees beside her mother's chair and took that astonished lady's hands in hers. "You see, I—I told you I was going shopping, and then to an astronomy lecture, but in fact, I stole away to Bartholomew Fair. I know it was very wicked of me, but perhaps you can forgive me after all, since everything has worked out so well? For it was there that I first met Philippe, and if I had been a good, obedient girl, I never should have met Lord Markham—the *real* Lord Markham, that is—and I should not be making just the sort of match you had wished for."

Thus, Mrs. Fayre found herself on the horns of a dilemma. It would be a very unnatural mother indeed who would cavil at seeing her daughter marry so very advantageously—only a barony, to be sure, but Penelope would be a duchess one day, if only the French would stop beheading one another. And yet, to countenance such very improper behavior would surely be a dereliction of maternal duty of no small magnitude. In the end, she was obliged to dissemble.

"I vow, child, what I am to do with you, I'm sure I don't know! Perhaps *you* may contrive to manage her, Duke, for I'm sure *I* never could!"

And on this statement, she rose somewhat gingerly from the sofa and departed the room in measured steps, the very picture of outraged propriety.

"About that dukedom," Philip said, once he and Penelope were alone together, "I hope you won't set too much store by it. God only knows what, if anything, may be left of *Sainte-*

Margeurite by the time the war is over. I would not want to raise false hopes."

"I would marry you if you were a baron or a bootblack," she confessed, smiling radiantly up at him.

"And I'm very pleased to hear it," he said, taking her hand in his. "But I think we will be much more comfortable living here as Lord and Lady Markham."

"*You* might, perhaps," she retorted, only half in jest. "But, Philippe, I know nothing about the running of a house this size!"

"You shall put yourself in the housekeeper's hands, just as I shall put myself in my uncle's."

"Your *uncle's?*"

He laughed aloud at her dismayed expression. "My Uncle Reginald, Freddie's father."

Penelope considered with a puzzled frown this new and entirely unexpected branch sprouting on the Markham family tree. "But Philippe, Lord Markham said Freddie—Mr. Markham, that is—was his heir presumptive. If his father is still alive, wouldn't *he* have been your uncle's heir?"

"He would have, if he'd been a third Markham brother. I suppose he's actually Freddie's stepfather, although the nuances of kinship escaped me as a seven-year-old; Uncle Reginald was the man who dusted my cousin's breeches when his antics became too annoying—which equated to my young mind as a father, since my own father occasionally performed the same office for me. In fact, Freddie's father died when I was still in leading strings. There's a portrait of him in the second-floor corridor that is said to be very good, but I don't remember him at all. I don't remember much about my Uncle Reginald, either, but my father was Freddie's guardian until my aunt remarried, and he always said Reginald Wilberforce was one of the shrewdest men he knew." He grinned. "Pity it doesn't appear to have rubbed off on Freddie."

"I was introduced to Mr. and Mrs. Reginald Wilberforce during my Season, at a dinner at Devonshire House. And here I thought I was marrying a footloose swordsman from Bartholomew Fair! Pray, how many *other* relations must I learn?"

"I believe there are a couple of aunts, one of whom I found quite terrifying when I was a child." In a more serious tone, he added, "It will not be all midnight trysts in the library, my darling, but very hard work. Still, I daresay we will come about in the end."

"Yes, but—Philippe, I've only just realized—it all happened, just as the fortune teller said it would! A 'man of passion and danger,' and secrets—my own as well as someone else's—and marriage, and riches, and a—a lover." She faltered on this last, adding somewhat timidly, "Although perhaps I am rushing my fences, for you haven't said you loved me, have you?"

He gave her a warm look that promised a thorough, and thoroughly satisfying, discourse on this subject in the very near future. "Nor, for that matter, have I made you an offer of marriage. My dearest Miss Fayre," he continued, his tone suddenly formal, "I know you are sick to the teeth of receiving marriage proposals, but dare I hope you will entertain one more?"

"Perhaps." The reigning belle of the past Season turned away and threw him a coy smile from over her shoulder. "If it comes from a gentleman who will kiss me without apologizing immediately afterwards."

"I know just the fellow." He caught her from behind with his good arm about her waist, and when she turned in his embrace, he kissed her with a thoroughness that left her in no doubt as to the depth of his affections.

"No apology?" she asked rather breathlessly, when they drew apart.

"None. In fact," he said, lowering his mouth once more to hers, "I intend to do it again."

And he did.

Epilogue

. . .And of course Mama wanted us to wait until spring, when we could do the thing "properly"—which, in case you've ever wondered, means nothing less than St. George's, Hanover Square, with **miles** of white satin and lace, so it appears you and James were never "properly" married, either! What a disappointment we must be to poor Mama! But Philippe (yes, I know in England he should be called Philip, but I daresay he will always be Philippe to me) says, quite correctly, that his return from the dead will be enough of a nine days' wonder without adding all the pomp and ceremony of a society wedding.

In any case, we were both eager to marry without delay, so we had the banns read in church, partly as a way of reintroducing Philippe to his tenants, and Mr. Hatton, the vicar, read the ceremony immediately after the third reading. Since then, we have been holed up at the Grange, where the grounds look so beautiful under a blanket of snow! Perhaps you may come to us in the spring, when travel is easier, and bring Benjy with you so he can meet his new uncle—although I hope he will simply call him

Philip instead of "Uncle" Philip, for the word has such unpleasant connotations for me now that I daresay I shall never hear it without shuddering!

Philippe has just returned from visiting some of the tenants' cottages with the steward, so I shall close now, remaining as ever, yr loving sister,

Penny (or, if you prefer, Penelope, Lady Markham)

Post Scriptum: You were quite right. It is not disgusting at all!

About the Author

At the age of sixteen, Sheri Cobb South discovered Georgette Heyer, and came to the startling realization that she had been born into the wrong century. Although she probably would have been a chambermaid had she actually lived in Regency England, that didn't stop her from fantasizing about waltzing the night away in the arms of a handsome, wealthy, and titled gentleman.

Since Georgette Heyer died in 1974 and could not write any more Regencies, Ms. South came to the conclusion that she would have to do it herself. In addition to the bestselling John Pickett mystery series (now an award-winning audiobook series), she has also written several Regency romances, including the critically acclaimed *The Weaver Takes a Wife*.

A native and long-time resident of Alabama, Ms. South now lives in Loveland, Colorado.

www.ingramcontent.com/pod-product-compliance
Lightning Source LLC
Chambersburg PA
CBHW061429150726
47987CB00001B/142